WELCOME TO PENNYCRESS INN

SARAH HOPE

B

Boldwood

First published in Great Britain in 2025 by Boldwood Books Ltd.

Copyright © Sarah Hope, 2025

Cover Design by Head Design Ltd

Cover Images: Shutterstock

A CIP catalogue record for this book is available from the British Library.

Paperback ISBN 978-1-83617-446-2

Large Print ISBN 978-1-83617-445-5

Hardback ISBN 978-1-83617-444-8

Ebook ISBN 978-1-83617-447-9

Kindle ISBN 978-1-83617-448-6

Audio CD ISBN 978-1-83617-439-4

MP3 CD ISBN 978-1-83617-440-0

Digital audio download ISBN 978-1-83617-441-7

This book is printed on certified sustainable paper. Boldwood Books is dedicated to putting sustainability at the heart of our business. For more information please visit https://www.boldwoodbooks.com/about-us/sustainability/

Boldwood Books Ltd, 23 Bowerdean Street, London, SW6 3TN

www.boldwoodbooks.com

For my children.
Let's change our stars
xXx

1

This was it! The first day of the rest of her life. The first page of a new chapter. A new year, a new her. She'd take all of those cringy clichés – all of them.

Laura Price closed the door of her rusty old Focus and half walked, half ran across the broken slabs towards the front door, pausing every few steps to untangle her ankles from the spindly overgrown lavender which grew alongside the cracked pavement through the front garden, the stringy stalks of the dormant plant a silvery, sage green against the blue of her jeans.

'Afternoon, Miss Price.' Ms Taunton, the stuffy but stunningly beautiful estate agent, checked her watch.

'Hi. Sorry I'm late.' Why had she said that? She knew she wasn't. She'd been forty-five minutes early and as soon as she'd seen Ms Taunton appear on the decking encircling the right-hand side of the inn, she'd run up here. Habit. That was why.

'Here are your keys. Spares are in the kitchen drawer.' Ms Taunton held out the keys dangling from a purple plastic teddy keyring.

'Wow! Thank you so much.' Trying hard to suppress the

excitement bubbling in her stomach and appear professional, Laura took the keys and fought the urge to give the estate agent a hug.

'You're welcome.' Ms Taunton shook Laura's hand briefly before turning on her overly high heels and sauntering down the steps and through the front garden to her two-seater BMW, avoiding the long stalks of lavender with much more finesse than Laura had, despite the height of her heels.

The keys! She had the keys to her very own inn! Pennycress Inn! She looked down at the small plastic teddy in her palm. Her new home and her very own business all rolled into one!

Stepping back down to stand on the cracked and uneven, but equally charming, garden path, Laura leaned her head back and peered upwards. This was really hers.

She swallowed, her mouth suddenly dry as she looked up at the yellow Cotswold stone building, the wooden window frames perfectly matching the lavender-coloured front door, framing the criss-cross of lead-paned glass. The large willow tree growing to the right was almost the same height as the thatched roof, which was adorned with a single straw cat seemingly inching its way across the ridge of the roof – the perfect addition to such an idyllic building.

Laura wrapped her arms around her middle as her stomach gurgled with a mixture of excitement and nervousness, the hard plastic of the teddy keyring digging into her side. Could she really do this? Could she really be responsible for a place as beautiful as this?

Of course she could. This was her fresh start, her chance to reinvent herself as the confident, independent businesswoman she wanted to be. Shaking the doubts away, she stepped up to the front door.

After unlocking it, she slowly turned the handle and inched

the purple door open, a lasting reminder of the colour the lavender would bloom in the spring. She wanted to savour this moment, to remember it forever.

Stepping into the vast hallway, she spun around slowly, taking in the elaborate oak staircase, the varnished oak floorboards and the rich green, pheasant-print wallpaper. It was hers. All hers!

She'd been dreaming of this moment since she had been a little girl. Every time her family had visited Cockleshell Inn in Whitby for their holidays, she'd told her parents that one day she'd open her own inn. Of course, as she'd grown up, her plans had become a pipe dream and she'd never thought it possible, until she and Harry had divorced and she'd found herself floundering, unsure which direction to take. Well, they said every difficult situation had a silver lining, and this was hers, the opportunity to take a leap of faith.

Two doors opened up from the hallway and she peered into the one on the left, which led into a large sitting room where guests would enjoy the morning papers and a freshly brewed cuppa, filling the time between breakfast and departure, or relax in the evening playing board games with family and friends or reading a novel borrowed from the bookshelf which stretched from one side of the open fireplace to the back wall. The room was even bigger than she remembered, and the large chesterfield sofas arranged in two groups gave guests the choice to mingle or to enjoy a game of Monopoly around one of the oak coffee tables.

Walking across the hallway, she reached the kitchen diner. The dark oak cupboards of the kitchen area complemented the pale yellow walls of the dining area, where four pine tables were positioned. French doors opened onto the decking which surrounded the back of the inn, steps leading down into the vast garden. At the kitchen end, a doorway led into a small utility area equipped with a washing machine, tumble dryer and a short washing line hanging from the ceiling.

As she walked towards the French doors, Laura ran her fingers across one of the pine tables before standing and gazing outside. Yes, she had a lot of work to do, but if she squinted her eyes against the low January sun, she could just about picture how it could look in the summer. She might need to replace the wooden benches and picnic tables which were scattered around the garden, but that would be a worthy investment to allow her guests to enjoy the flowers she would plant, as well as the view of the fields beyond the hedge at the bottom.

As her mobile phone began ringing, its cheerful tone echoing in the large hallway, Laura walked across to the reception... bar? Desk? Counter? – whatever it was called, which filled the space beneath the stairs, and placed the keys down on the dark varnished wooden top before answering. 'Hi.'

'Laura, sweetheart. We've got you on speaker. How's it going? Have you got your keys yet? Are you in?' Her mum, Ruth, fired off a million questions.

Laura smiled. 'Yes, I'm in. I have the keys and I'm in. I have my own inn!'

'Congratulations!'

'Congratulations, Laura!' Her dad's voice echoed down the line.

'Thanks.' Laura nodded. They'd changed their tune.

Her dad, Phil, cleared his throat. 'Look, about this morning, we only have your best interests at heart. You know that, don't you?'

'Yes, your dad's right. We just worry, and as your parents, that's our job.' Ruth's voice softened.

'I know.' Laura sighed. She knew it was only because they

cared about her, but they never questioned Richie's or Jenny's every decision.

'Good. Just as long as you know that what we were saying was out of love. We're proud of you for taking on this huge venture all on your own.'

Laura smiled. She couldn't remember the last time her dad had told her he was proud of her. Probably the morning of her wedding to Harry. Shaking her head, she closed her eyes, pushing all thoughts of Harry from her mind. This was her day, her fresh beginning, and she wasn't about to tarnish it by giving him a second's thought. Opening her eyes again, she looked up at the lovingly cross-stitched sign hanging on the wall above the reception desk – *Welcome to Pennycress Inn*. 'Thanks.'

'I am too, sweetheart. Very proud.'

'Thanks, Mum.' Laura ran her fingers across the wallpaper as she circled the hallway. Pausing, she tried to smooth a bump in the paper which loosened beneath her fingertips and peeled at the join. Oops. She'd have to get some super-strength glue on that.

'And just so you know, we do have a pot of savings we can dip into if you need it.' Her dad's voice had returned to the quiet authoritative tone she knew too well.

'That's right, sweetheart. And your brother and sister won't need to know about it. You can still tell everyone you've done it on your own.' Her mum's voice was hushed, as though Richie or Jenny were right in the next room.

'Yes, our little secret.'

Here we go again. Laura rolled her eyes. Now they could no longer try to convince her to withdraw from the purchase, they were trying to throw money at her instead. 'I don't need your savings. I'm perfectly capable of doing this myself.'

'Of course you are. We know you are. We just want you to remember you have options. That's all, isn't it, Phil?'

'Yes, yes. Options. And if you need to put the place back on the market and come home, then we can cover the mortgage until it sells.'

Laura gritted her teeth as she unfurled another piece of wallpaper she'd noticed was beginning to peel. She lowered her voice, hoping her words sounded more confident than she was currently feeling. 'I don't need you to do that. I know what I'm doing. I didn't go into this lightly. You know how much research I put into it. Besides, Pennycress Inn was up and running until a few months ago. The regulars will be back as soon as I reopen, I'm sure.'

'We're not doubting you. Far from it. We know you're now a strong independent woman. We're just offering a safety net, nothing more, nothing less.' Her mum's voice was kind despite what she was inferring.

'Thanks, but I don't need it. Any of it. I've got this.' Laura jumped back and failed to stifle a scream as a lump of plaster crumbled beneath her fingers and fell to the floor.

'Are you okay? What's happened? Do you need your dad to drive down?' Her mum spoke quickly, her voice full of concern.

'No, no. I just...' Laura looked down at her trainers, a dusting of plaster having turned the black fabric to white, before she focused on the wall again. Tentatively, she pulled the wallpaper back a little more, revealing cracks and dips in the plaster. Why hadn't she noticed this before? During the viewing? Because she'd been so excited at the prospect of owning her very own inn that she'd failed to notice, that's why. Now she'd just have to deal with it herself unless she wanted to give her parents the opportunity to utter those words – 'I told you so'. The words they'd made it clear they expected to say to her. Well, she wouldn't give them the chance. No, she'd show them that they could, they should, believe in her, that she was capable of this. 'I almost dropped my phone, that's all.'

'Okay. Well, we'll be off now. Jenny has just this minute popped over with the twins. Speak soon and remember, if you...' Her mum's voice trailed off as the phone line suddenly filled with excited screeches from Jenny's children and Ruth turned her attention to greet her youngest daughter and grandchildren before returning to the phone. 'Sorry, sweetheart. Jenny wants a quick word.'

'Hi, Jenny.' Taking a step back, Laura tilted her head and perused the wall. Would the problem area be just that little patch of plaster beneath the wallpaper she'd pulled back or would she need to get the whole wall skimmed? Surely it would just be that little patch, wouldn't it?

'Hey, sis, the innkeeper!' Jenny, now in full control of the phone, laughed down the line. 'I can call you that now, can't I? Innkeeper? It just makes you sound so weird – and old!'

'Haha, thanks.' Looking down at her fingers, covered in white plaster, Laura rubbed them together before wiping the powdery crumbs down the leg of her dark blue jeans.

'Everything all right? You sound distracted.'

'Yes, yes. All good.' Taking a step forward again, Laura went to pull back more of the wallpaper before thinking better of it. She'd have a proper look at it later. After the phone call. 'Just taking a look around, that's all.'

'And how is it? Is it—' A child's scream interrupted Jenny's voice, followed by the line going quiet momentarily. 'Sorry about that. Tammy and Toby are hell-bent on trying to kill each other. I blame the fact that Rob woke them up at five this morning when he went to work early.'

'Ouch.'

'Exactly. You did the right thing in choosing to buy an inn rather than having kids.' Exasperation laced Jenny's voice.

'Well, I wouldn't...' What was the point? She knew her younger sister was only venting at her. Jenny was very aware that the decision Laura had had to make hadn't actually been between having children and buying Pennycress. She'd had to decide whether to stay with Harry or not. Having kids with Harry hadn't been the right choice, but having children at all? Well, she'd longed to be a mum ever since she could remember. She sighed. 'That's super early. No wonder the twins are tired. You must be shattered as well.'

'Oh, you've no idea. What Rob forgets is that I've got to work too, in addition to running these two horrors to school and back and entertaining them until he gets home from the office.' Jenny's voice became distant again. She was probably trying to cajole the two six-year-olds into being kind to one another.

'Right, well, I'll let you go now then. It sounds as though you've enough on your plate.'

'Yes, yes. Okay. We'll have to pop by, and you can give us the grand tour. Love you.'

'Love you too.'

Ending the call, Laura perched on the bottom step of the large ornate staircase and tapped the edge of her phone against her palm. She hadn't wanted children with Harry, but she'd wanted them. She still wanted them. She always had. But definitely not with Harry. She hadn't been able to see a future with him for years now. Seven-year itch? Maybe. They'd been married for seven years. Maybe that's why he'd begun to close down, to emotionally shut down their relationship, to push her away.

Yes, about a month before she'd made the move from their marital home and slunk back to her parents' house, he'd suggested they start a family, but she'd known a baby would have only acted as a sticking plaster. And not for long either. Besides, that had been the final nail in the coffin in making her mind up to leave. She'd realised then that he'd been grappling at straws. He'd felt it too. He'd realised their marriage was over as much as she had.

And this place – Pennycress Inn and her vision for it – wasn't *instead* of starting a family. She hadn't even dreamt of running her own business when she'd walked away from her marriage. No, this wasn't a consolation prize, as Jenny suggested. This was the next chapter in her life. She couldn't hang around waiting until her Prince Charming came and rescued her from a life of living back home with her parents and rocking up to her overly dull admin job every day. No, she didn't have that luxury. She was on her own and she had to carve out a life for herself now. She had to be independent. To survive.

Leaning back on her elbows, she looked up at the ceiling. The beams etched with history were every bit as beautiful as she remembered when she'd first viewed the inn. Yes, she was going to be happy here. She just had that feeling.

'Argh!' Laura groaned as she unfolded herself from the dusty sofa in the guest sitting room. Every single bone and muscle in her lower back and legs ached, and she immediately regretted her decision to camp out here instead of staying up late and washing the bedding from the small owners' suite upstairs.

Sitting up, she reached her arms above her head and stretched to one side. Did her back just crack? She wouldn't be surprised, but whatever had just made that noise, she now felt marginally better, so it couldn't have been anything too bad.

She looked across at the large stone fireplace and the oak mantelpiece above. The previous owner really had left everything. A golden carriage clock stood centre stage, flanked by two photo frames holding small sketches of the inn. She hadn't noticed those before. Judging by the lack of foliage and how small the willow tree in the front garden was in the drawings, they must have been created years ago. Perhaps when the previous owner had moved in.

Being new to all of this – owning and running an inn – the fact that Pennycress Inn had been a combined house and contents sale had really been what had swung it for her. The other two properties in the running had been offered unfurnished and she'd felt so out of her depth, facing the prospect of having to buy everything – from the beds the guests would sleep in to the salt and pepper shakers for the tables – that the fact Pennycress was ready to go really had been an opportunity too good to pass up.

After slowly straightening her back, Laura gingerly took a step forward. Yep, washing the bedding had to be first on her list of tasks to do today. After that, she'd take a proper look at the wall in the hallway and assess the situation before making a start at cleaning.

Maybe later she'd even have the chance to sort through the reception desk and see what supplies she needed to buy, as well as taking a look at how the books had been kept. Of course, she'd been given the chance at the viewing to take a cursory look over them, but she hadn't really quite understood what she should have been focusing on. Now, after weeks of research, she thought she'd stand a better chance of truly comprehending them.

Although sinking all her money from the divorce and the sale of their marital home into buying an inn had been a somewhat snap decision, during the time it had taken for the estate agent and solicitors to do their thing, she'd researched the heck out of running a place like this and she was looking forward to putting all of her research into practice. All being well, she'd be welcoming her very own guests to Pennycress Inn by this time next month, giving her the spring months to ease into her new role before the busier summer months, when she'd hopefully have each of the four guest rooms filled continuously, if the information she'd gleaned from the inn's records of the previous years' bookings was anything to go by.

The ringtone of her mobile pierced the silence in the room. Please don't let it be her parents checking in on her again. Picking it up, she slumped her shoulders in relief. It wasn't her parents; it was Richie, her older brother. 'Have Mum and Dad told you to ring me?'

'What? No, of course not. Hi yourself too.' Richie's voice was laced with amusement.

'Sorry. Morning. You can't blame me for assuming. You know what they're like.' Laura relaxed.

'I do. And I suppose I should admit that, yes, they asked me to check how things are going, but I was going to ring to congratulate you on the big move, regardless.'

'Ha, knew it!' Walking through to the hallway, Laura averted her eyes from the problem wall and instead began climbing the stairs, running her hand across the beautiful oak banister as she did. She'd never tire of seeing the intricately carved roses and vines. It reminded her of something out of the fairy-tale castles of her childhood.

'You sound all echoey.'

She grinned as she turned and looked down at the hallway below. 'It's this hallway. It's huge! And beautiful.' Apart from the small pile of crumbled plaster on the floor.

'When do I get my invite, then? It's all been very secretive.'

'Not secretive. Just quick. I needed to get out of my post-divorce rut and change my life, you know that.'

'I do. I'm only teasing you. And I'm happy for you that you're moving on, even if it is in a completely different direction than anything you've ever done before.'

Feeling herself automatically tense, Laura let out a slow, long breath. Richie had always been the perfect image of the big brother. Fiercely protective, always there for her – and also always thinking he knew best. 'I know it is, but I've got this.'

'I know you have. I just want to help, that's all. I...' Richie wavered, obviously trying to decide whether to say what was on the tip of his tongue or not.

Laura walked across the old-fashioned but classic red and gold patterned carpet and pushed open the door to the owners' suite. Here, the luxurious carpet was quickly replaced by a plain cream one, a little threadbare and with intermittent brown and red stains. Coffee and red wine, that's what the previous owner must have been partial to, or that's what she'd tell herself. 'What?'

'I don't know what you mean.'

'Uh-huh. Just get on with it. I can take it, Richie. Tell me what you really want to say.' She blew a loose strand of hair from her face as she eyed up the small queen-sized bed by the window. The whole suite – bedroom area, sitting area and the tiny kitchen to the left – was painted a very boring magnolia and in contrast to the classic and tasteful furniture in the guest bedrooms and downstairs, here the furniture was unmistakably flatpack. And old – not in a good way like the other furniture was, but in the marked and slightly wobbly fashion. Which was fine. Of course it was. She'd be the only person who would see inside this suite, and she could decorate it and update the furniture, in time, once the inn itself was perfect.

'It's nothing bad. All I was going to say was that since you split with Harry, I've been worried about you. We all have. And now you've taken on this enormous project! Well, I just wish you'd have let me and Dad come round to check it out before you'd put an offer in, that's all.'

Yep, just what she thought he was going to spout. 'I'm thirty-eight. I'm more than capable of running my own life and making my own decisions. Besides, you didn't go and view Jenny and Rob's house before they put an offer down.' Standing in front of the window next to the bed, which looked out over the overgrown front garden, Laura braced herself for what was to come.

'Well, Jenny has Rob to look out for her, you don't have...' She could hear him clearing his throat, possibly realising what he'd been about to say.

Quickly walking out of the room, she closed the door to the owners' suite and made her way across the landing to the guest bedroom opposite before looking out of the window towards the large willow tree which grew slap-bang in the middle of the vast back garden. It was bigger than the willow in the front garden, its branches reaching metres across the lawn. A couple of birds flittered from branch to branch before making their way to the hedge hugging the edge of the patio area. She made a mental note to brush up on her wildlife identification skills. She'd need to sound knowledgeable if any of her future guests asked her something about the local flora and fauna.

'Laura? You're not mad at me for worrying about you, are you?'

'Not for worrying, no, but for not trusting my instincts, my decisions, you bet I am.' She exhaled sharply. None of her family believed in her. Everyone else had their lives completely sorted. Jenny had her business, husband, and the gorgeous twins. Richie worked in the City doing some important job in finance – not that she'd ever been able to fully understand what it was he did, but he brought in enough money to support his wife, Jane, and their equally gorgeous children. They'd had their third baby only a couple of months earlier.

Whereas she, Laura, what did she have? She was thirty-eight, the middle child, newly divorced and until recently working in a dead-end, mind-numbing job she'd hated with a passion but had stuck with just to give her parents a pittance for rent and cover her mobile bill. Perching on the edge of the four-poster bed, she coughed as a plume of dust filled the air. When she thought about it like that, who could really blame her family for not trusting her choices?

'I do trust you. We all do...' Richie tailed off, his voice becoming distant before he addressed her again. 'Look, sis, I've got to run, I've got a meeting I need to be in, but believe me, I trust you. It's the other people I don't trust.'

'Bye.' Speaking quietly into the phone, she ended the call. It meant the same thing, didn't it? He'd just admitted he didn't trust her ability to see through people. She hadn't with Harry. She'd married him, believed all the promises he'd made, fallen for the plans he said he had for the two of them, and where had that led? Her having to make the decision to leave him, that's where.

But then, maybe that was where her family's concerns stemmed from. After all, they all still had a soft spot for Harry. Of course, they wouldn't admit it. Not now. They all told her they supported her decision to end the marriage, but whenever his name was brought up or her failed marriage referenced in passing, their unspoken words hung in the air, the confusion as to why she'd walked out.

And it had been Richie, her own brother, who, whilst she'd been on the phone with him in tears at the side of the road after her car had started to smoke because she'd forgotten to refill the leaky water tank, had uttered those words. 'If you'd still been with Harry...' She knew it had been a slip of the tongue, something he'd taken back milliseconds after saying them, but it had given her more than a little insight into how her family felt about her situation – her 'self-imposed' situation.

Shaking herself from her thoughts, she stood up, pocketed her mobile and walked back into the owners' suite to begin stripping the bedclothes off the bed. The best thing she could do to avoid wallowing in self-pity was to get back to her tasks, to focus on building her perfect future running this place.

She grimaced as she bundled the bedding into her arms, the thick dust covering her white T-shirt. How long had Ms Taunton said the inn had been empty for? She couldn't remember, but she hadn't thought it had been long enough for the dust to build up this much.

3

After stuffing the washing machine full, Laura stood and reached for the washing powder, once again thankful that literally everything had been left here for her. It reminded her of one of those old ships she'd learned about in a secondary school History lesson, found bobbing up and down in the ocean, everything seemingly normal except for the small matter that the entire crew had disappeared into thin air. She remembered being told by her favourite teacher, the one who all the kids had looked up to, Mr Hudson, that the people who had boarded the ship had found the tables laid, meals half-eaten and everything in its place. As far as she knew, the crew's disappearance still remained a mystery to this day.

Setting the half-full box of powder back down, she spun the dial and pressed 'start'. Of course, there was no mystery with Pennycress; the owner had merely wanted to hang up her or his innkeeper's apron and retire. Still, however handy it was, Laura had to admit a small part of her found it a little eerie that everything, from personal effects such as ornaments to the more businesslike items such as the pens at the check-in desk, had been left behind for her. Still, it was her gain and perfect for a novice like she was.

Tilting her head, Laura listened. Had she heard something? Yes, there it was again, a weak, intermittent, dainty tune. Was that the doorbell?

Walking out of the utility room and through the large kitchen towards the hallway, she made another mental note, this time to buy some new batteries for the doorbell. She'd need that working properly if she wasn't going to miss any guests turning up.

As she pulled the heavy door open, Laura quickly glanced down at her grubby jeans and T-shirt. This wasn't the first impression she'd been planning on giving to the people of the beautiful Cotswold village of Meadowfield, but it would have to do.

'Hello, I'm so...' Her words trailed off, her first ever greeting in the village halted. It wasn't one of her new neighbours standing on the doorstep ready to welcome her, nor was it some potential guest wondering if she were open. No, the person standing there, mouth agape, was neither of those things.

'*Jackson?*'

'Laura?' She watched as, shaking his head, his dark curls danced above his furrowed forehead.

'What are you doing here?' She flared her nostrils. She knew exactly why Jackson Scott was here. Richie. It obviously hadn't been enough for her brother to ring and quiz her, remind her that he didn't believe in her. He'd sent his best mate round, too.

'I...' Jackson held his hand aloft, a large wicker basket swinging at his hips.

Laura swallowed, her mouth suddenly dry, anger rising from the pit of her stomach. She was a fully grown adult! How many times did she have to remind her parents, her siblings, that she was an independent and capable woman? She didn't need checking up on, keeping tabs on, just like she hadn't needed anyone to view Pennycress Inn with her. She could do this! She began to close the door.

Jackson stubbed his foot against the wooden door, preventing her from shutting the world of disbelievers out, and grinned. 'This is *your* new place, then?'

Glaring down at the large brown boot partially inside her hallway, she looked back up at him, trying to control her voice. The last thing she wanted to do was have a go at him and for him to tell Richie that she was stressed and not coping. Relenting, she threw the door wide again, holding it open with her own foot before crossing her arms. 'Obviously. And you don't have to do this.'

'Do what?'

She waved her hand between them both before tucking it around her middle again. 'This. You and I both know why you're here. We both know who sent you and why.'

Without missing a beat, Jackson answered, 'I'm here because I live in the village. Right next door, as it happens.'

Letting her arms fall to her sides, it was Laura's turn to be left open-mouthed. 'You live next door?'

'Yes.' Twisting on the front step, Jackson indicated the conifers marking the inn's boundary. 'Just beyond there.'

'Seriously?'

'Would you like to see my driver's licence?' Jackson pulled his wallet from his back pocket with his free hand and, with one deft movement, used the same hand to slide his licence out.

'No!' Laura pinched the bridge of her nose. 'But... Richie never said you lived in Meadowfield.'

'Richie doesn't do details. He just knows I live in the Cotswolds.' Jackson shrugged.

True. If it wasn't anything to do with money, numbers or any aspect of finance, Richie's attention span was close to 2.06 seconds long. Nevertheless, this couldn't just be a coincidence. Someone must have known Jackson lived here. He'd basically been part of the family since he and Richie had met in infant school.

Her parents. Maybe they'd put him up to this. Kept it quiet from her that Jackson lived in the same village as Pennycress Inn. They'd have loved it, knowing that she thought she was gaining her independence, doing something totally alone, and yet Jackson lived right next door. She could just imagine them sitting on their sofa grinning and rubbing their hands together in glee that they'd got one over on her, that they could protect her whilst appearing to be the innocent party. 'Typical.'

Shaking his head slightly, Jackson chuckled. 'Thanks for the warm reception.'

'You know what, I've just about had it with my family's games. I really have.' Narrowing her eyes, Laura huffed and went to close the door in his face again.

Placing his palm on the door, Jackson held it open. 'Wow, thanks for that. I come round to do the neighbourly thing and I get the door practically slammed in my face.'

'Ha, that's funny.' He wasn't going to admit it, was he? He wasn't going to admit that he was in on their game. It was clever. She'd give them that. And the fact not even her mum had let anything slip... 'Yep, you just keep that up.'

'You're not even going to take my basket, then?'

Gripping the door handle tight in her fist, Laura tried and failed to suppress her anger, instead feeling it bubble over. This wasn't going to go away, was it? Her parents would continue to do their very best to interfere one way or another, so she might as well let him in, let him report back. She swung it fully open again, flinching as it knocked into the wall and a small slab of plaster fell to the floorboards. Great. 'Go on then, you might as well come on in. I can give you a tour if you like?'

'Okay...' Jackson glanced towards the street behind him before stepping inside and loitering by the open doorway.

'Don't be shy. Here, grab a notebook and pen. You might as well take detailed notes. That way, you won't forget anything. You can even make some sketches. They'd like that, my parents. They were always fans of your artwork.' Reaching across the reception desk, she pulled a notebook and pen from the shelf before holding them out to him, wriggling them in her hand as if to encourage him to take them. She knew she was being childish but she just couldn't help it, the frustration she felt was towards her parents, but they weren't here. He was. All she'd wanted was for them to believe in her, to be proud of something she'd achieved, and yet her new venture was seemingly some sort of game to them.

Stepping forward, Jackson gingerly took the notebook and pen from her, still gripping the basket with his other hand. 'Your parents?' His voice was wary, guarded.

'Yes, that's why you're here, isn't it? And that's why my parents didn't mention you lived here in Meadowfield. You're here to spy, so spy! Feed back to them to your heart's content.' She flung her arms out, encompassing the hallway, the doors, the stairs.

Breaking into a smile, Jackson chuckled.

Pursing her lips, Laura scowled at him. She'd always liked Jackson Scott. She'd even had a stupid teenage crush on him. What she used to see in him, she didn't have a clue. Well... He'd always been there for her. He'd been the one she'd turned to when she'd had her first kiss, and her first broken heart. She'd been too embarrassed to confide in Richie. And Jenny, well, by the time Laura had her first kiss at sixteen, teenage sweethearts Jenny and Rob had already met and fallen in love. Huh, Laura had always been a lousy judge of character by the looks of things.

'You think Richie or your parents have sent me here? Why? To tell them what you're up to?' After placing the notebook and pen on the edge of the reception desk, Jackson rubbed the back of his hand across his eyes.

'You're laughing at me.' Crossing her arms again, Laura leaned against the desk.

'I'm not laughing at you.' Despite trying to keep a straight face, Jackson's mouth quivered.

'You are.' Laura took a deep breath. She could see it in his eyes.

'Okay, okay. I am, but can you blame me? You seriously think your family has sent me round as a spy? How would that even work? You think they bought up the house next door and forced me to move in just so I could keep tabs on their daughter?' Jackson raised his eyebrows.

'No, of course not.' How stupid did he think she was? 'It's obvious that they just didn't tell me you lived in Meadowfield on purpose. They must have been so relieved when I told them I'd put an offer in on Pennycress and not on any of the other places I was looking at.' She shook her head. 'What would they have done then? Ha, probably have tried to put me off the idea of running an inn all together.'

'Well, you're wrong. They didn't put me up to this. They haven't asked me to spy on you. Jeez, I've not even seen Richie since I moved and...' Jackson let out a small sigh. 'And I bet that's why I didn't get your parents' usual Christmas card: I forgot to tell them I was moving too.'

Laura watched as he swapped the basket to the other hand. Had she misjudged him? Jumped to the wrong conclusion because of how her parents were making her feel?

'I know your parents are overprotective and all, especially now you're single, but still, it would seem a little extreme to have someone follow you around.'

Feeling a blush course up her neck, Laura looked down. 'Richie told you my marriage was over?'

'Richie told me you left that eejit, yes.'

'I thought he liked Harry.' Laura frowned.

'He does. It's me that calls him an eejit.' Jackson gave a quick grin, mischief lighting his blue eyes.

'Huh.' Laura nodded slowly, her anger suddenly seeping away.

'Do you believe me now?'

'I guess.' Laura shrugged. But if her parents really hadn't orchestrated this whole situation, then she'd literally just moved in next door to Jackson. What were the chances of that? 'So, this *is* just some crazy coincidence?'

'It seems to be, yes.' Jackson looked down at the basket before holding it out towards her. 'And this is the real reason I stopped by, to welcome my new neighbour with a food hamper.'

'Thanks.' Mumbling, Laura stepped forward and took the basket, which was heavier than Jackson had made it look, before placing it on the counter. 'Sorry about—'

'No need to apologise.' Taking a step towards her, Jackson held his arms out. 'Does Richie's sis still have a hug for me?'

'Haha, always.' Sinking into Jackson's bear hug, she wrapped her arms around him, breathing in the familiar earthy aftershave. He'd not changed in that department then. His hugs were still the best. Stepping back from the embrace, Laura shrugged. 'Sorry again for jumping to conclusions – and thanks for the hamper.'

'No worries.' Nodding, Jackson walked towards the front door, pausing before stepping outside. He indicated the fallen plaster. 'I can pop by and take a look at that for you, if you like? I'm on shift this afternoon, but I'm free tomorrow morning.'

'It's all under control. Thanks.'

'Okay.' Frowning, Jackson held his hand up in a wave. 'See you around then.'

After watching him walk down the garden path, she shut the door firmly behind him before making her way across to the reception desk and sinking her chin to her elbows. However nice it was to see Jackson again, this had been her new start and with him living next door – next door! – how was she supposed to assert her independence and show the world she was a capable adult, with him right there breathing down her neck? How was she supposed to prove herself to her parents? To Richie? To Jenny?

She glanced back at the door. To Harry?

Everyone would just think Jackson was helping her. They still wouldn't believe in her. And she needed that. After the divorce and being forced to move back into her parents' house, after her world falling apart, she needed people to see her for who she really was again. She'd had enough of the pity, of the treading on eggshells; she was ready to be herself again, to build herself back up. To be better, to show everyone she could do it, that she didn't need to rely on others. On anyone.

But Jackson was here. And, by suggesting he pop by to fix the plaster, he was already offering to help.

Forcing herself to open the basket, she had to admit the aroma of freshly baked food was enticing at least, and a definite plus of having a chef as your neighbour. She rooted through the basket, pulling out and lining up the various home-baked gifts. Still, all the lavender shortbread or cheese and jalapeño rolls in the world wouldn't make up for the fact that her dream of a fresh start away from anyone and everyone she knew had been crushed.

4
───────

The bedding! Laura had forgotten to pop it in the tumble dryer. Shoving the last of Jackson's lavender shortbread into her mouth, she made her way into the utility room as the buttery goodness melted against her tastebuds. Good job she'd remembered, or she'd have been sleeping on the sofa again tonight.

Looking around, she located a washing basket in a tall cupboard by the sink. She'd had quite a productive day in the end. After spending the morning scrubbing and cleaning the owners' suite upstairs, she'd begun unpacking her clothes. It hadn't taken too long – the unpacking part anyway. After all, she'd not brought that much: a couple of bin bags full of clothes, a box of books and her parents' battered old suitcase holding trinkets and such – photo frames of her late grandparents, pictures of family from her childhood and a photograph of her and her family on the day of the twins' Christening – about the only image she owned of herself with her siblings and parents which didn't also have Harry in.

She sighed. Maybe she shouldn't have agreed Harry could keep so many of the possessions they'd accumulated over the seven years of marriage and three before that of living together, but after cohabiting alongside him in the house which had once been their home whilst it was on the market and then in the months it actually took for the couple who had put an offer in to complete their chain, she'd grown to associate the once-cherished items with indifference, contempt even.

The dining table and chairs which they'd finally sourced after traipsing around at least ten different flea markets and they'd both spent two weekends restoring had suddenly transformed from somewhere they'd sit around hosting dinner parties, playing cards or sketching out designs for the garden to the surface upon which she'd filed for divorce, the place she'd sit for hours in the evenings, reading, attempting crosswords, anything to avoid venturing into the sitting room to sit in stilted silence with the man she'd once loved as he flicked from TV channel to TV channel obviously feeling just as awkward in her company as she was in his. The sofa they'd spent evening after evening cuddled up on chatting about the holiday they'd take next year or simply engrossed in a movie or TV series had changed from a comfortable sanctuary to where she had told Harry their marriage was over, where she'd later sought her parents' approval of her decision and was instead met with the realisation they thought she was making a mistake.

No, she'd made the right decision, she'd needed this fresh start, not to be surrounded by inanimate objects which reminded her of a time she'd rather leave in her past.

After placing the washing basket on the floor in front of the machine, she rubbed at her eyes. Even just thinking about the items she could have brought with her caused the familiar sting of tears in her eyes. At the time, it had made sense for Harry to take charge of the household goods. He'd moved into his flat, she into her parents' house. She'd have only had to pay to store it all.

Pushing all thoughts of that strange, murky period of transition between marriage and divorce from her mind, Laura tugged on the washing machine door, pulling until the latch released before shrieking and jumping back. Water cascaded down the front of the machine, pooling on the floor beneath her feet. Shaking water from her now drenched socks, she bent down and reached inside the drum, emptying the bedding into the wash basket. It was sodden. Literally sodden. Looking down, she watched the water seep from the bedlinen through the holes of the plastic basket, joining the puddle on the tiles before she piled it back into the washing machine again.

It obviously hadn't spun. Stepping out of the puddle, Laura tore off her soaking-wet socks and ran through to the kitchen to grab the towel before making an attempt to mop it up.

With the floor now a little drier, she turned her attention back to the machine. She just needed to put it on a quick spin and then she could still get everything dried in time for bed. There: she turned the dial to the spin cycle and jabbed the 'start' button again.

Standing back, she watched the machine splutter to life with a groan. Hmm, it still wasn't spinning. It was making all the right noises as it tried to empty the water, but the drum wasn't moving an inch.

Okay, she'd seen this before. The belt must have broken. Her parents' machine had stopped spinning just after she'd moved back into their house and her dad had managed to fix it himself. All she needed was a new belt and a screwdriver to get the back of the machine off. She could do that.

Not tonight, though. The village may be a treat for tourists, but everything but the local pubs and restaurants closed at five. Yes, after another night curled up on the sofa, she might regret not making the twenty-minute car trip to the nearest retail park and DIY shop, but right now her muscles were aching after all the cleaning, and besides, it would be nice to have a wander into the centre of the village tomorrow. She'd be able to meet some local residents and maybe grab lunch somewhere too. Yes, an early night and an early start tomorrow.

* * *

Lifting her head, Laura looked around the room. With her eyes dazed from sleep and the room dark, all she could make out were shapes and shadows and it took her a moment to realise the noise that had woken her hadn't been in her dream. An almighty continuous splashing noise almost silenced the pounding of rain against the windows. It sounded just as though someone was standing next to the sofa pouring bucketful after bucketful of water down around her.

Another minute passed, and it dawned on her that the noise must be coming from outside. The guttering must be broken or something, causing the rain to run in torrents down the window before splashing onto the ground below.

Turning over, she covered her head with a cushion, hoping to dull the sound, and closed her eyes again. *Just another hour. Please.*

* * *

Laura pulled her coat on before checking the large clock behind the reception desk for the seventh time in as many minutes. It had to be almost nine now. Yes, quarter to. The shops must be opening soon. She'd have fifteen minutes to amble the short way into the centre of the village and locate a hardware store, or anywhere that might sell a washing machine belt. Hopefully they'd have one and she wouldn't regret the decision she'd made yesterday to support local businesses rather than just ordering online or going to a chain store.

She rubbed the top of her arms, relieving a little of the ache from her muscles. After being woken once again by the rain gushing through the broken guttering at about half past three and lying awake staring into the darkness of the sitting room, she'd given up trying to fall back to sleep, even when the rain did stop. Instead, she'd begun deep cleaning the bathrooms, a task which had felt like a good idea at the time but which now she was regretting due to the aches and pains of reaching into the top cupboards combined with sleeping on the sofa.

Stepping outside, she locked the front door before turning and pausing on the porch. With the rain having relented at about four in the morning and the low morning sun trying to make an appearance between the dark clouds, it really was rather beautiful. Or else she could see that it would be. At the moment, the garden resembled a mud bath with a thin covering of grass that had seen better days, punctuated by the silvery lavender bushes and dark green ground ivy. Now that would be a pain to remove. A sheen of rainwater glistened across the cobbled driveway to the side of the inn, leading to the small car park around the back, but she could visualise what it could – what it *would* – look like. With a little work and a lot of perseverance, she could make it beautiful again.

She walked down the broken slabs of the garden path, wrapping her scarf around her neck as her ankles brushed past the lavender stalks. Pennycress Inn might be a little more run-down than she remembered from her viewing, but that didn't matter. It was still a stunning building and gardens and the amount she'd paid for it made it a positive steal.

Closing the wrought-iron garden gate behind her, she turned right and began her walk towards the cluster of shops huddled around the village green at the centre of Meadowfield. Slowing down to a snail's pace, she looked at Jackson's house next door. It was a lot smaller than Pennycress. Obviously it would be, Pennycress had undergone extensive alterations and extensions over the years to convert it into an inn and had grown to accommodate the increasing number of guests, whereas it looked as though Jackson's house might well have the original footage. It looked well-kept, though. From the immaculately cut lawn and tended hedges to the freshly painted front door and window frames, it was a million miles away from the condition of Pennycress.

Catching a glimpse of movement in one of the upstairs windows, Laura hurriedly looked down at the ground. The last thing she wanted was for him to think she was watching him. Or worse, dropping by to take him up on his offer of help.

Laura pulled her mobile from her back pocket and scrolled through to Richie's name before pressing the Call button. 'Hey, Richie.'

'Sis. Twice in two days? Well, I'm honoured.' Richie's voice was punctuated by noises around him. 'I'm just about to get on the Tube so I can't promise you I won't cut out.'

'No worries. It was only a quick thing, anyway.' She took a deep breath. She knew she should let it lie. She was ninety-nine-point-nine per cent sure Jackson had been telling the truth yesterday, but she just wanted to be sure. 'Do you know where Jackson is living now?'

'Jackson? Somewhere in the Cotswolds, I think. He moved sometime in the autumn. Why?' A loud beep sounded as the Tube door closed. 'Hey, you could give him a call. His new place might not be far from you.'

He didn't know then. Jackson *had* been telling the truth; she hadn't been set up. 'It's not.'

'No? That's brilliant. How far away is he from the inn?'

'Let's put it this way. I could probably throw a stone from my front porch and break his window. Pay him back for smashing the glass on Dad's greenhouse.' Laura grinned. Now that had been a fun weekend. Jackson had spent the weekend at their house, as he often had to get away from his parents, and after a particularly lively game of football with a half-rotten potato their dog, Rufus, had dug up from the vegetable patch, they'd spent the rest of the time trying to prevent their dad from doing the one thing he loved most to do of a weekend – gardening – in the hope that they could enjoy the time off school before he uncovered the damage and punished them. As it happened, their plan failed, and they'd spent the Sunday knee-deep in manure and bulbs.

'Ha, seriously? He lives opposite you?'

'Next door,' Laura mumbled.

'Next door? No way! What are the odds of that?' Richie's contagious chuckle filled the line.

'Yes, next door.' She supposed it was quite funny and maybe she'd be able to see it that way soon. Infuriating at the same time, mind. She had still been robbed of her fresh start, but maybe she'd be able to come up with a solution, even if she didn't have a clue what that could be.

'You sound annoyed.'

She took a deep breath, he'd asked, so she'd just have to tell him. 'Honestly? I am. This was my chance to make a new life for myself. To prove to myself and everyone else that I could do this. That I can turn my pitiful existence around and cope on my own. I—'

'Take a breath, sis. You don't need to prove yourself to anyone.'

'I do, though, don't I?' She fixed her gaze on a tree ahead, its twisted branches almost touching the car parked on the side of the road beneath it. 'You and Jenny both have your lives sorted – like, really sorted. You're both married, got gorgeous children and jobs or businesses. And then there's me. I lived my life for Harry, didn't give a crap about working my way up the career ladder and now here I am.'

'Yes, there you are. You've just bought an inn!'

'A decision that no one supported me in.' She hated voicing it, accusing him, but it was true. No one had. Every single person she'd spoken to about her idea had tried their best to talk her out of it – her family, her friends, heck, even Bob who ran the local chippie back home had basically told her that running an inn would be a money pit and too difficult to do on her own.

'We do support you. It's just such a huge task for you to take on alone, that's all. We're just looking out for you. That's all.'

'I know. I just wish you believed in me. There was never any of this when Jenny told everyone she'd decided to quit her job and use her cooking skills to start up her own business making organic dog food. That was a huge decision for her, a huge risk, and yet everyone sang her praises for taking the leap.' She sounded like a whining child even to her own ears, but it was how she felt and she'd been bottling it up ever since sharing her dream.

'That was completely different. You know it was.'

'Umm, I don't see how. Apart from the fact that Jenny's old job used to pay really well, whereas mine paid a pittance. Surely, she had more to lose than me and yet everyone encouraged her.' She felt like crossing her arms and pouting as it all came out, instead she stuck her free hand in her coat pocket.

'After running the logistics in her old job, Jenny had the skill set. She knew what she was doing, whereas...' Richie grew quiet.

Laura could feel her face redden. So that's what everyone really thought then. They had supported Jenny's decision because they'd believed she'd known what she was doing, because they'd believed she was capable of building her own brand. But her?

Nobody thought she was capable of doing anything remotely successful.

'And Jenny had Rob's wage to fall back on,' Richie mumbled.

'Don't try to backtrack now, Richie. I've heard it all.'

'Hey, Laura, wait, let me explain—' The line cut out.

5

Laura held her mobile away from her and stared at the screen. The call had been cut off. The train must have gone through a tunnel or something. Well, good. She didn't need that negativity in her life. She didn't need any of her family's negativity. They could keep it and she'd show them. She'd show them she could do it. She'd open Pennycress Inn and the guests would flood in. Business would be good. She'd be a success. She would.

'Hey, wait up.'

Jackson.

With her heart sinking, she stopped walking and turned around. Maybe he wouldn't be so easy to avoid after all.

'Morning.' As he jogged up to her, he gave her one of those killer grins which would have had the teenage Laura buckling at her knees.

'Hi.'

'How's life as an innkeeper treating you so far?' He pulled his dark blue rucksack higher on his shoulder as she began walking again and he matched her pace.

She shrugged. 'Okay.'

'Only okay? Aren't you supposed to still be feeling the lofty high of moving and buying your own business?' He looked over at her.

'Yes, I mean it's great.' She held up her mobile. 'But I've just been on the phone to Richie.'

'Oh really? I've been meaning to catch up with him for a couple of months now. By the sounds of it, he's knee-deep in nappies and toddlers.' Jackson chuckled.

'Yes. That and working in London. He got promoted a couple of weeks ago, so...' She shrugged.

'I didn't ask yesterday, but how are your parents? And Jenny? I keep meaning to join you all for one of your mum's monthly roast dinner events, but what with my shifts and other stuff...' He shrugged. 'I take it she still does them? That she still guilt trips you all into going home for dinner on the first Sunday of every month?'

Laura nodded. Her mum had always been a stickler for tradition and her 'rule' of making a large roast for the family on the first Sunday the month had been going ever since Richie had moved out when he'd been nineteen.

'I hope I've finally been forgiven for breaking away?' Jackson gave a quick smile.

'Ah, yes, that was quite the scandal.' Laura remembered when Jackson had first started going out with his long-term girlfriend, Angie, who had been more into weekend country retreats than travelling to rainy Lincolnshire to sit around a table with a family who weren't hers or Jackson's. 'Nobody dares utter the name Angie around my mum to this day.'

'Ha.' Jackson looked upwards as the sky grumbled, reminding them that thunder was forecast.

'I'll have to pop by and say hi to her.' Not that she wanted to.

She'd rather run a million marathons than have a cuppa with the snooty Angie.

'That'll be a tad difficult seeing as she's currently thousands of miles away.' Jackson grimaced. 'She got a transfer with her job to the US about eight months ago.'

'Oh, right. And you didn't go with her? I would have thought that'd be right up your street, having the opportunity to travel and live abroad?' She turned to him as his jaw flexed. They'd been dating for what? At least three years and she'd never seen Jackson quite so besotted with a woman before. Plus, he'd always spoken about travelling. Something must have happened.

'No. We weren't right for each other in the end, and besides, I had other responsibilities.' Jackson pointed across the road to the whitewashed pub with a battered old sign swinging in the breeze. 'That's me. That's where I work. Pub chef, bartender and general dogsbody until we get some more staff. See you around.'

'Ah okay. Yep, see you.' He was still a chef then but by the sounds of it, Angie moving away had set him on a different path too. Much like her with the divorce.

Giving him a quick wave, Laura turned in the opposite direction towards the village green and the shops. Yes! There was a hardware store. Perfect.

She glanced across the road as Jackson disappeared through the pub door. He'd tell her if he wanted to.

The bell above the door tinkled loudly, announcing her arrival, and she watched as the handful of people in the store turned and looked at her. Smiling broadly, she walked down the first aisle of racking displaying tools and other DIY paraphernalia. Here, these looked as though they were washing machine belts. She picked one up and turned it over, catching the eye of the man standing behind the counter, his arms folded as he sported an array of wood shavings in his beard. She could ask him for help.

Grabbing two different packs from the small silver hooks, Laura made her way towards the counter.

'Excuse me, please?'

As soon as she'd started to speak, the man turned, apparently oblivious to her question and to her presence, and called towards an elderly couple who had just walked in. 'Janette, Pat, over here. Your new mop head came in with yesterday's delivery.'

'Oh, lovely. We were hoping it would have, weren't we, Pat?' The woman turned to Pat as he closed the door behind them, the bell tinkling again.

'Yes, yes. Especially after having Susan's boys over yesterday.' Pat nodded as they began walking towards the counter.

'That's right, what a mess they decided to make.' Janette shook her head.

Laura shifted from foot to foot as she watched this exchange. The man behind the counter – Neil Parsons, if his name badge was to be believed – suddenly appeared to be very interested in Janette and Pat's kitchen floor as they detailed every little thing that Susan's boys had spilt on it yesterday. She forced herself to hold her smile and reminded herself that these were her neighbours, fellow villagers, and she wanted to make a good impression rather than hurrying them up and cutting into their conversation. Still, it was crazy that she was standing close enough to the counter to be able to read Neil's name badge and yet he was acting as though he hadn't laid eyes on her, let alone watched her walk over towards him.

'Thanks again, Neil. You're one of the good ones.' Janette took the now-bagged mop head from Neil before looking pointedly at Laura and turning back to her husband.

Stepping forward, Laura placed both the belts on the counter, waiting there for a full two minutes before clearing her throat.

Neil slowly turned to her and raised his eyebrows.

'Could you help me with these, please? I'm not sure which one I need.' Laura picked up the two packets from the counter.

'No idea.' Shrugging, Neil picked up a pen and began scribbling on a notepad.

'It's for my washing machine.' Could she have said anything else to sound more incompetent? Of course it was for her washing machine. She wasn't likely to buy a washing machine belt to hang a picture from, now was she? 'I have a photo of the machine...'

Sighing heavily, Neil looked at her. 'Are you going to buy them or not?'

Frowning, Laura slumped her shoulders. Why had he been the perfect shopkeeper with the couple who had come in and yet he really couldn't be bothered to even try to answer her question? She pulled her purse from her bag. 'I'll just take them both, please?'

Once Neil had slid the change across the counter, she mumbled a quick 'thank you' and left, relief sweeping over her as she stepped outside into the cold.

Well, that hadn't exactly been a welcoming start to village life. Still, maybe he had assumed she had been a passer-by or something, someone he obviously felt he didn't need to try to assist in any possible way.

On the plus side, she had her washing machine belt – two of them in fact, so one must fit. She'd be able to spin the bedding before putting it in the tumble dryer and fixing the guttering. From what she had tried to work out, the problem was above the bay window, and if she was lucky, it would only be blocked or need to be clipped back together – an easy fix and one she'd seen her dad do a dozen times in the past.

As she walked past the village bakery, her stomach rumbled, reminding her she'd skipped breakfast. Turning towards the window, she looked at the delicately decorated cupcakes, the over-flowing cream doughnuts and the thickly covered chocolate flapjack. She'd deserve a treat after fixing the guttering, and all of the lavender shortbread Jackson had left yesterday had somehow disappeared.

This time, the door buzzed as she entered, the warmth and aroma of freshly baked bread and cookies pulling her in. Letting the door swing closed behind her, Laura scanned the room. A long bakery counter lined one wall with a handful of tables and chairs squeezed into the back of the shop. The yellow decor and lovingly painted canvases of the front of the bakery and a selection of bakery goods made it inviting and cosy.

Laura smiled as she stepped up to the counter and began studying the baked treats behind the glass. If she didn't have so much to get done at the inn, she'd have been tempted to sit down and order a bacon buttie. But now she was living in the village, she could do that any time. Maybe she could even make it a weekly treat for herself, or else once the inn was open, she could bring some paperwork here and set herself up on a table in the corner for a couple of hours. She grinned at a woman sitting at one of the tables tapping away on her laptop. It looked like a nice, relaxing atmosphere.

'Can I help you?' The woman behind the counter took Laura by surprise with her curt tone.

'Yes, please. Could I have… umm…' What was it she wanted?

The door buzzed again, announcing a new arrival, and the woman behind the counter held her hand up to wave, her face lighting up with a friendliness which had been absent when Laura had walked in.

Glancing from the woman behind the counter to the mum and small child who had just entered, Laura felt hurried and pointed towards a cupcake. 'I'll take one of those, please? Thought

I'd treat myself before the thunderstorm comes.' She laughed nervously, trying to lighten the mood.

Without saying a word, the woman passed the cupcake to Laura and as soon as Laura had tapped her card against the machine; she turned towards the woman and child. 'Morning, you two. What can I get you both today?'

Taking her cupcake, bag not included, Laura headed towards the door, listening to the two women chatting and laughing. She closed the door quietly behind herself before heading out of the centre of the village towards the inn. Was she being paranoid or were people being hostile towards her? She certainly wasn't getting the warm welcome she'd hoped for from the village community.

She wiped a fingerful of pink icing from her cake and licked it off. She was being paranoid. As if people would shun her on purpose. But the cold reception she'd received in both the hardware store and the bakery hadn't been her imagination. She was sure of that. Did the village community just hate outsiders? That was a thing, wasn't it? You heard about places like that. Trust her to have chosen this particular small village in the Cotswolds above every other place.

Gently pulling the paper casing from the cake, Laura bit into it. It was good. So good. Almost worth going in there again and facing the same cold welcome.

A loud guffaw of laughter caught her attention, and she glanced across the road towards the pub. Jackson was there standing in the doorway chatting to another man, telling jokes by the looks of the other man's reaction and loud laughter.

So Jackson had settled in okay then and been accepted. He'd only moved in just before Christmas, hadn't he? Maybe the villagers were quick at accepting newcomers after all then. Maybe she wouldn't have to withstand the chilly atmosphere for long before the ice would begin to thaw.

Yes, people were just wary. Just like when someone new started at work. People would be eyeing them up, making sure they were a good fit. Things would settle. Besides, it wasn't as though she had time to socialise at the moment and wouldn't for the foreseeable future. Once the inn was up and running again and she had a bit of time to join a book club or a craft group or something, then people would get to know her. They would be happy for her to join. She just needed to give them time. That was all.

6

Laura jammed the legs of the ladder she'd found in the shed into the wet mud and leaned it against the wall of the bay window before gripping it and giving it a shake.

Yep, that was solid. It wasn't going anywhere. She looked up. It was still a long way up to be able to reach the guttering. Twelve rungs of the ladder, at least.

She shook her head. That wasn't high. Heck, it had always been her job to go up into the loft because Harry had been absolutely petrified of the enclosed space and, of course, his claustrophobia had trumped her fear of heights every single time. She could do this. She needed to so she could show herself she could at least do something.

Looking down at the grease covering the front of her T-shirt, she sighed. After getting back from her walk into the village centre, she'd attempted to fix the washing machine, but even after scrolling through hundreds of YouTube videos and following at least a dozen strong men demonstrating how easy and simple it was to change a belt, she still hadn't been able to succeed. After two and a half hours of stretching the thing and placing it in what looked to be the correct position, each and every time she'd turned the machine on again, the damn belt had sprung straight back off. She'd tried both. And both belts had been a complete waste of money.

Just as she began to climb the ladder, her mobile rang out and she jumped down and pulled it from her pocket. 'Hello?'

'Afternoon, this is Washing Machine Repairs Limited. I'm returning your call.' A gravelly voice filled her ear.

'Oh great! Thanks for ringing back. The belt on my washing machine has broken and needs replacing. I've given it a go, but to be honest, I don't have a clue what I'm doing and could really do with some help.' Her knight in shining armour had returned her call! After her dismal failure at attempting to fix the thing, she'd given in and rung for professional help.

'No problem. Should be an easy fix.'

'Fantastic. Thank you! I don't suppose you have any time free today, do you? I could really do with getting it up and running.'

'Absolutely, not an issue. In fact, I have an hour late afternoon I could fit you in. What's your address and I'll pop by?'

'Amazing.' Laura grinned. She might just be able to get a good night's sleep tonight after all. 'It's Pennycress Inn, down Wisteria Lane in Meadowfield.'

'Pennycress Inn, you say?'

'Yes, that's right. Thank you so much for fitting me in so quickly. I really appreciate it.' Laura looked at the ladder, feeling all the more determined to fix that gutter so she could have a night of peace cocooned in a clean bed.

'I'm so sorry, but I'm not going to be able to help you.'

'What? Why? Sorry, I mean, I thought you just said you could.' Her heart sank.

'No, I've been looking at the wrong day. Fully booked today, I'm afraid.' Was it her imagination or had his tone changed? Gone was the friendly voice who had rung her, instead he sounded distant, dismissive and a little curt.

'Oh, what about tomorrow? That will be fine.' It would have to be.

'Nope, not tomorrow either. In fact, I'm pretty much booked up for the time being. Sorry.'

'But...' It was no good. The line was silent. He'd hung up. Great.

Turning around, she perched on the third rung of the ladder and pulled up the internet, scrolling through to another local plumber's number. The company wasn't based in Meadowfield but was still only a few miles down the road.

'Hello, Utility Services. How can I help you?' The woman on the other end of the phone sounded cheery.

'Hi, do you fix washing machines please?'

'We certainly do. Can I ask what the problem seems to be?'

Phew, the day wasn't over yet. 'Yes, it's the belt. It's snapped.'

'Great, that's half the battle knowing what the issue is. If you give me your address, I can get someone out to you by this evening.'

'Thank you. It's Pennycress Inn, Wisteria...' Laura paused and listened to a series of mumbles. It sounded as though the woman was having a conversation with someone else. 'Hello?'

'I'm sorry. There are no appointments left.'

'Okay...' Shaking her head, Laura ended the call before ringing the next repair company on the internet search list. Something wasn't right here.

'Afternoon, Village and Town Repairs and Services.'

'Hi, can I book for a washing machine belt to be fixed at Pennycress Inn, Meadowfield—'

'Sorry, we've no appointments available.'

Jabbing the End Call button, Laura pinched the bridge of her nose. What on earth was going on here? Did no one out there want to earn money by fixing a washing machine belt? It wouldn't take long for someone who knew what they were doing, she knew that. She remembered it had only taken her dad a few minutes, so it wasn't as though it was one of those tricky jobs that no one wants to do, so why wouldn't anyone come out and help her?

A large raindrop landed on her phone, and she watched it roll down the now blank screen before pooling at the edge along the rim of her phone case. Great. She really needed to get a wriggle on and sort that guttering before the clouds opened again. Wiping her phone dry on the leg of her jeans, she placed it in her back pocket before thinking better of it and pulling it out and setting it on the ground by the foot of the ladder. Knowing the way her luck was going today, it'd fall right out of her pocket as she was climbing and then she wouldn't even have a phone to research and ring another repair company. After all, there must be one who had availability and would be willing to help.

Checking the ladder was still stable, she began to climb, forcing herself not to look down and to focus on the rung above her. She was hardly off the ground. The most damage she'd do if she fell now would be to twist her ankle. Or break her back. That was possible, wasn't it? To just land funny and end up with the most awful, unrecoverable injuries?

Gritting her teeth, Laura continued to climb. She was letting her fear of heights run away with her and she needed to focus. She needed to remember why she was doing this... for a good night's sleep. Everything felt better after a good night's sleep. Heck, maybe she'd be able to tackle the washing machine again and actually fix it. There'd be no stopping her.

There, she'd been right. The two lengths of guttering had become unclipped. An easy fix. Taking a deep breath and holding herself very still, she released her hands from the death grip on the ladder and held on to the guttering, manoeuvring each piece to try to clip them back together.

Yes! Done. She'd done it. She'd actually fixed something herself. A large grin spread across her face. She could do this. She could maintain and open the inn. She literally could. She'd show all the doubters. She relished the feeling of pride washing over her.

Just as she was about to begin the descent back down onto solid ground, she looked across the top of the bay window. It looked as though one of the tiles was loose right against the wall. It was sticking up a little and at a funny angle. That would need sorting before it started to let in rain. The last thing she wanted was for a guest to be lounging in the sitting room below and get a big, fat raindrop on their head, or worse the ceiling to come down. Now, that wouldn't be good for business. Not at all.

Taking another step up the ladder, Laura stretched her right arm out towards the tile. Nope, it was no good. She couldn't reach it. Keeping her eyes fixed on the tile, she took another step up the ladder before pulling herself up onto the roof of the bay. The tiles were cold beneath her hands and slippery from the downpour last night, but she'd made it this far and had fixed the guttering all by herself and this was just the next thing. If she could inch across the roof towards the loose tile, she'd likely be able to slip it back into position.

Easy.

She bent her knee and swung her left leg over the top of the ladder and onto the roof, clinging with her hands to the good tiles and using the grips on the soles of her trainers to secure herself. She probably wouldn't even need to hoist herself all the way up. If she just leaned a little further, she'd be able to reach the tile with her other leg still on the ladder. It would take ten seconds at the most. Probably five.

As she reached out again, a loud noise from below startled her and she froze. There it was again, something thudding against the ground, the swish of plants being parted. What was it?

Turning, she caught her breath as she looked over the edge of the roof towards the ground below, something she'd promised herself she wouldn't do. She inhaled deeply as she tried to fight the dizziness of disorientation, but how she felt wasn't what worried her the most...

What on earth?

No.

She closed her eyes, squeezing them tight before opening them again. Huh, her mind hadn't been playing tricks on her. It was a sheep. A white fluffy cloud barging its way across her garden, leaving a trail of destruction behind – a hole in the hedge, trodden-down lavender and muddy hoofprints on the path. A length of ground ivy trailed behind the sheep, having got itself caught on its woollen fleece.

What was worse was that it was heading this way. Right towards the ladder.

As fear gripped her stomach, Laura shouted out, a strange, strangled noise escaping her lips before she could form coherent words. 'Oi, away! Go!'

What was it doing? Was it going? She couldn't see it now. She'd lost sight of it. It must have found its way out of the garden.

Just as she exhaled the breath she'd been holding, she watched with horror as the ladder tilted and the leg which was still standing on it was tugged outwards. Pulling her leg up onto the roof, she watched as the top of the ladder disappeared from view and listened to the clatter as it fell to the ground.

Her scream got caught in her throat as she watched the sheep race out of the garden, back the way it had come. Whilst lying down, keeping as much of her body against the roof as she possibly could, Laura slowly slid her way across to the edge and peered over the now-fixed gutter and ladderless wall.

There it was, lying on the ground, a mixture of lavender and ivy poking up through the spaces between the rungs of the metal ladder. And the ten-foot drop to reach it.

What now? What was she supposed to do? With her knuckles turning white, she leaned further over the edge. It wasn't so far down. And she'd land in the garden if she were to fall. It would be a relatively soft landing compared to the decking, which began on the other side of the front door and wrapped its way around to the back of the inn. And at least the earth would be soft after all the rain.

No, what was she thinking? She couldn't just jump down there. She couldn't even lower herself over. She just couldn't bring herself to. Who would? She'd just have to... What? Ask for help? Ring someone? Who? Jackson?

She scoffed. Nope, that was off the cards. If she asked him for help, she'd never live it down when her family found out. And they would. Richie would likely ring Jackson now he knew he lived next door to her just to get the gossip, to find out how she was coping, and then it would filter through the family, and everyone would nod in agreement because they had known she'd taken on too much. And they'd be right, they'd told her she wouldn't be able to cope.

Nope. Not Jackson. Who then? A local company? A window cleaning business, perhaps? She could ask them for an urgent clean and when they got here, they'd be able to rescue her. Or anyone, for that matter. She could ring anyone. She had the ladder. She just needed someone to prop it back up. It would literally take a matter of seconds. Heck, she could see the ladder...

She groaned. And her phone. She could see her phone, the

corner of the bright orange case peeking out from beneath one rung of the ladder.

So not only did she not have her phone on her – why had she left it down there? – she also now probably had a cracked screen. Great. Absolutely great. What else could possibly go wrong today?

A low rumble filled the air as a large raindrop splattered her square on the back of the neck.

Rain. And thunder. That was what else could go wrong.

Sliding her body towards the wall, she gripped the window ledge above her head and pulled herself into a sitting position before bringing her knees up to her chest. Now, if only the wind was blowing in the other direction, the wall behind her would offer some protection, but as it was, the wind was blowing the rain right into her face. She'd be soaking wet in less than five minutes. And so would the tiles, making them even more slippery than they currently were.

She was so stupid. Why had she thought she could do this? Despite the cold, her cheeks burned with embarrassment. Everyone would soon discover she was as useless as she'd always known she was. She swiped her eyes with her sleeve as her tears mixed with the rain. She'd failed before she'd even opened the place.

Lowering her head to her knees, she closed her eyes. She knew she was feeling sorry for herself, but she couldn't help it. Who wouldn't if they were in her position – stranded on the roof in the middle of a thunderstorm with no way of getting down and little chance of anyone turning up to help?

The only thing she could do now was to wait and hope the postman passed by or a delivery driver got lost and meandered down the garden path. She curled her shoulders, making herself as small as she possibly could and shielding as much of her body against the now pelting rain. She should have worn her coat;

she'd been chilly when she'd started this mission, but she'd thought it would just get in the way and that it would be safer not to have it on in case it got caught on the ladder. Well, now she had no coat, no ladder and no phone.

The rain slid from her hair beneath the neck of her jumper, freezing her skin as it did so. She was soaking already, and it had barely been two minutes since the weather had changed.

Laura looked up towards the dark clouds as a flash of lightning streaked across the sky. Was she even safe here? Would the lightning strike her, or would it hit the roof of the inn first? Surely the latter. That's what she'd been taught – that lightning struck the tallest object – not that knowing this fact put her mind at rest at all. There were always exceptions to every rule, weren't there?

As the wind picked up and the rain continued to hammer down, she felt the tiles beneath her become more slippery and she reached out, pulling herself back up towards the window. How long could she stay like this? How long before she just slid right off the bay roof and landed in a broken heap on the ground below? And how long would it be until someone found her? Her body could be lying there, crumpled for hours, days, weeks, months. Forever.

No, her family would call her and at some point, they'd become suspicious and wonder why she wasn't picking up. At some point, they'd make the two-hour journey down to the Cotswolds and discover her body, likely half-eaten by that damn sheep.

Did sheep eat meat? Were they carnivores? Or was it just grass and hay they ate? She'd never seen a sheep eat meat. The ones she'd seen just lived in a field with grass. Maybe she'd be okay then. Maybe the runaway sheep wouldn't get to her. Maybe it would just be the crows.

She shuddered. What had a sheep been doing in her garden, anyway? Yes, she knew it was overgrown, but come on...

7

Was that the sound of an engine? Straining her ears, Laura tried to pick out any other sounds apart from the relentless splattering of rain. Yes, there was definitely a rumbling noise. And thankfully it wasn't the thunder returning. There was life beyond the garden gate.

Straightening her back, she gripped the window ledge above her and took a deep breath in, screaming as loudly as she possibly could, 'Help! In here! In the garden. Help!'

Nothing.

She yelled again, desperately trying to project her voice as far as possible, 'Help! In here! At the inn.'

Keeping her eyes fixed on the garden gate, Laura listened. The rumble of the car engine had disappeared, the torrent of rain the only sound filling the air around her again. Curling back up, she wiped the rain from her eyelashes before closing them, her slither of hope quickly disappearing.

'Laura? Laura, did you shout?'

Flinging her eyes open again, Laura watched as Jackson opened the garden gate before letting it swing shut behind him.

He'd always been the sensible one of him and her brother and today was no different. He was wearing a dark blue coat with the hood pulled up right over his dark curls.

All she wanted was to call out, alert him she was there, and get down into the heat of the inn, but the nagging thoughts of what her family would say, of what this would prove to them, whirred in her mind. Maybe someone else would come by? Maybe she'd be able to shout again if she heard someone walk past?

She watched as he jumped the stairs to the decking and hammered on the front door. He hadn't seen her. He wouldn't see her. Not with his hood up and the ladder half camouflaged by the undergrowth.

But if she let him walk away, this might be her last chance – her only chance – of a rescue. She'd either have to risk broken bones and get down herself or spend the night stranded up here. She'd certainly catch pneumonia and then wouldn't be able to get the inn up and running.

Either way, her parents, her family, her friends would be right. They'd know she couldn't cope. Heck, she couldn't even get someone out to mend the damn washing machine and every single repair company she'd spoken to had said it was an easy fix. Surely that meant it would be easy money for them? A five-minute job they could charge a hundred pounds for. So why wouldn't anyone help her?

And why had everyone been so snooty towards her in the village?

She swiped at her eyes, almost laughing at herself. Tears, rain-water, it didn't matter; she was soaked anyway.

She watched as Jackson retreated back along the garden path before pausing and turning to look back at the inn – a look of confusion sweeping across his face.

It wasn't until his hand was on the gate latch that Laura

snapped out of her pity party and took a breath. 'Jackson, up here.'

Turning back once more, Jackson surveyed the garden.

'Here. Up on the roof.' What was the point anymore? Her parents had been right, everyone had, and the sooner she admitted that, the sooner she'd be able to get inside and dry off.

Pushing his hood down, Jackson shielded his eyes with a hand and looked up, his eyes widening as he met her gaze. 'Laura. What on earth are you doing up there?'

'Trying to get a mobile signal.' She swallowed, her throat hoarse from screaming and the sarcasm lost on even herself. She looked pointedly at the ladder. 'There was a sheep.'

'Jeez.' Running back up the path, Jackson lifted the ladder and repositioned it against the roof of the bay.

After rubbing her eyes, Laura slowly inched towards the top of the ladder as Jackson's face appeared, his hand stretching out to her.

'Here, take my hand.'

Reluctantly, she reached out to him, his skin warm against hers as she made her way across the tiles.

'Here, mind yourself.' Gripping Laura's hand tighter, Jackson guided her until her feet were on the rungs of the ladder, his body shielding hers from the rain as they made their way down to solid ground.

With her feet back on solid ground, she looked at him, wanting nothing more than to be the receiver of one of his famous bear hugs, for him to tell her that everything was going to be okay, just as he had when she'd caught her stupid teenage boyfriend kissing her best friend behind the bike sheds at school. But that wasn't going to happen. She needed to show him that she was an independent adult now. That she didn't need his help. Apart from being rescued from the roof, that was. She needed to show him she was capable.

She stood a little straighter and rolled her shoulders back, putting on what she hoped was a show of strength. 'Thank you.'

Shaking his head, Jackson blinked. 'What happened? What were you doing up there? You're terrified of heights.'

'No, I'm not.' Each time she tucked her sodden hair behind her eyes, she missed a strand clinging to her nose. She stood still as Jackson gently took it between his finger and thumb and curled it behind her ear. She looked across at him. There was a slight tinge of red on his cheeks and he locked eyes with her. Swallowing, she looked away.

'You're telling me it was always mine, Richie or Jenny's job to clamber up the old oak tree in your parents' garden to knock the football from the shed roof because you found it funny to watch us fall and scrape our knees?'

'Yes... no.' Taking her eyes from the garden gate, she looked back at him, his eyes still on hers. 'The gutter clip had come off and then I saw a loose tile.'

'Why didn't you just ask me to pop round? I'd have sorted it in no time.' He indicated the front door. 'Let's get inside out of this rain. You'll catch pneumonia if you're not careful.'

'Okay.' Bending down, she retrieved her mobile from the ground and realised that by some small miracle the screen hadn't cracked after all.

Once inside, she stepped out of her wet trainers and took the towel Jackson had run through to the cloakroom to give to her.

'Thanks for helping me down and for this.' She held the towel up.

'Any time.' Jackson glanced down at the floor before looking back up at her. 'Not that I hope you'll need rescuing down from a roof again. Not any time soon, anyway.'

She gave him a quick smile before towelling her wet hair into a damp mess.

'But, seriously, any time you need anything, just shout. I'm only next door and more than happy to pop round to help. In fact, the weather is supposed to be drier tomorrow, so I'll pop by before work and sort out that loose tile you mentioned.'

'No!' The word came out harsher than she'd meant.

'No?'

'I don't need your help.' Again, she could hear her tone was harsh, and looking across at Jackson, he'd noticed the way she'd spoken to him too.

'Okay.' His voice was quiet, his expression sullen.

'Sorry, I don't mean to sound so rude. Or horrible. Or...' She sounded as though she was twelve again, annoyed at the way Richie and Jackson had barged into her bedroom whilst she practised make-up on the plastic head her parents had bought her for Christmas. She hadn't meant to come across so young, so brattish. But she had. Without warning, tears began streaming down her cheeks and she buried her face in the damp towel.

Without saying a word, Jackson stepped towards her, drawing her into one of his bear hugs, the ones in which the world melted away. Only it didn't, not this time. Jackson had come to her rescue and all she'd done to repay him was shout at him.

'I'm sorry. I really am. I'm just... I'm just tired.' And overwhelmed and not coping. Just as everyone had predicted.

But she couldn't say any of that. She couldn't tell him in case he then went and told Richie, who would tell Jenny, who would tell her parents and then, before she knew it, they'd all arrive and take over. Or else utter the words she knew they were itching to say, *I told you so.*

'I bet you are. I can't imagine you've had much sleep, what

with the rain and the broken guttering.' Jackson's words were soft, his breath warm on her damp hair.

She closed her eyes, letting the pent-up tears continue. She knew it was just that she didn't have anyone to talk to about it all, about her problems at the inn. No one to vent or rant to about the way she'd felt shunned in the village. She'd bottled it all up and now... now Jackson was here and bearing the brunt of it. 'I'm sorry.'

'Hey, no need to apologise.' Jackson held her by the elbows, leaning back to look her in the eyes. 'Moving is stressful. I should know, I've done it enough times.'

'Yes, yes, it is.' She looked up at him, his blue eyes dark with concern. Drawing the towel roughly over her face, she dried her eyes. 'I shouldn't be taking it out on you, though. You don't deserve me yelling at you. Or crying on you.'

'I don't think I'd have called it yelling.' Jackson tilted his head and grinned. 'It was more like a reprimand.'

Laughing softly, Laura looked down at the towel in her hands and ran her index finger along the edge of it. It was well worn. And a little stained. Another thing she'd have to add to the list of things to source, buy and replace.

'I mean it about helping out, though. I'm more than capable of turning my hand to most things. Next door will be the fourth house I've bought, refurbished and sold on when it's complete.' He nodded in the general direction of his house.

'Really? You're not staying in Meadowfield?' Her voice was like a whine. She closed her eyes and cleared her throat. 'I mean, I didn't know you were in the property business. You said you were a chef at the pub; do you do both?'

'Yes, that's right, but I'll leave the pub job when the house is complete, buy another one and find some work close by.'

'Oh, right.' So he wasn't going to be hanging around. That was something. She frowned. That should be something. It should be positive news. She could have her fresh start then. 'How long do you think you'll be living in Meadowfield for?'

'Ha, are you trying to get rid of me already?' Jackson raised an eyebrow.

'No, I...' She sighed. 'I just wanted a fresh start, that's all.'

'And then I rocked up on your doorstep? No wonder I didn't receive such a warm welcome.' He gave a lopsided grin.

Wringing the towel in her hands, she couldn't work out why she suddenly felt a knot in the pit of her stomach. Him only being here for a while was a good thing. It was. So why did she feel as though she wanted to feel his arms wrap around her again? 'Sorry, just ignore me. I'm just t—'

'Tired. Yep, you said that.'

She turned, leading the way into the kitchen, grateful for the few seconds' break in conversation to try to get her thoughts in order. She'd hurt his feelings. She shouldn't have said what she had. She sank onto the long wooden bench which ran along the length of the largest table and turned to him again. All she wanted to do was change out of her wet clothes and warm herself up, but first, she needed to put right what she'd said. 'I didn't mean to sound ungrateful. It's just with Richie and Jenny having their perfect lives and juggling children, houses, successful marriages and good jobs, and then there being me... I'm not even the youngest.'

'You're comparing yourself to Jenny and Richie?' Jackson swung his leg over the bench, sitting and facing her, his arm resting on the table between them.

She shrugged. 'I should have my life together by now.'

'Why? Because they have?'

She nodded. 'I'm just such a failure. I couldn't even keep my husband, my career – if you can actually call it that – has always been a sinking ship and I'd been living with my parents for a whole year before moving here.'

'Well, if you're a failure, that makes two of us.'

Narrowing her eyes at him, she dried her forehead with the towel, her damp hair still clinging to her skin. 'You're not a failure. You could never be a failure.'

'By your standards, I am. I'm two years older than you, haven't settled down, don't even have anyone I can call my girlfriend and move around the country every few months.' He ticked the reasons off with his fingers.

'No, but you've always been successful in whatever you do.' She reached out, touching the tips of her fingers against the sleeve of his coat.

'That's your perception.' He looked down at her fingers lying on his arm.

Pulling her hand away quickly, she shook her head. 'No, it's the truth. And that's why I snapped at you when you offered to help. I need to do this myself. I need to prove that I can.'

'You don't need to prove anything to anyone.' Jackson shook his head slowly. 'You really don't.'

'Oh, I really really do. No one wanted me to buy this inn. Not my parents or Richie or Jenny. Or anyone else I told my plans to, for that matter. No one believed I could.' She looked around the vast kitchen, her eyes resting on the large gas cooker, or Aga... or whatever it was. She had never even used gas to cook and everywhere needed a good scrub and clean. Plus, if the washing machine saga was anything to go by, would the oven, Aga thing even work? 'I can't do this. They were right. They were all right.'

Taking her hands in his, Jackson looked her in the eye. 'You're just tired. After a good night's sleep in a warm bed, you'll feel better in the morning and ready to take it all on again.'

'Ha, but I can't even do that! The damn washing machine belt has come off, so the bedding is sitting in a pool of water inside the drum.' She looked down at their hands, his still holding hers.

'I'll take a look at the machine. If it's just the belt, then it will take all of five minutes to fix.'

'No, no. I need to stand on my own two feet.' She shook her head. There wasn't anything she wanted more in the world than to let Jackson fix the machine, be able to spin the bedding and get to bed tonight.

'Honestly, it's an easy job. They'll rob you if you call in a repair company.'

'I tried that. I rang round like three, four companies and they were all too busy.'

Jackson frowned slightly before taking his hands from hers and standing up. 'Then let me do it. It'll be done in a second. You don't have anything to prove to anyone. So what if people voiced concerns? That just shows that they care.'

Sighing, she stood up and followed Jackson through to the utility room. She didn't have the energy to argue anymore. Besides, he was right, she needed a good night's sleep and this, allowing him to help this one time, would give her that. She leaned against the doorframe as he knelt down.

'Looks like you've done most of the work.' He placed the back of the machine, which she'd left off, aside and twisted it towards him.

She nodded. She'd done her best. She'd tried. She was just incompetent. Or that's how she felt.

'Honestly though. You really don't have to prove yourself to anyone.' Jackson looked up at her as he tugged the belt into place. 'You've done an amazing thing, taking the leap to buy your own inn. You should feel proud of yourself, nothing less.'

'Huh, but I've still got to get it ready and open it, haven't I?' She wiped the towel over her forehead as a droplet of rain dripped down onto her nose. She obviously couldn't even dry herself properly. Why did she think she could take on a task as big as this? 'I should have listened to Dad, to Richie, when they offered to come and view it with me, but no, I wanted to do it myself, be independent, and as it turns out, they were right.'

'In what way?' Jackson looked up at her.

'Well, look at it.' She glanced around her, encompassing the space. 'I thought it would be ready to just clean up and open to the guests, but it's not. The washing machine was broken, there's plaster crumbling from the wall in the hallway, the guttering, the loose roof tile. I should have noticed it. I should have realised what I was getting myself into.'

Jackson breathed out through his mouth before standing up and facing her, screwdriver still in hand. 'Look, you've not done anything I haven't in the past. Things aren't always visible during a viewing. Estate agents want a quick sale, owners want the same and so defects, things which need fixing, aren't pointed out, or worse, they're hidden.'

Glancing down at the floor, Laura shifted position. 'But I should have known what to look out for. I should have been able to spot the telltale signs. They would have – Dad and Richie – they'd have spotted them.'

'Not necessarily. You should have seen the first house I bought to do up.' Jackson gave a lopsided grin, the dimple in his left cheek drawing Laura's attention to him. 'It was a right state. I'd been in a hurry, bought it at auction after only going to have a look at the outside of the property and, well, it cost me more to do it up than I got back.'

Laura nodded. 'But I bet you've never made that mistake again.'

'No, but this is your first time buying an inn.'

'I should still have known what to look for. I was just impatient.' She shrugged. She had been. As soon as she'd decided what to do, she'd been desperate to make a start on her new life. She'd wanted to move out of her parents' and her childhood town as soon as she could. She'd wanted that fresh beginning where people didn't know her family, didn't keep asking about how her sister and brother were, pointing out how well they were doing and thereby highlighting how rubbish her life was.

'Pennycress Inn is beautiful.' Placing the screwdriver on top of the washing machine, Jackson held his hand out for her and led her into the hallway. 'Look up. Look at all of the original features, the beams, each and every mark on them a memory. This place is stunning.'

His skin was warm against hers as she watched him point out, with his other hand, the features which had made her fall in love with the property in the first place. Looking across at him, she smiled. His eyes were wide, enthusiastic, his smile genuine. He really liked this sort of stuff. She'd forgotten how into history he'd been at school, how immersed he used to become on homework projects. Whereas Richie would always just sit there on his bed throwing a tennis ball in the air, Jackson would be at Richie's desk, his body bent over the books he was reading, the information he was lapping up.

'It is, but it's still falling apart.'

'It's old. That's all. It needs some care. Some love. And it will be just as stunning as it once was.' Jackson released his hold on her hand and turned to her, his eyes still full of the wonder of history. 'And I think you're the perfect person to do this.'

'Now I know you're just saying stuff to try to make me feel better.' Still, it was sweet of him and seeing how mesmerised he'd been with the features of the inn had done something for her. It had made her realise that if she could pull this off and reopen the inn, then it *could* be really beautiful.

That was a big 'if' though. She still only had the same measly amount of money in the pot for repair work – repair work she hadn't envisioned and money she'd planned to use as a buffer whilst she was building up bookings.

'No, I'm not. You always had an eye for the creative when we were growing up.'

'That was a long time ago. I haven't as much as been to an art gallery in the past fifteen years and I'm not confident I could tell one end of the paintbrush from the other anymore.'

Jackson chuckled. 'You'll do a great job with Pennycress. You just need to start believing in yourself, that's all.'

'Hmm.' Laura sighed. She could hear how negative she was being but she couldn't help herself, there was so much to do, to overcome, before she could even dream about the inn becoming a success.

She followed him back through to the utility room, where he knelt once again and replaced the back on the machine before shifting it back into place.

'Thank you.'

'No worries. I told you it wouldn't take long.' Standing up, he placed the screwdriver on top of the machine. 'Now, go and get out of those wet clothes before you catch pneumonia.'

'I will. No, I mean thank you for talking to me, for telling me you believe I can do this.' She smiled. 'As well as for fixing the machine and rescuing me from the roof, obviously.'

'Haha, no problem.' Walking towards the front door, Jackson pulled it open, pausing in the doorway. 'Just shout if you need anything else.'

'Thank you.' She wouldn't. The stubborn streak of wanting to be independent was still very much alive in her, but it was sweet of him to offer. Standing in the open doorway, she watched as he pulled his hood up whilst walking away.

8

Pulling a string of ivy from the front of her jumper, Laura grabbed her secateurs before turning to the rather overgrown hedge separating the front garden from the path. After her chat with Jackson last night, she felt a lot more positive and having had the best night's sleep she'd had since moving in, again thanks to him for the fresh bedding, meaning she was able to spend her first night in the bed, she felt as though she could achieve anything. Or at least more than she had the previous days.

Laura threw another bunch of twigs into the heap behind her before standing up and looking around the front garden. She'd only been working out here for a few hours, but she could already see the difference she'd made. She'd trimmed the lavender back from where it had been encroaching onto the narrow garden path, pulling the ivy from between the plants as she went. She was about halfway up from the gate along the hedge and although it was by no means perfect, it looked a lot better than before. Maybe when she was up and running, open and earning money, she'd be able to employ a gardener.

A noise from behind the row of conifers drew her attention away from her thoughts and she glanced over in the direction of Jackson's house. It sounded as though his front door had banged shut. Throwing the secateurs down next to the heap of twigs and weeds, Laura ran out of the gate and onto the street. She'd been half listening out and half hoping she'd hear him leave so she could thank him again for yesterday and apologise for crying at him.

As she walked along the pavement she paused. She could hear his and another voice, a child's, laughing and chatting. Whose kid could that be? He hadn't mentioned anything about looking after a child. Although she'd been so wrapped up in her own drama that she hadn't given a thought to what was going on in his life. That was something else she needed to apologise for, but this probably wasn't the right time.

Turning, she began making her way back towards her gate. She'd catch him later.

'Laura!' Jackson's voice rose, catching her attention.

Oops, too late. She turned and smiled as he walked up to her, a little girl who must have only been about five or six held his hand and skipped along next to him. 'Morning.'

'Morning. Laura, this is my niece, Eden. Eden, this is my good friend, Laura.' Jackson grinned as he introduced them.

'Hello, Eden. That's such a beautiful name.'

'Thank you.' Eden tugged on Jackson's hand before looking up at him and pointing at the grass which ran beneath the trees along the path next to the road. 'Can I pick the flowers?'

'Yes, of course you can.' Letting go of her hand, Jackson smiled as Eden knelt down and began picking the daisies, which, thanks to the mild winter, were still going strong.

'Sorry, I didn't mean to interrupt or anything. I was just going to come and say thank you again for yesterday and apologise for...' Laura held her arms out, 'everything.'

'No worries, it was good to catch up.' Jackson grinned at her.

Laura looked at Eden as the young girl held up the daisies she'd picked, showing Jackson before turning back and gathering some more. Jackson's only brother had left home as soon as he'd turned sixteen, leaving Jackson to deal with his parents alone from the age of twelve, and she had never heard him talk about his brother since. 'Your niece?'

'Yes. You remember Billy? He reached out and got in contact with me about a year ago.' Jackson shrugged. 'We spoke about things and we're pretty close now. I look after Eden the occasional weekend and, like today, for an hour or so in the mornings before school when Billy and his wife, Jane's, shifts overlap.'

'Oh right. That's great he got back in contact.' She touched his forearm. She still remembered the day Jackson had run round to their house in floods of tears because Billy had left, only leaving him a scribbled note. It had been the day that Laura's parents had set him up a bed in the spare room and offered for him to move in. Of course, Jackson being Jackson had stayed only a handful of times, preferring to go back home to check his parents hadn't drunk themselves into so much of a stupor that they'd be in danger of setting the house on fire, or worse.

'Yes, it is.' Jackson nodded, a huge grin on his face as he watched Eden begin to make a daisy chain from the flowers she'd picked. 'It really is. He's in a good place now and only lives half an hour away, which means I can help out with childcare when needed.'

'I'm really pleased for you.' Jackson deserved happiness. He was one of those people who would do anything for anyone else, no questions asked. He always had been.

'Thanks.' Jackson looked back at her.

'Oh, I meant to ask you yesterday, although I'm not sure if I should or if I'm going to sound completely crazy...'

'Go on.'

'As I think I said yesterday, it was a sheep that pushed my ladder over, which is why I ended up becoming stranded on the roof.' She frowned. 'I know that sounds impossible and even now, as I say it, I'm doubting myself and wondering if I hallucinated or something, but I swear, there was a sheep in my garden. It came barging out of the hedge and ran across the lawn.'

'Oh, that'll be Claudette.' He spoke as though it was the most normal thing in the world for a sheep to pass through the garden.

'Claudette? There really is a sheep then? I wasn't seeing things?'

'Haha, no. You weren't imagining things. She escaped from one of the farmer's fields outside the village and the whole village has been trying to capture her for over a month now.'

'A sheep is running amok in Meadowfield.' Laura let out a laugh. 'Sorry, I shouldn't laugh, but is this what village life is like? Sheep causing chaos?'

Jackson chuckled. 'It seems to be. Old Mrs Pritchard down the road was the first one to spot her and managed to corner her in her shed, or so she thought, so the village mayoress, Miss Cooke, rang round a few sanctuaries and found her a place, but by the time someone came to collect her, the sheep was nowhere to be seen and the whole village was doubting Mrs Pritchard's sanity. It wasn't until Claudette had rummaged through some shopping bags Phillip McGuire had left on Paddy's back step for him that people began to take poor Mrs Pritchard seriously.'

Laura covered her mouth as a loud guffaw escaped. 'I can just picture Claudette running around the village, making her way from house to house.'

'Exactly!' Jackson wiped his eyes as he tried to compose

himself again. 'I probably should have warned you about the village sheep when I first saw you.'

'Haha, yes you should have!' She dried the tears of laughter from her cheeks with the sleeve of her coat. 'Won't the farmer just come and collect her?'

'I shouldn't think one sheep is worth his time. Besides, as stern as Miss Cooke can be with us villagers, she's a different person when it comes to animals and she figured Claudette has made the escape and deserves to live her life out someplace she won't end up on someone's plate.' Jackson shrugged.

'Fair enough.' Laura smiled at Eden as the young girl walked up to her uncle with the daisy chain she'd made draping from her hands.

'Look, Uncle Jackson. Do you like it?'

'Aw, that looks lovely, Eden.' Jackson grinned as he looked down. 'Do you want me to help you put it around your neck? You could wear it as a necklace.'

'No, it's for you. You wear it, Uncle Jackson.' Eden stood on her tiptoes as Jackson bent down, allowing her to hang it around his neck.

'Thank you. I love it.' Straightening his back, he high-fived Eden.

'You'll wear it at work today?' she checked.

'I will indeed. I'm sure it'll make my customers very happy.'

'All day?'

'All day.' Jackson held out his hand before looking back at Laura. 'On which note, we should get going, as Eden is coming to help me at the pub until her mummy picks her up in a few minutes. See you later.'

'That sounds fun. See you later.' Laura waved before watching as Eden took Jackson's hand, unable to turn away. Jackson must have said something funny to his niece as Eden looked up at him, her uncontrollable giggle filling the air. Laura smiled. She didn't think she'd ever seen anything sweeter. He'd make an amazing dad one day.

Sighing heavily, she forced herself to spin on her heels and head back to her garden. Why had that thought even popped into her mind?

9

_____

Placing her mug of steaming coffee on the kitchen table, Laura sank onto the wooden bench. After spending the rest of the morning and most of the afternoon gardening, muscles she didn't even realise she possessed ached. She rolled her shoulders back before picking up her mug and wrapping her hands around the hot ceramic. Thanks to Jackson fixing the washing machine last night, she'd managed to get the throws and cushion covers from the sitting room washed today too. It actually felt as though she was getting things organised, taking a step closer to being able to open.

Just as she savoured the last sip of coffee, the doorbell rang, letting out its feeble tune. That's one thing she'd forgotten to do today – buy batteries. She'd have to remember to write it on the list.

Standing up, she made her way to the door, raking her fingers through her hair before she pulled it open.

'Surprise, sis! I hope you don't mind, but we were heading down to Rob's parents and the twins were desperate to see you, so we thought we'd pop by.' Without waiting for an invitation, Jenny bustled into the hallway and drew her in for a hug.

'Hi.' Laura spoke into Jenny's pale pink cashmere jumper as she watched the twins, Tammy and Toby, run up the garden path, slowly followed by Rob. She was sure Rob's parents lived in Stratford-upon-Avon, at least an hour away from Meadowfield by any route they could have taken to reach there.

Jenny unwrapped her arms and stepped away from the embrace before turning slowly on the spot and looking around. 'This is the famous Pennycress Inn, then?'

'This is Pennycress.' Laura jumped out of the way as Tammy and Toby barged past her, their eyes on each other and seemingly in the middle of a very serious game of tag.

'Hello, Laura. Lovely to see you and your new place.' Rob hugged her quickly around the shoulders. 'We won't stay long because my parents are expecting us for dinner, but Jenny was desperate to come and see how you were getting along.'

Ha, she'd known they must have taken a special detour.

Laura nodded. 'No worries. Are you staying at your parents' for the weekend?'

'No, we're not.' Jenny grinned as Laura closed the door behind them. 'The twins are. Rob's booked us a nice weekend away, haven't you, Rob? Down in Bourton-on-the-Water. I can't wait.'

'Oh, that'll be lovely then.' Laura smiled. Her sister worked so hard on her business and looking after the kids and house – not that she ever made it look hard. No, she was like a swan gliding across the surface of the water, she made everything look easy. Anyway, however hard she worked or didn't, she deserved a night away.

'It's an anniversary treat. Our big one, ten years.' She looked down at her shoes. 'Are we doing shoes on or off?'

Laura looked across to where the twins were sliding down the banister, their trainers firmly attached to their feet. 'Shoes on is fine. I'm so sorry, I completely forgot about your anniversary. I've not even got you a card. Or anything.' How could it have slipped her mind? She'd been so focused on the inn, on her problems, that she'd completely forgotten about what was going on in her sister's life, her family's lives. How was she supposed to juggle it all? Business and family? Jenny could. She had her business and two kids and still managed to keep up with what everyone else was doing. Laura though, she just couldn't do anything right at the moment.

'Don't worry about it, sis.' Jenny walked further inside. 'Shall we get the kettle on? I'm parched.'

'Yes, of course. We can have a coffee before I show you around. Come on through to the kitchen.' Holding her hand out, Laura indicated the way. 'I still can't believe I forgot to even text to congratulate you.'

'I'm sure it's a date in your diary you'd rather forget at the moment.' Rob looked at her sympathetically before doubling over as Jenny elbowed him in the ribs. 'Ouch!'

'Ouch yourself! I told you not to bring it up.' Jenny scolded Rob before laying her hand on Laura's forearm. 'Men, they have no tact whatsoever.'

Laura took a deep breath as it dawned on her what Rob was referring to. Break-up day. The day she and Harry had gone their separate ways, the day everything had come to a head and she'd told him it was over. In retrospect, she probably shouldn't have broken up with him on Jenny and Rob's anniversary, but at the time she hadn't realised, she'd had so much going on, so much to think about that the date of their special day had completely slipped her mind. And now, it seemed, she'd forever be reminded of the day she'd called off her marriage.

'Sorry, I shouldn't have mentioned anything,' Rob spluttered as he sat down at the table. 'I was warned not to.'

'Yes, you were.' Jenny, sitting opposite him, glared at him.

'Honestly, don't worry about it.' Laura filled up the kettle before flicking the switch and busying herself with getting the mugs. 'In truth, it had completely slipped my mind. I hadn't realised what the date was. Every day has just merged into another since I moved in.'

'I'm glad this place is doing what you'd hoped then. Giving you a new start and something to focus on.' Standing up, Jenny took the milk from the fridge and handed it to her sister before sitting back down.

'Yes, yes, it is.' After taking the mugs of coffee to the table, she sat down next to Jenny. 'There's more to do than I'd first thought, and although I researched loads, I still need to get my head around the advertising side of things before I open up, so it's definitely keeping me busy.' Not to mention the hallway wall she needed to repair, the roof tile and anything else she hadn't yet discovered. But she wasn't about to point them out.

'That's good then. Less time to mull over your divorce.' Rob lifted his mug.

Raising her eyebrows, Jenny pursed her lips before turning to Laura. 'Tell me all about what—'

The twins flew into the kitchen, pulling the cupboard doors open. 'We're hungry,' they said in unison.

'Stop, stop, I have food here.' Rummaging in her oversized handbag, Jenny pulled out two Tupperware tubs of cucumber and carrot sticks.

'Yuck, hasn't Auntie Laura got any *real* food?' Tammy let the cupboard door swing shut with a bang and walked across to the table.

'I don't suppose she's had time to get much in.'

Laura shook her head. 'I might have something. I'll have a look.' Standing up, she began searching through the snacks she'd bought on her way down to the Cotswolds and pulled out two chocolate bars. Her favourite, but after being saved from an awkward conversation about her and Harry's break-up, the twins could have what they wanted.

'Thank you, Auntie Laura.' Tammy took the treats before passing one to her brother.

Taking the chocolate bar, Toby glanced at it before looking across at his mum. 'I thought these were Uncle Harry's favourite? He was eating one the other day.'

The other day? Had they met up with Harry and not told her? Why wouldn't Jenny have mentioned it? Laura frowned as she sat back down at the table.

'Mummy said we're not allowed to call him Uncle Harry anymore.' Tammy punched Toby's arm.

'That chocolate is Auntie Laura's favourite, Toby. Harry just likes them too.' Laura shifted on the bench. 'Why don't you two go and explore? Take a look around.'

'Okay.' Taking Toby's hand, Tammy began leading him back out of the kitchen before turning and throwing something in the direction of the table. 'We found this too. I think it's a money card and I wanted to buy that unicorn teddy I've been wanting, but Toby said we couldn't take it with us.'

'Okay, thanks.' Leaning down, Laura picked up the card. Tammy had been right, it was a credit card, but not one she recognised. She turned it over in her hand. It was Jackson's. It must have fallen from his pocket last night.

'Sorry. I did tell them he's not their uncle anymore,' Jenny offered as way of explanation.

Laura waved the apology away. If she was honest, it hadn't even occurred to her that her niece and nephew had lost an uncle because of her actions. Had they been upset? 'Don't worry. You met up with him though? With Harry?'

'We didn't meet up with him, no. We ran into him at the supermarket and, well, you know how difficult he is to get away from.' Jenny grimaced.

'And the way you chat, too.' Rob took another sip of his coffee.

'Well, okay, yes, but I didn't feel as though I could just blank him, either.' Jenny focused on Laura again. 'You two were together for what, ten years? Besides, I had the twins with me. It would have confused them even more if I'd just walked right past him.'

'Still, you didn't need to chat with him for quite as long as you did. I think the twins were more upset about the fact their ice lollies had melted by the time we got to the checkouts.' Rob shook his head softly.

'Yes, well, you swapped them for new ones, didn't you? So no harm done.' Jenny twisted, so she was facing Laura again. 'You don't mind me talking to Harry, do you? I just wasn't sure what I was supposed to do and then he got talking in the rambling way he does, and I just couldn't see a way out of the conversation without appearing super rude.'

'No, of course not.' That was one of the main reasons she'd wanted to move away, so that she didn't keep running into him too. He'd been a huge part of their lives, part of the family. She couldn't blame them for not completely cutting all ties. And Jenny was right. It would have seemed really odd to the twins if her parents hadn't spoken to their former uncle. She held her mug up to her lips and mumbled behind the rim. 'Did he say what he's up to?'

'Same old stuff as far as I could tell. Work, snooker, drinking down the pub with his mates. It didn't sound as though anything's changed.' Jenny shrugged.

'And he's still with Dina?' She shouldn't have asked. She didn't want to know. She took a gulp of her coffee, immediately wishing she'd remembered to buy some sugar as the bitter taste hit the back of her throat.

She'd been pleased to hear he'd found someone else. Even if it had only taken a month after the marital home had sold and they'd finally been able to go their separate ways, but she still couldn't get over the fact Dina was his ex from before Laura had met him. She was happy for him as she'd felt awful being the one to make the decision to end their marriage, but she couldn't help wondering if he'd always felt something for his ex. Had he always harboured feelings for her? Throughout their marriage? If so, had their marriage been doomed from the start? Had Laura been second choice all along? She shuddered as she thought of the possibility that Harry may have been seeing Dina for longer, seeing her whilst they'd still been living together, maybe even before they'd separated. After all, she knew Dina had frequented the same pub as Harry; anything could have happened. She gripped her mug tighter, her knuckles turning white.

'No, he's not actually. That was one thing he did say. They split up a few months back.' Jenny turned to her husband. 'Can you remember how long he said it's been since their break-up? Four, five months?'

Rob shrugged. 'I must admit I was more focused on trying to stop the twins from filling up the trolley with junk food than listening to him.'

Laura stifled a laugh. That sounded like Rob. He'd never been one for small talk.

'Well, four or five months, something like that, anyway, so it didn't last long.'

'No, it didn't, did it?' Laura braced herself for the bitter taste as she took another sip of her drink. She wasn't quite sure how she felt after hearing the news that her ex-husband was single again.

Part of her felt upset for him, another relieved. But why? It wasn't as though she wanted him back. She was still sure that walking away had been the right decision but the fact he'd moved on so easily to another serious relationship had made her feel as though their marriage had meant absolutely nothing, that she was so easily replaceable. So, hearing he and Dina hadn't worked out after all suggested that maybe, just maybe, she'd jumped to the wrong conclusion and he wasn't finding their separation quite the walk in the park she'd thought he was.

'You're just not that easy to replace.' Jenny grinned as though she'd read her mind.

'Mummy, Daddy, quick!' Tammy ran full pelt into the kitchen, skidding across the floor and narrowly missing running headlong into the cupboards as she slipped on the tiles.

'What is it?' Jumping up, Jenny and Rob followed her out into the hallway, Laura shortly behind.

'Toby!' Jenny's scream filled the hallway before Laura had even stepped out of the kitchen.

Rob sprinted the few short steps to where Toby lay in a heap at the bottom of the stairs, crying and holding his ankle, pieces of the wooden banister scattered around him. 'Toby, are you all right? Are you hurt?'

Standing and watching as Jenny and Rob fussed over him, Laura opened and closed her lips silently, struggling for words. A large chunk of the beautifully engraved oak banister had splintered off, lying in pieces across the floor. 'Is he okay?'

'My ankle! My ankle hurts. It hurts, Mummy. It hurts.' Holding his ankle, Toby rocked back and forth as Jenny tried to look at it.

'Can you wriggle your toes?'

Looking down at his foot, Toby tried to move his toes before screaming again. 'It hurts.'

'I think we need to get him checked out at a hospital.' Rob

picked him up in his arms before looking down at his daughter. 'Tammy, go and fetch yours and Toby's coats. There's a good girl.'

Standing up, Jenny stroked Toby's hair as he buried his face in his dad's shoulder. 'It's okay, sweetheart. You'll be okay.'

'I'm so sorry. I don't know what to say.' Laura held her arms out. If Toby had broken his ankle or something, she'd never forgive herself. 'I didn't realise there was anything wrong with the staircase.'

'It's not your fault. We've both told them time and time again not to slide down the banister.' Jenny drew Laura in for a quick hug before holding the front door open.

Stepping outside, his son still in his arms, Rob glanced back. 'It looks like woodworm. I'd get that checked out before you get it replaced.'

'Right. Okay, thanks.' Laura nodded as she closed the door behind them. Woodworm. Great, now that sounded expensive.

Turning, she looked at the aftermath of Toby's accident. In the short time since she'd moved in, the hallway had gone from looking mostly okay, maybe needing a little spruce-up, to crumbling plaster from the walls and now a broken banister and a possible case of woodworm. But that wasn't what was important, as long as Toby was okay she'd be able to deal with the rest.

Sighing, she returned to the kitchen and sank onto the bench before pulling her coffee towards her. Staring into the cold drink, she just couldn't get the image of poor Toby lying in pain and crying out of her head. What if he really was hurt? What if he had broken his ankle? Blinking, she picked up her phone. There was nothing she could do for Toby but wait for news, but she could try to distract herself from her worries by focusing on what she could control, trying to get the banister repaired. There must be a woodworm specialist near here. What would a woodworm specialist even be called? Did she need a carpenter? What did she need to look up? Pest control?

She took a long glug of the disgusting coffee. What if the whole building was infected? Was that even the right word, infected? Overrun? Or infested maybe? Is that what happened? Did it spread? Did she even have enough savings to cover something like this?

10

With the packet of sugar in her hand, Laura closed the door to the small grocery shop, glad to be outside. The atmosphere inside had been tense, to say the least. No one had returned any of her smiles or cheery 'hellos', not the other customers and not the man who had served her. And it hadn't been her. She was sure of that. Yes, she was worried about the woodworm and how she was going to deal with it after ringing around numerous local pest control specialists who had all told her they were busy before she'd even had the chance to explain or ask for advice or anything, but she'd tried to be friendly in the shop, and she thought she had. There might be something odd about Meadowfield, the locals either hated outsiders or were just generally grumpy, but at least Jackson was here.

She shook her head and smiled. That was a thought she didn't think she'd be having. Not after discovering he lived next door and all hopes of her fresh start had been squashed, but, at the moment, he was her only friend here, the only person who even seemed to want to utter two words to her.

Laura tapped her pocket, checking she still had Jackson's

credit card on her. At least she'd receive a warm welcome in the pub.

Reaching the pub, she swapped the sugar to the other hand. Despite the thick wooden door, she could hear the raucous laughter and chatter of people enjoying themselves inside. Pushing it open, she stepped into the warmth of the old place. Letting the door close softly shut behind her, she looked around. The highly polished bar ran across the back of the room and a fire roared in the fireplace at the far end. It was busy. The tables were almost all full and a cluster of people were standing around the bar. She glanced at her watch. It was already six o'clock. No wonder it was packed.

She pulled the card from her pocket and began weaving her way through the tables and chairs towards the bar. She frowned, her eyebrows knitting together. With each step she took, it was as though the pub grew quieter and she could feel people's eyes upon her. Coming to a stop at the bar, she turned around, trying to catch somebody's eye. Anybody's eye. But as she looked about, she saw people turn away and talk to their companions, their voices low, too quiet for her to overhear.

Turning back, she looked across at the barman, trying to catch his attention. With each shop or, in this case, pub that she entered, she felt more and more uncomfortable. What did the local residents have against newcomers? She'd been the only one who had put an offer in at Pennycress, so it couldn't be that someone else had wanted to buy it. She hadn't bid above asking price or anything. In fact, she'd been told it had been languishing on the market for over six months and she wasn't aware of there being any other interest. Normally, estate agents made it obvious if there was: they pushed for a quick sale and tried to hurry you to make a decision. That hadn't happened with Pennycress. If anything, Ms Taunton had been laid-back, disinterested almost.

Placing the packet of sugar on the bar, Laura shook herself. People would warm to her. They'd soon see that she was here for the right reasons. It wasn't as though she was part of a huge chain of hotels and had bought Pennycress to turn it into a carbon copy of another. No, she was here to open Pennycress Inn as it was. Well, once she'd cleared the garden, sorted the crumbling plaster, fixed the loose tile and got the rest of the roof checked. Oh, and got rid of the woodworm.

She sighed as she watched the barman walk past her and serve the man standing next to her. That was fine. He'd probably been waiting longer than her. She was just being paranoid.

She glanced up and down the bar. A couple were sitting on bar stools at the end, seemingly immersed in a private conversation. A group of three men chatted to each other to her right, one of them glancing at her before indicating an empty table by the window. After nodding in agreement, the other two picked up their pints and followed him.

Laura smiled as she noticed another customer who had been hidden behind the group of men. At last, a friendly face. Well, not especially friendly, but at least someone she recognised, Ms Taunton. She held up her hand. 'Hi.'

Pursing her lips, Ms Taunton nodded in her direction before picking up her glass of wine and focusing on that, the conversation clearly over before it had begun.

Laura looked away. Ms Taunton's reaction to her hadn't been anything out of character. In all her dealings with the estate agent, Laura didn't think she'd once seen her smile.

A door behind the bar swung open and Laura recognised Jackson's voice before she saw him.

'Two beef wellingtons and mash.' Stepping out into the area behind the bar, Jackson held up two plates of food, steam rising from them, and passed them across to the barman.

'Jackson.' Ms Taunton held her glass towards him, her face relaxing at the sight of him.

Laura watched as Jackson walked across to her, chatting quietly. Had that actually been a smile? Had Ms Taunton smiled at him? She waited as Ms Taunton spoke to him before Jackson glanced up and down the bar area, his eyes meeting hers before a grin slowly spread across his face.

Turning back to Ms Taunton, Jackson said something before walking across to her. 'Hey, Laura, decided to check out the local pub then? What can I get you?'

'Oh, I've just come to give you this.' She quickly looked across at Ms Taunton, who met her gaze and glared at her, before passing across the card. Yep, she definitely wasn't about to stay and order food. Or even a drink, for that matter. 'It must have fallen out of your pocket or something when you were helping with the washing machine.'

'Oh fab. I wondered where that was.' Taking the card, Jackson pulled out his wallet from his back pocket and slipped it inside. 'I'd assumed Eden had picked it up when she'd been playing shops earlier.'

'No worries. Sorry, I would have brought it down earlier, but I only realised it was there because Tammy found it.'

'Oh, Jenny's visited?' Placing his elbows on the bar, he leaned his forearms across the wood.

'Yes, they popped in very briefly earlier.' Laura shifted position. 'It didn't end well though, poor little Toby—'

'Jackson, two pie and mash and another beef wellington please, mate.' The barman held his hand up and brandished a small slip of paper.

'Right, boss.' Jackson held his hand up, indicating he'd got the orders before straightening his back. 'Sorry, I'd better get on. Tell me about it later, though?'

'Yep, of course.' Nodding, Laura turned.

'Oh, hold on. You have...' Jackson spoke softly and reached across the bar, pulling something from her jumper.

Turning back, she grimaced as she realised it had been a strand of ivy Jackson had pulled off. She must have been walking around with it hanging from her since doing the gardening. No wonder she'd been getting funny looks.

11

'I'm sorry. *How* much?' Laura placed her hand against the wall for support as the pest control specialist looked up from the floor where he'd been surveying the pieces of banister. She knew she should be grateful to have finally managed to get someone round to take a look, but after charging an extortionate call-out fee because he'd travelled half an hour from where he was based, the quote was ridiculous.

Standing up, the man rubbed his beard, leaving splinters of wood in the brown fuzz, and repeated the amount. 'Sorry, that's just how much it's going to cost. These things are complex and there's no easy fix. Of course, you can call in someone else, get another quote.'

Laura sighed. As if it were that easy. She was beginning to think Pennycress was cursed, the number of people she'd rung for help with the washing machine, and now this. 'Thanks. I'll get back to you soon.'

'Okay, suit yourself. I wouldn't leave it too late, though. You don't want it spreading through the rest of the house.' He took a last look at the staircase before leaving, nodding at Laura on his way out.

Closing the door firmly behind him, Laura placed her forehead on the stained-glass window in the door. Maybe she'd underestimated just how expensive this whole thing was going to be. Her dad and brother had been right. She should have let them look around, or at least paid for a proper survey, but, no, she'd known best, she'd wanted to go it alone. And, of course, because she'd been trying to save money she'd only opted for the survey the mortgage company had to complete.

Lifting her head up again, she let it fall back to the cool glass. Maybe she could just stay like this? Just stand here and forget it all. Forget about the stupid woodworm, forget about the strange atmosphere which seemed to follow her around whenever she ventured into the village centre, forget all the dirty looks Ms Taunton had given her – what was going on there, anyway? Was there something going on between her and Jackson? The estate agent wanted there to be, clearly, but were her feelings reciprocated?

'Argh.' She closed her eyes tightly. Why did it matter? It wasn't anything to do with her. In the slightest. Jackson could get into a relationship with whoever he wanted. Even if it was with the haughty Ms Taunton who couldn't crack a smile for anyone.

Ha, but she did for Jackson, didn't she? So that proved her theory – Ms Taunton did hold a special place in her heart for Jackson. A tiny little slither only occupied by people she deigned worthy enough to smile at.

But was he into her too? Laura tried to think back to how he had acted around her in the pub earlier. She'd hadn't been able to hear what they were saying, but she'd seen their body language. She'd been leaning towards him. Heck, Laura was pretty sure the woman would have been right up sitting on that bar if she could have. But him, what had his body language towards Ms Taunton shown? Had there been any hints at how he felt?

Stop. Laura, stop.

Lifting her forehead from the window, she walked into the guests' sitting room and flopped onto the sofa, drawing one of the floral cushions onto her lap. She wasn't thirteen with a huge crush on her brother's best friend anymore. Heck, she'd been married! And she was a grown adult. The stupid teenage crush was long since dead.

And it wasn't as though she hadn't seen Jackson since they were teenagers. She had. They'd spent many a family Christmas dinner and summer BBQ together. Plus, her mum's monthly roasts up until recently, and she'd never questioned her feelings towards him like she was doing now.

Pulling the cushion down, she placed it on the far side of the couch. She knew what the problem was, and it wasn't because that long-buried crush had suddenly resurfaced. No. It was because he was the only human being in Meadowfield who looked at her without scowling.

Yes, that's what it was. Her emotions were just playing with her.

Her phone pinged, and she grabbed it. Maybe it was Jackson thanking her again for giving his card back. After all, he had been called away before they'd a real chance to talk.

Oh, Jenny.

> Hi, sis. Just thought I'd let you know that we're out of A&E and Toby is fine. His ankle isn't broken, thank goodness! It's just a bad sprain xxx

That was great news. Laura nodded. She should have been

thinking of Toby instead of trying to decipher her stupid feelings. She tapped back quickly.

> What a relief! So glad it's not broken and I'm so sorry that it happened here xxx

Not your fault. The twins shouldn't have been playing on the stairs or sliding down the banister. They know better xxx

> Still, I feel awful. You'll have to come round again. I didn't even show you around properly xxx

Yes, definitely. Think we'll wait until it's not so much of a health hazard, though! Haha xxx

A health hazard? Is that what Jenny and Rob thought of Pennycress? If they thought it was a health hazard, what would her paying guests think?

> It's not a health hazard. Just rotten luck and rotten wood…

Laura deleted her words. Yes, it was rotten, both wood and luck, but it had still happened. Toby had fallen, and it was because the banister had woodworm. If the same thing had happened to a guest, she'd have been sued, wouldn't she?

She tried again.

> Okay. Hope it doesn't spoil your weekend away xxx

Laura held her phone against her chin as she awaited a reply. Did Jenny blame her? She'd said it was just bad luck, but after the comment about her keeping the twins away, did she blame her?

We'll stay with the twins tonight to make sure Toby's all right, then we'll go in the morning. Still one night away :) xxx

And that made her feel even worse. Jenny and Rob were supposed to be spending the weekend celebrating their anniversary.

Keep me posted as to how he is and hope you have a great night away xxx

Thanks, sis xxxx

Great. That was it then. She'd ruined Jenny and Rob's weekend getaway and she had a hallway which, between the rotten banister and the crumbling plaster on the walls, was barely holding itself upright. Perfect.

A clatter of metal sounded from the hallway. Post! Her first post here at the inn. Laura stood up and went to investigate.

She'd been right. The noise had been the letter box. She checked the time on her watch. It was a bit late for the post, wasn't it? Bending down, she retrieved the flyer from the doormat. It wasn't a letter, after all. No wonder it was so late, it would have just been someone walking past who had delivered it.

Turning it over in her hand, Laura frowned. It was an invitation. An invitation to a village meeting. And it was for tonight. She groaned. After the day she'd had, the last thing she wanted was to drag herself out in the cold again, find the village hall and go and sit with a bunch of strangers who she was pretty certain hated her.

Yuck.

But if she didn't go, she'd become even more ostracised. And looking at it a different way, this might just be perfect timing. She could go and show her face, maybe even try to contribute to whatever was being discussed – what did a small place like Meadow-field have to discuss, or plan anyway? And if she came across as friendly and happy, then maybe, just maybe, it would show people what she could bring to village life.

Yes. She had to go. However much it filled her with dread just thinking about walking into a hall full of the people who had been less than welcoming, she needed to do it. But first she needed to brush her hair and slap a bit of make-up on. Oh, and make sure she didn't have more ivy stuck to her.

12

She was here. She was at the village hall. Laura looked down the street. Trees lined the road on one side, fields stretching out towards the horizon beyond, cottages built with the famous yellow Cotswold stone on the other side. This was picture-postcard perfect and one of the many reasons she'd moved here. Besides escaping her parents' house and a town where Harry seemed to lurk around every corner, she'd chosen to make Meadowfield her new home and the place to build her business because of views like this.

She jumped aside as a family walked past her, immersed in conversation. She had been standing there for at least ten minutes now, watching people file into the village hall. There must have been at least fifty people in there now, maybe more, maybe even a hundred. She wasn't sure. She should have counted. It would have given her something to do, taken her mind off the worry of walking in there alone.

Another group of people walked past her, this time not seeming to see her at all as she was practically forced to step down from the kerb into the road to give them more space. She recognised some of them, the man from the hardware store and the woman from the bakery. That other woman, with the long red hair, pushing a buggy, she'd been in the bakery too, hadn't she? Yes, she was sure she had. That would explain why the two women had chatted away then, because they knew each other.

Laura held her hand up towards them and smiled. Lowering it again quickly as she got zero response apart from a quick glance from the younger woman. They had seen her then. Maybe they were thinking she shouldn't be there. That she had no business attending the village meeting. Was it just for residents who had been there longer or were on a special committee or something? The leaflet that had been posted through the door may have been a mistake. Maybe she shouldn't have come after all.

Pulling the flyer from her pocket, she smoothed it out and reread the information. No, it definitely said 'all Meadowfield residents welcome and encouraged to attend'. She was meant to be here.

But she couldn't go through with it. It had been a silly idea. She'd greeted those people politely and had nothing in response. Who was to say when she went in there that anything would be different?

Nope. Nope. Nope. She wasn't ready. She'd keep going into the village centre and trying to befriend people that way, try to show them she wanted to be a part of Meadowfield life, that she was here to stay. But all in one go like this? She couldn't.

Turning, she pushed the leaflet back into her pocket as she began to walk away, straight into the path of someone else, someone who she collided with. Now that definitely wasn't the impression she'd wanted to give. Reaching up to rub her arm, she kept her eyes down. If they didn't catch a full look at her, they might not report back that she'd tried to attack a fellow villager or something equally daft. She mumbled, 'So sorry,' as she dodged out of the way and began walking again, only to feel the person grip hold of her coat and pull her back.

'Whoa. You're going in the wrong direction.'

She relaxed. She knew that voice. Turning, she raised her head. 'Sorry, Jackson. I wasn't looking where I was going.'

'No, apparently not because the village hall is that way.' Jackson released her coat and indicated the hall in front of them.

'Oh, I'm not going in there.'

'That's why you're here though, isn't it? You have the leaflet.' He pointed to the corner of the leaflet sticking up out of her coat pocket.

Laura shook her head firmly. 'I was, but I'm not anymore. I've changed my mind. I'll come along to one when I've been here a little longer.'

Taking a step back, Jackson crossed his arms and looked at her. 'Why?'

'Why? Well, no reason.' She glanced towards the hall as more villagers arrived. She hadn't realised Meadowfield was so big. Where were all these people coming from?

'Umm, that's not washing with me.'

'Okay, I just don't think it's a good idea, that's all. I'm new to Meadowfield, and I just don't think I'll be very welcome.'

'Of course you'll be welcome! Everyone has been really good to me since I've moved here.'

'To you they might have been.' She looked towards the hall again and lowered her voice. 'To me, though, I get the distinct impression I'm not expected to turn up. Or wanted.'

'To the meeting?' Jackson raised his eyebrow.

'Yes. No. Everywhere. To the village.' She shook her head. She was probably being daft. After all, Jackson was a newcomer and he felt welcomed. 'I don't know. Maybe I'm just seeing things differently.'

'I'd say so. People around here really are lovely.' As if to prove a point, Jackson held his hand up to wave at the two women from the bakery who had paused outside the hall, chatting to someone else. In return, they both smiled and raised their hands back, whilst the man they were with called across, 'Hello, Jackson.'

Laura sighed. Yep, Jackson had definitely been welcomed into the Meadowfield community. The problem must just lie with her. 'Come on then, let's go in and get this over and done with.'

'Okay!' Holding out his arm, Jackson waited until she'd looped hers through his before leading the way into the village hall.

Pausing in the entrance whilst people were ushered to their seats, Laura looked around the vast room. Wooden beams adorned the ceiling whilst large, framed photographs of the village from previous years hung between beautifully stained-glass windows. 'Wow, it's beautiful in here, isn't it?'

'It sure is. I was talking to Mrs Pierce the other day, who owns the bakery, and she told me that the hall had been in disrepair only about forty years ago and the entire village had joined together to set up a series of fundraising events to rebuild it. Think the beams had suffered from woodworm or something.' Jackson shrugged. 'Anyway, ever since then they've held monthly village meetings to keep the residents up to date with anything which may concern them.'

'Umm, maybe that's where my woodworm came from then. A village legacy.' She laughed.

'Evening, Jackson.' The man who had shunned her both in the hardware store and outside just now, nodded as they walked past.

'Evening, great night for a village meeting, isn't it, Mr Parsons?' Jackson looked back at her. 'Your what?'

'Oh, the banister at the inn collapsed, taking poor little Toby with it and apparently it's woodworm.' She shrugged as they slipped into a row of chairs before sitting on the uncomfortably hard wood.

'Toby? Is he okay? He wasn't hurt, was he?' Jackson furrowed his brow, concern etched between his eyes.

'No... well, yes he was, and Jenny and Rob had to rush him off to the hospital, but it turns out he's just sprained his ankle.' Laura slipped out of her coat, draping it over her lap. 'I'm just relieved he hasn't broken anything. He was in that much pain, bless him.'

'Ouch, sprains can still be painful. Let's hope he makes a quick recovery. Sorry, that's what you began to tell me earlier at the pub, wasn't it? Did all of your family visit?'

'No, just Jenny and Rob, and the twins, obviously. They were on their way down to Rob's parents' house.' She stood up, allowing a couple to exit their row before sitting back down again. 'They were supposed to be leaving the kids and going away for the weekend, but after the accident, they're all staying at Rob's parents' tonight and will just go away tomorrow.'

'Oh, that's a shame. I can't imagine they get much time to themselves. Not with Rob working all hours and Jenny running her own business.'

'No, I don't suppose they do.' Laura frowned. If she was honest, she'd always felt quite envious of Jenny and Rob's relationship, as they always seemed so happy together. Still in love after all this time, whereas she and Harry had fallen into the trap of friendship, or, towards the end of their marriage, only just about being able to tolerate each other. She hadn't really thought about Jenny and Rob not having that much time together. Jackson was right, though, and her damn banister had just robbed them of the precious little couple time they did have.

'Still, at least no permanent damage is done and the lovebirds still get to spend one night away on their romantic getaway.'

'True.' Leaning forward, Laura peered around Jackson. The

seats next to him were empty too, just like the ones on her side of the row now the couple had gone and sat somewhere else. She looked around the hall, most of the other rows were full and those which weren't only had one or two chairs empty.

'But woodworm? You really think it was woodworm which made the banister collapse?' There was the creasing of his forehead again.

'Yep. Definitely woodworm. Rob said as much and then I managed to get someone to come and take a look and he confirmed it.'

'As much as I love Rob, DIY is not his greatest strength, but if you've had a professional come and take a look, I suppose he'd know.' Jackson shrugged.

'I'm just hoping it hasn't spread elsewhere in the inn. By the way he was talking, it's going to be an expensive job just to eliminate it from the hallway. I dread to think how much it'll cost if the whole inn needs to be fumigated and treated.' She watched as a woman bearing the large golden chain of mayoress took to the small stage at the front of the hall.

'It's odd, though. Checks were made on all the properties within the original village when this hall was treated. That I remember because that was something Mrs Pierce stressed when she was talking about the hall being rebuilt and I wondered if that was normal practice or if the village were particularly worried about it.' Jackson shook his head. 'Although I guess it must have returned.'

'Lucky me.' Laura looked across at the stage. 'I'm guessing the meeting is run by the village mayoress then?'

'That's right and a small but well-respected group of long-term village residents.' Jackson leaned in towards her. 'I say long-term, but what I really mean is people who are likely the descendants of the original settlement hundreds of years ago who are either too proud of their heritage or too scared of the outside world to leave.'

Laura giggled.

'And by well-respected, I mean they think they're well-respected, when, in fact, everyone else is just too scared to piss them off in case they don't approve the seven-inch fence they want to erect around their front garden or the porch they need planning permission for.'

'Ah, aka the school bullies?'

'Nah, they don't really have as many powers as they like to think they do, and for the most part, they're good people. If you have a problem and go to them, you know it'll pretty much get resolved.' Jackson leaned back in his chair and crossed his arms. 'I think these village meetings add to the charm of the place. I've lived in many areas, and I've got to admit Meadowfield has a nice community vibe to it. The best I've come across.'

Laura sighed and turned to Jackson. 'If I wasn't sitting with you right now, in this hall and knew you were referring to the people here, I'd honestly think you were talking about a completely different village.'

'You've got that wrong. These people are good. They're not snooty to us outsiders like a lot of places, they're just happy people want to come and live here, be a part of their community.'

Nudging her elbow into his side, she indicated the empty chairs next to her and to the side of him. 'That's why we've been abandoned, then? Ostracised within the charming community?'

Following her gaze, Jackson sighed before shaking his head. 'It doesn't mean anything. Someone put out too many chairs, that's all. It's just coincidence.'

She twisted in her seat and looked behind her. At least a dozen people were standing along the back of the hall, leaning against the wall or perching on the long table which ran the length of the back wall. Hmm, she wasn't sure if she believed Jackson about the chairs. Still, it was good that he had been welcomed into the Meadowfield community with open arms. But then, who wouldn't like Jackson? Everyone liked Jackson, they always had. Despite his difficult home life growing up, he'd sailed through school and luckily for her as on more than one occasion he'd used his influence to help her out of sticky situations.

'Honestly, give them a chance.' Jackson lowered his voice as the mayoress shuffled her papers behind the lectern and cleared her throat, ready to address her village.

'I will.' Laura turned as the mayoress began to speak. And she would give people a chance. Or another chance. She just hoped it wouldn't take long for them to begin to accept her. She wasn't sure how long she could keep up the pretence of being happy to the people she met, how long she could pretend everything was fine to her family when they asked.

13

'And now to the serious matter of Gertrude.' The mayoress, Miss Cooke, shuffled her papers as a murmuring swept through her audience.

'Gertrude?' Laura looked at Jackson quizzically. She'd not heard that name since arriving here.

'The sheep.' Jackson whispered. 'That's what—'

'Florence!' a young woman called from behind them.

'Davina!' 'Freda!' 'Roselyn!' A group of teenagers to the left called out.

'Yes, yes.' Miss Cooke quietened the crowd.

Huh. How many fugitive sheep were there in the village? Had it been a mass escape from the farm? She'd just assumed Claudette had been a Lone Ranger, a lucky one.

'Officer Huntley will update us on this issue.' Miss Cooke's voice grew louder, bringing the attention back to herself before she stepped aside and a man in a police uniform took her place at the lectern.

Clearing his throat, Officer Huntley nodded to Miss Cooke before looking out across his audience. 'The operation to remove the sheep is ongoing, and we are dealing with it as a matter of urgency. I am aware that chaos has been caused on the village green and the snowdrops planted by our students at the primary school have taken a bashing—'

'What about the allotments? My fences are down. Again. Who's going to repair those? I've already done it once.' A man with a long beard and flat cap stood up, waving his hand to grab the police officer's attention.

'That's right, we've had numerous reports detailing the destruction at the allotments,' Officer Huntley continued.

Laura tugged on Jackson's coat to get his attention. 'Destruction? Chaos? Vandalisation? We are still talking about the sheep, aren't we? Or have I missed something and they're now discussing an unruly gang of criminals?'

Covering his mouth with his hand, Jackson muffled a chuckle. 'You know these farm animals, a dangerous bunch they are.'

'What with bandanas covering their faces in fear of recognition and carrying baseball bats for protection?' Laura grinned.

'Exactly. Who wants to come across one of them in a dark alleyway?' Jackson's eyes creased with suppressed laughter. 'Although you could have fallen from the roof, remember? So the point is proven that the devastation caused by an escapee can have dire consequences.'

'Oh yes, if I had, I guess this would now be a murder investigation.'

'I should think so.'

An elderly woman in the front row stood up. 'I just hope this matter is resolved before the spring. I spent hours planting bulbs. I would hate for anything to happen to my daffs when they begin to grow.'

'The blighter was in my garden again last night, came right through the hedge she did, leaving a gaping hole and muddy paw prints all over my patio.' A man shook his fist, his face growing a deep shade of red.

'Paw prints? A sheep with paws? Like with fur and pads and everything?' Jackson spoke behind his hand.

'Don't. I think I'm going to burst out laughing in a moment.' Laura swallowed, her shoulders beginning to shake as she tried to keep a straight face.

Jackson shrugged. 'You and me both.'

'As I've said before, please continue to report sightings and I'm hopeful that one day in the near future we'll be able to locate the sheep's refuge.' Officer Huntley stepped back from the lectern; a flush of relief evident on his face.

'Thank you, Officer Huntley. Very reassuring to know that you're still on the case.' Miss Cooke took her position again. 'And I'll reiterate what Officer Huntley has said, any and all sightings must be reported and hopefully we can get this case closed and Gertrude off our streets.'

Leaning across to Jackson again, Laura lowered her voice. 'What about Claudette? Or the other sheep? Why aren't they going after them too?'

Jackson looked back at her and grinned. 'They're—'

'Lovely to see you, Jackson. I didn't realise you were sitting behind me.' Turning in her chair, Ms Taunton reached through the gap between her chair and the person next to her and laid her hand on Jackson's knee.

Clearing his throat, Jackson nodded at her as she turned back around.

Searching his face, Laura noticed his cheeks had pinked.

'And that brings us to the final matter of the evening, the upcoming craft fair.' Miss Cooke cracked a smile. 'The village council have been working tirelessly to recruit stallholders from our village and the surrounding ones and the variety of goods which will be on offer sounds divine. We do still have a list of volunteers needed though, so I'll pass you over to Jill Davies.'

Jill, a red-haired woman with a young toddler clinging to her leg, stepped onto the stage and opened a small notebook. 'Evening, everyone. I apologise for the clingy, exhausted toddler, we're transitioning from having naps to no naps, and, yep you guessed it, this one sneaked in a nap today, so rather than leaving him at home to disrupt bedtime for the other kids, he's here with me.'

Miss Cooke rubbed the toddler's back before stepping back. 'I'm sure you'll be a good boy while Mummy talks, won't you?'

'You have more faith than me.' Jill smiled at Miss Cooke before turning back to the villagers. 'It's looking as though we're going to have some really marvellous handcrafted creations on offer for our first craft fair of the year, but there are a few voluntary positions we're hoping to be able to fill this evening. First off, we're hoping to sell tea and coffee from the kitchen here and...'

Laura turned and glanced towards the back of the hall. A door led off to the side, with a wooden hatch next to it.

'...Which brings me to the reason I'm standing in front of you tonight.' Jill leaned down and picked up her toddler, positioning him on her hip before continuing. 'Well, one of the reasons. The first was to update you all, the other is to plead for volunteers who would be willing to put an hour's work in serving drinks and cakes in the kitchen and helping set up the stalls in the morning and tidy up after the event.'

Now, Laura thought, this might just be the perfect opportunity for her to contribute towards village life and to prove to people that she was in it for the long haul, that she meant to stay living in Meadowfield and that the inn wasn't just a money deal for her. Before she could back out, she raised her arm in the air.

Jackson nudged her side and raised his hand, too. 'I'll join you.

Might even bring Eden along. She'd love helping out and serving cake.'

'Aw, that's a good idea.' Laura smiled. He was so sweet thinking about his niece.

'Fantastic! What a response!' Jill high-fived her toddler's tiny hand. 'I'll just pop your names down. Please keep your hands in the air until I've said your name.'

Miss Cooke stepped back to the lectern and took Jill's notebook. 'I'll take the names down. Thank you, Jill.'

'Great. Thanks again, everyone. It's so lovely to see we've got such a great support in Meadowfield for these events.' Jill stepped down from the stage and made her way back to her seat in the front row as her toddler waved to the audience.

'Aw, such a sweetie,' Jackson whispered across to her as he waved back to the small child.

'Yes.' Laura smiled. She hadn't seen this side of Jackson before, not before moving to Pennycress and seeing him with his niece. Yes, he'd always been the 'fun uncle', as Richie called him, to Richie and Jenny's children, or he had when she'd last seen him with them at a family roast before he'd stopped coming, but this was different. Was he broody?

'Penny for them.' Jackson leaned closer, the fragrance from his aftershave tickling her nose.

'Well, if you must know, I was wondering if you'd reached that time in your life when you were thinking about—'

'Ron, thank you.' Miss Cooke jabbed her pen towards the raised hands in the audience before scribbling in the notebook. 'Lesley, again, thank you.'

'If I was what?' Jackson's voice was quiet, his eyes focused on Laura as Miss Cooke continued to call out to the volunteers.

Laura shifted in her seat, suddenly feeling self-conscious. What if he thought she was insinuating that she and him...? She shook her head. Where had that thought even come from? With one arm still raised, she tugged on the collar of her coat. It suddenly felt quite warm in the stuffy old hall.

'Susanne, thanks, love. Rachel, great help.' Miss Cooke's pen would soon be in danger of running out of ink, the list seemed to be growing that quickly.

'Broody.' She blurted the word out louder than she'd meant to and cringed as Ms Taunton and the couple sitting in front of them turned around, their eyes wide and their mouths gaping. She covered her face with her free hand and inwardly groaned.

Seemingly oblivious to the attention they'd gained, Jackson answered, 'Maybe. I'd like kids one day, that's for sure.'

'Right,' Laura muttered under her breath, a fierce heat still flooding her face.

'Freda, amazing,' Miss Cooke continued.

'And you?'

'Me?' Could this conversation get any more awkward? Not that she should be feeling awkward with Jackson. They used to speak about anything and everything, but... 'Same as you. One day.'

Nodding, Jackson grinned before nudging her again with his free elbow and indicating Miss Cooke on stage. 'If this list of volunteers gets any longer, I don't think there'll be anyone left in the village to go and buy the crafty bits on sale.'

'Haha, you're right.' Thankful for the change in conversation, Laura felt her shoulders relax, though she kept one arm resolutely raised.

'Jackson, lovely to have you in our group of volunteers.' Miss Cooke abruptly closed her notebook, entrapping the pen inside. 'And I think we have all the volunteers we need. Many thanks to the kind souls who are willing to give up their time for the greater good of the community.'

Huh, that was it? They'd got to Jackson and suddenly all the voluntary roles were filled? Laura lowered her arm slowly and looked around. Was she the only one in the position of being passed over to volunteer? It looked like it. 'Great... My warm welcome into village life continues.'

'Shhh!' The woman from the couple in front of them twisted in her seat again and glared.

'Sorry,' Laura mumbled and resisted the strong urge to roll her eyes.

'Aw, don't take it personally. They've got half the village as volunteers already.' Jackson tilted his head towards her.

'Erm, then one more wouldn't have made a jot of difference, would it? I tell you, I'm not welcome here.' She crossed her arms and sank lower in her chair. 'No one wants me here.'

'Are you pouting?'

She narrowed her eyes at him. She could see the twitching in the corners of his lips, could almost hear his internal chuckle. 'It's okay for you. Everyone loves you. They always do.'

'Laura?' Jackson gave her a look which reminded her of her college tutor.

She shrugged and whispered back, 'It's true.'

'And that's all for tonight's meeting. Thank you for coming.' Miss Cooke's voice cut through the audience and just as soon as she'd finished uttering her last word, people started to stand and file out.

14

'Come on, let's get you out of here before you decide the whole county has turned on you.' After standing up, Jackson held his hand out towards her and grinned.

'Okay, but on our way out, watch how people react to me.' Taking his hand, she let herself be pulled up.

'I will.'

Letting go of his hand, she followed him outside and pulled her coat tighter around her. She'd forgotten how cold it was. 'Watch this, then.'

'Watch what?' Jackson slowed his pace as they walked through the small garden of the village hall.

'This.' Pausing, she scrutinised the huddles of people: a group of women clustered around Jill Davies beneath the tree just outside the garden; a group of older people, mostly couples, gathered around Miss Cooke, their voices low and serious; a couple who were bending over their newborn in a pram. Now, who did she choose to prove her point? Not Miss Cooke. With the external hard shell of a tortoise, she would be an obvious choice. Not the couple. They were too busy cooing over their offspring to pay any attention to anyone, let alone a newbie. The group of women then. Perfect. Putting on her sunniest grin, Laura waved towards them as she and Jackson walked past. 'Evening! Great meeting.'

'Hi...' Jill spoke up, but abruptly broke off as a woman with jet-black hair nudged her.

Turning back to Jackson, Laura drew in a deep breath. Despite being overtly shunned, she at least felt victorious. Maybe now he'd believe her. 'See?'

'Well... They may have just been busy discussing the upcoming craft fair?' He rubbed his hand across his face before looking over his shoulder at Jill and her friends.

'Seriously, Jackson? Did you really not see that? How that other woman stopped Jill from speaking to me? They're ignoring me, they really are.' She shoved her hands in her pockets. She knew what she'd seen and tonight had given her the confirmation that she wasn't being paranoid. Something was going on. Whether or not Jackson could see it.

'Okay, I admit, something was a little off, but...' Jackson glanced back at the group. 'They were probably just engrossed in their conversation, that's all.'

Raising her eyebrows, she looked across at him. Judging by the way he was frowning, he'd definitely noticed something too.

'Look, if you're still worried, I'll ask around at work. See what I can find out.'

'Thank you. I just don't understand it. Mind, you've been seen at the meeting with me tonight. They might not be talking to you tomorrow.' She followed Jackson as he crossed to the other side of the road.

'You mean it might be contagious?' He chuckled.

'Whatever "it" is.' She curled her fingers around the word 'it'. 'Yes, maybe.'

'I really—'

'Jacks, there you are!' Catching up with them, Ms Taunton placed her hand on Jackson's arm.

'Evie? Hi.' Pausing, Jackson looked from the estate agent to Laura and back again.

'Can I have a quick word?' Ms Taunton glared at Laura. 'In private?'

'Oh, sure. I need to get back, anyway,' Laura mumbled.

'No, I—'

Jackson's voice was lost as the other woman began speaking again. 'Thank you.'

Turning, Laura began walking down the street. Evie? Ms Taunton's name was Evie? But Evie was such a pretty name. Not that Ms Taunton – Evie Taunton – wasn't pretty, she was. Stunningly so. But she was also harsh, and from what Laura could see, unless she was around Jackson, she was... sour. That was the only word Laura could think of. In all of her dealings with her – the viewing, the negotiations, even when she met her to collect the key – Evie Taunton had never once cracked a smile or even shown any hint of humanity towards her at all. She had never even offered her first name, instead referring to herself as Ms Taunton.

Taking her gloves from her pocket, Laura pulled them on as she turned down Wisteria Lane. She could see the willow tree in her garden from here.

And 'Jacks'? Ms Taunton had called him 'Jacks'? Jackson had always been Jackson. No nickname had ever stuck with him, and Laura and her siblings had tried a few.

'Hey, hold up.'

Turning, she paused as Jackson jogged towards her.

'You survived then?'

'Survived?' Slowing down to a walk, Jackson fell in step with Laura as she continued along the path.

'Ms Taunton. She didn't attempt to kidnap you and take her

back to her evil lair.' She rubbed her gloved hands together. It somehow felt colder here in the Cotswolds than it had back home. Maybe it was because Meadowfield was a village. Was that a thing? Less pollution. More chill factor?

'Haha, Evie's not so bad when you get to know her.' Jackson chuckled.

'And it seems you know her very well. *Jacks*.' Laura gave him a sidelong look, her eyebrows raised.

'You got me.' He held his hands in the air, palms towards her. 'We were actually together a while back.'

Laura opened and closed her mouth, unsure if he was being serious or pulling a stunt. 'Together as in together, together? Like a couple? You and her?'

'Yes. Why is that so hard to believe?'

'For so many reasons.' Laura took a deep breath in, trying to picture him and the sour estate agent together. As a couple. 'One, you've only just moved to Meadowfield and you're telling me you had a relationship with her "a while back"? I'm assuming it was a very quick relationship...?'

'No, no. We were together seven months, actually.'

'Seven *months*? How?'

'She's sold me a few houses now. Yes, I've only recently moved to Meadowfield, but I've been flipping properties around here in the Cotswolds for a couple of years. Ever since Angie and I broke up, actually.'

'Right. She's sold you a few houses? Oh, you didn't move to Meadowfield to be closer to her, did you?' Did she really want to know the answer?

'No! No, I didn't. The house I'm refurbing now was a steal. Nothing more, nothing less. Besides, our relationship was over well before I bought that place.'

'She wanted you close so she could reignite the relationship.'

Laura nodded. That made sense. 'She helped you get the house at a good price so she could try to move in on you again.'

'What? No!'

'Yes.'

'Absolutely not! We're nothing more than friends now.' Jackson set his jaw, his expression serious.

'Or that's what you think.' She was right. She knew she was, even if Jackson couldn't see it.

'Ha, it's what I think because it's true.' He walked closer to her and nudged her with his arm, causing her to step to the side before he pulled her back to him.

'Uh-huh. I'll rephrase that statement then.' Linking her arm through his, she leaned up towards his ear and stage-whispered, 'She still has a crush on you.'

Coming to a stop, Jackson looked over at her and grimaced. 'Oh, she really does not. We both agreed it wasn't working. Besides, she quickly got with someone else.'

'And she's still with this boyfriend?' Both agreed? Laura would bet her last pound on the fact Evie hadn't wanted the relationship to be over.

'Well, no, they broke up about a month afterwards.' Jackson shook his head. 'But Evie does not have still have feelings for me.'

'You just keep telling yourself that.' Laura laughed. It felt good to be able to have a laugh with Jackson. Yes, for not the first time, she was actually glad she'd bought the inn right next to him. 'Do you know something?'

'I know a lot of things.' Jackson pushed out his chest, his expression serious but his lips twitching. 'But enlighten me.'

'When I first opened the door of Pennycress to find you standing there with your welcome basket, I never in a million years thought I'd be saying this now, but I'm actually pretty pleased you're here in Meadowfield.'

'You are?'

'Yep. I am. I mean, there's still a little bit of me which is beyond annoyed I don't get to have my completely fresh start.' She held her thumb and forefinger millimetres apart. 'But if someone had to be here, I'm glad it's you.'

Jackson stopped and looked at her, his eyes illuminated by the light of the moon. 'If it means anything, I'm pleased you're here, too.'

Laura glanced down at the ground before meeting his gaze, his blue eyes holding hers, the world around them coming to a stop.

Blinking and breaking eye contact, Jackson pointed forward. 'We'd best get home. Billy is dropping Eden off before school again tomorrow morning so I need to make sure I get up in time to cook her something nice for breakfast as well as get set for work.'

'Right. Yes. Homeward bound.' What had just happened between them? That look. That hadn't been a friend's look.

As they began walking again, Laura looked up at the moon. It was full and hanging low in the sky, its white glow lighting the street ahead of them with an unearthly radiance. It must have just been a friend's look. This was Jackson. He was her brother's best friend, a family friend, her friend. Nothing else. Just a... friend.

With his eyes fixed firmly on the path ahead of them, Jackson kicked at a stone, watching as it ricocheted off the low garden wall to their right and rolled to a stop perilously close to a blue Mercedes.

Laura looked across at him quickly before focusing ahead again. She needed to bring the conversation back to life, to feel normality again. She needed to suppress the feelings of lust which were growing in the pit of her stomach. If that was what they were. Which, of course they clearly weren't. She couldn't be feeling that way towards him, towards Jackson, could she?

Pushing all thoughts of how she felt about him from her mind, she laughed. 'What are you cooking for breakfast then? You might as well tell me, so I don't need to stand out in the front garden and sniff the air.'

'Ooh, I was thinking French toast.' Jackson plunged his hands in his pockets and grinned, seemingly glad of a chance to talk about what he loved most, cooking.

'Fancy! You know, I'm still not quite sure what French toast actually is.' She felt her shoulders relax. 'I used to be convinced it was just a posh name for eggy bread.'

Dropping his jaw, Jackson gave a dramatic gasp. 'I can't believe you just said that! That needs to be rectified as soon as possible. One day I'll make you some.'

As they came to a stop in front of Pennycress, Laura raised her eyebrows at him. 'Is that a promise?'

'Of course.' Jackson ran his fingers through his hair.

'Great.' Laura glanced towards the gate as heat flooded across her neck towards her face. She needed to get inside. Tugging off her scarf, she turned and fumbled with the gate latch. 'See you around.'

'Yes, see you. And don't worry about the weird reaction from that group of women. I'll try to get the intel at work tomorrow.' Jackson stepped forward and clicked up the latch with ease, his fingers brushing against hers on the cold iron gate.

'Great. That would be great. Super great, thanks.' What was this? A 'squeeze as many "greats" into one conversation as she could' competition? His fingers brushing against hers... had that been intentional? Of course it hadn't. He was Richie's best mate, a family friend, a friend. She repeated the mantra in her head as she walked down the garden path, the lavender still brushing against her ankles, the sweet earthy perfume filling the cold night air, but fewer strands of unruly ivy tangling around her trainers after all the gardening she'd been doing. Yes, think about the gardening, Laura. There was still so much to do. The flowerbeds needed to be replanted, the willow tree needed cutting, trimming, pruning, bulbs...

'Laura?' Jackson's voice cut through her thoughts.

Slowly turning, she hoped the moon's glow and the light from the streetlamp behind weren't enough to show just how quite bright red her face was. Although she felt so hot that quite possibly her skin had taken on a glow of its own. She dug in her pockets, drawing out the purple plastic teddy keyring before gripping it in both hands. 'Yes?'

'Your scarf.' Taking a few long strides down the garden path towards her, Jackson stood in front of her, the scarf draped across his hands. 'It must have fallen.'

'Oh, right. Thank you.' She glanced down at her bunched hands; the teddy digging into her palms, suddenly a little unsure of what she might do if she were to reach out to take her scarf. Why was she feeling like this about him?

Standing there, a mere few inches away from her, Jackson tilted his head before reaching forward and gently laying the scarf around her neck, the two ends still in his grasp as he stood in front of her.

Laura looked into his eyes. His pupils were dilated, his irises deep and dark in the moonlight. She could almost feel the air between them tingle with electricity before Jackson dropped the ends of her scarf and stepped back quickly, the spell dissipating.

Blinking, Laura watched as he dithered on the spot for a moment, his eyes searching hers before he ran the palm of his hand over his face and turned slowly on his heels.

'Jackson?' Her voice was unsure. She could hear the rise and dip as she mumbled his name.

He spun around to face her again. 'Yes?'

Clearing her throat, she indicated her scarf. 'Thanks.'

With a quick nod, he turned and hurried back down the path.

Half walking, half running the few short steps to the porch, Laura unlocked the door and slipped inside, grateful as the darkness of the inn embraced her. Had that just happened? Had he felt it too?

Shutting the door firmly behind her, she leaned her back against it, the back of her head lying against the cool of the stained-glass window. He must have. The moment had been brief, fleeting even, but it had been there. She'd felt it, and judging by his reaction, by the speed with which he'd walked away, he had too.

She slid down to the floor, her legs outstretched on the doormat beneath her. It was wrong. So wrong. She took a deep breath and muttered her mantra. 'He's Richie's best mate, a family friend. Just a friend.'

Closing her eyes, she spoke her words louder each time she said them, with the hope that the louder and more clearly she spoke them, the greater would be her conviction. 'He's Richie's best mate, a family friend. Just a friend. He's...'

Covering her eyes with her hands, she pressed. She couldn't be having these feelings for him. It wasn't right.

She lowered her hands and looked around. She could pick out the dark shadow of the reception desk opposite her, the banister rising behind it, the broken pieces of wood kicked to the side of the wall. It was all unfamiliar, but she could just about make out the little bits she could see in the dim moonlight fighting its way through the stained-glass window.

Letting out a loud laugh, she grinned. That was it. She was

only having these so-called feelings for Jackson Scott because he was the only familiar person she knew in Meadowfield. She wasn't lusting after him; her teenage crush wasn't resurfacing. No, it was a feeling of familiarity. She was clinging onto him – metaphorically speaking, of course – because he was here. It wasn't even because he was Jackson. She'd likely be feeling the same way if it had been any of Richie's friends, or any bloke she already knew. She was just hankering after a safety net, someone familiar, and the way she'd been treated by the so-called welcoming residents of Meadowfield had only amplified these mixed-up feelings.

And Jackson hadn't acted strangely because he was feeling the same way, because he 'felt' something too. No, he'd acted the way he had because he'd been confused. Because she'd been weird with him, awkward.

Tucking her hair behind her ears, she reached up to the door handle behind her and pulled herself to standing. She just hoped he hadn't guessed how she'd been feeling. Or how she thought she'd been feeling at the time. With him her only companion, her only constant in a sea of unfamiliarity, the last thing she wanted was to push him away over nothing.

15

Laura shifted her canvas bag higher on her shoulder. The carton of orange juice was still digging into her side and as much as she tried shifting around the items in her shopping bag, she couldn't get things comfy.

She glanced back at the small grocery shop. If it wasn't for the chilly atmosphere she'd just escaped from, she would have popped back in to ask for another bag, but if she didn't step foot inside there again, it'd be too soon. The look Miss Cooke had given her when she'd walked in and picked up a basket would give her nightmares for weeks, and the man on the till had been no better, tapping the small screen to indicate how much she owed rather than even muttering the amount out loud to her.

She sighed. That was it. She'd had enough. From now on, she'd shop elsewhere. There was a big retail park with every shop she could need just a half-hour's drive away and a supermarket closer than that.

Yes, she'd tried to spend her money in the local shops to support local businesses and local people, but they'd made it crystal clear they didn't want her, so she'd take her money somewhere else, she'd line the pockets of the big chain stores if she had to.

She looked up as a big fat raindrop splattered on her forehead and dribbled down her nose and picked up her pace as the heavens opened, releasing a torrent of rain. Pulling her hood over her head, she looked down at her bag, the mint green canvas quickly turning a deep evergreen. If she didn't get a move on, the bag of flour she'd bought would soon turn to a gloopy mess and the croissant she'd treated herself to, a mound of sodden dough.

As she turned the corner, a clap of thunder vibrated through the sky, shortly followed by a flash of lightning. Fantastic. More rain and more thunder, even the weather was making it obvious she wasn't welcome. That's all it seemed to do here – rain. She spotted the pub as the rainfall increased and the thunder rumbled around her again. She'd run in there and take shelter before venturing out again.

Yes, she'd have to face Jackson, who she'd been hoping to avoid for the day at least, but if she was honest, it would be good to see him and realise all the mixed-up feelings from last night had been just that – mixed-up. She might even be able to get a good night's sleep tonight after seeing him and setting to rest any notion of there being anything between them, because she certainly hadn't slept well last night.

Ha, it would kill two birds with one stone, so to speak: quieten the ridiculous feelings she was having about Jackson and provide a shelter from the storm as well.

She crossed the road, jumping over the puddle forming against the kerb before she pushed the heavy wooden door open.

It was the warmth from the open fire which hit her first; that and the dry. She reached up to yank her hood down, but then froze. She noticed the frustrated tone of Jackson's voice before her brain deciphered the words he was speaking. The tone caught her off guard. This was Jackson. Forever the calm one, the even keel. Not today though. She hadn't heard him sound so angry for years, not since Mike had cheated on her and broken her heart in college and she'd caught Jackson having a go at him down the alley which ran behind the supermarket in their hometown.

'...And you really think you're one to preach? You moved into your place after Will was sent to live with his daughter. And you, Ron, didn't I hear you'd...' Jackson's voice trailed off as Ms Taunton stood up from her bar stool.

Holding the edge of her hood, Laura peered across the pub floor. It sounded as though Jackson was in the middle of an argument, but with who? A group of five or six people were gathered around the bar, Evie Taunton to the side.

She began walking, weaving through the tables, suddenly eager for him to have someone on his side.

'Jacks, I don't know why you're getting so het up about it. She's just a newbie and the sooner she takes the hint and moves out of Pennycress Inn, the quicker things can go back to how they were.'

Pennycress Inn? She? Were they referring to her? Laura stopped short and pulled her hood lower, shielding her face and identity from them.

'That's right. It should never have been sold,' the man Jackson had referred to as Ron took a sip from his pint glass before continuing. 'We need to stick together.'

'No, you all need to butt out and give Laura a chance. I know it's an adjustment with the inn being in new hands, but Laura is a good person and she'd be a valuable asset to the village if you just let her.' Jackson took a deep breath. 'The way each and every one of you shunned her yesterday, you should be ashamed of you behaviour.'

He had noticed then.

'Hey, no need for that, Jacks. We're only trying to do the right thing.' Evie rubbed her fingers across Jackson's hand.

'No, you're really not.' Looking down at the bar, Jackson shook his head and pulled his hand away. 'This is no way to behave, and you all know it. Drop the stupid pact and grow up.'

'Now...' Ron pointed his pint glass in Jackson's direction. 'We welcomed you to the village with open arms. You know there's more to this than her being a newcomer.'

Pulling the tea towel from his shoulder, Jackson threw it onto the bar before turning and disappearing into the kitchen.

As the group huddled closer and lowered their voices, Laura stood still and held her breath. Was he going to come back out?

One man turned, holding up his hand to the group and raising his voice. 'Back to work I go. Catch you later.'

As if being shocked into moving, Laura turned quickly and walked to the door, her head down, trying desperately not to draw any attention to herself. They hadn't noticed her, had they? As the man reached the door before her and held it open, she shuffled through, glad she'd escaped unnoticed.

Outside, she headed back to the inn, oblivious to the rain drenching her coat and bag, the rumble of thunder around her. What had just happened? What had she witnessed?

As she reached the top of Wisteria Lane, her hood slipped from its position, but she continued, the rain quickly soaking her hair, strands sticking to her wet cheeks. She didn't care. She'd been right. At least she hadn't been paranoid. A strangled laugh escaped her lips. That was a good thing, wasn't it? She wasn't going crazy, she was just being shunned in an attempt to... what? Make her sell up? Run back to her parents' with her tail between her legs?

Letting the gate swing closed behind her, she hurried down the garden path towards the porch. Her first instinct was to flee.

To pack up her bags and escape. To give the villagers what they wanted. But what then? Where would she be? Homeless and penniless, living with her parents again. Without a job and with no prospect of moving on.

Of course, it wouldn't be forever. It would only be until Pennycress sold, and she found somewhere else. Somewhere more welcoming. Somewhere without crumbling plaster. Without woodworm. And preferably with a bog-standard electric oven too.

Huh, maybe it would be a good thing in the long run. She'd at least know a little more of what she was looking for.

She closed the door behind her and made her way into the kitchen, placing her bag of wet shopping on the table. Shrugging out of her coat, she headed out into the hallway, into the sitting room, before taking the stairs. As she wandered around the guest bedrooms, she ran her fingers across the golden wallpaper in one room, the large roses emblazoned upon a cream background in another, the path of raised vines on the feature wall of another room.

She didn't want to leave. She loved this place. Despite there being more work involved before she could open than she'd ever imagined there would be, there was something about it. About the bones of the place, about the building.

She'd fallen in love with Pennycress, and she wanted to stay.

Sinking to the top step of the ornate staircase, Laura bundled her wet hair into a messy bun. Those people wouldn't run her out of Meadowfield. She'd just have to make them see she was a good person who only wanted the best for the inn.

And that needed to start right now.

Standing up, she ran down the stairs and grabbed her car key. She'd start with fixing the plaster and as she now knew there was no chance of getting a professional in and why she'd been turned down by them all, she'd do it herself. How hard could it be? There were YouTube videos for everything, right?

16

Laura wiped the back of her hand across her forehead, feeling a smear of wall filler against her skin. Yuck. Standing back, she crossed her arms, getting yet more white goo across her T-shirt, and surveyed the hallway.

Strips of wallpaper lay strewn across the floor, with small mounds of crumbled plaster mixed in. And the dust! The fine white powdery dust covered everything: the reception desk, what was left of the woodworm-riddled banister, as well as herself.

Her plan of only filling in the gaps in the plaster which she'd discovered during the previous days had soon turned to ripping the wallpaper from the whole of the hallway. She'd begun filling in the first patch which had crumbled when she'd been on the phone to her parents, but every time she'd brought the little scraper up to the wall to smooth the wall filler, more of the old stuff had crumbled away and before she'd known it she'd uncovered a patch the size of a dinner plate and then a large oven tray, until she'd taken off a whole metre square of wallpaper and the wall was still crumbling beneath her fingers.

Still, it needed doing, and it needed doing right. And now,

with the wallpaper on the floor, she could see where the worst of the old plaster was crumbling. She squeezed the last of the ready-mixed wall filler from the tube and threw the empty container onto the heap of three other empty ones behind her before beginning to smooth the blob.

Laura took the final tube of wall filler from where it was sitting on the reception desk and cut the sealed top off. In hindsight, if she'd known how many patches there were, she'd have looked into replacing with plasterboard. Although, of course, she'd have only been back to the same old problem of struggling to find a professional willing to fix it for her.

No, this way, although she was certain it was probably more awkward and time consuming, at least she'd have it done in one day. And she'd have done it herself, too. She contemplated taking a photo to send to her parents but, catching sight of her hands, decided that gloating wasn't worth ruining her phone for.

Running a palm over the final section of the wall, she winced as yet more plaster snowed down. Still, at least the dodgy patches were flaking off easily, apart from this one patch about halfway up the wall at shoulder height, where the hole was deeper than she'd discovered elsewhere, and yet there was still more plaster coming off.

She pulled out the screwdriver she'd been using, which she'd found where Jackson had left it on top of the washing machine, and had stashed in her back pocket. Then gently tapped the small section. She just needed to get to the solid stuff. Nowhere else had been a problem, the plaster had finished crumbling a few millimetres beneath the surface.

Jabbing the screwdriver in a little harder this time, Laura screamed and jumped back as a spurt of water sprayed her in the face.

'No, no, no!' She couldn't have hit a pipe. She couldn't have.

The hole didn't go that deep, just a centimetre or two at the most. There wouldn't be a pipe there, and if there was, where would it be going? It was the hallway, not the kitchen or a bathroom.

She lifted her hands, quickly replacing them again as water shot out. She'd definitely hit a pipe, and it was definitely water. What now?

Pulling her mobile from her pocket, all thoughts of getting the screen covered with gloop gone, she kept one hand over where the water was escaping while attempting to scroll through the search engine to find a local plumber. Stabbing the call button, she held the phone against her ear.

'Hello, Heale Plumbers Limited.'

'Hi, I've got an emergency and need someone to come out now, please.' She took a deep breath. She might as well tell them where she was ringing from. She really didn't have the time to go through their pleasantries if they were just going to put the phone down on her once she'd told them. 'It's Pennycress Inn, Meadowfield.'

'I'm sorry, all our plumbers are bus—'

Ending the call, Laura scrolled through to the next one and the next one and the one after that, with all the same conclusions. Each either cutting the call dead or making excuses as to why they couldn't send anyone to help.

She screamed, her voice echoing around the hallway. This could not be happening. She hadn't done anything to deserve to be treated in this way. She hadn't hurt anyone, she hadn't turfed anyone out into the streets when she'd moved in. The inn had been empty for six months – empty! Why were people behaving this way towards her?

Laura raised her hand, ready to throw her mobile to the other side of the hall before thinking twice and holding its cool screen against her forehead. Taking deep breath after deep breath, she willed the gut-wrenching anger in the pit of her stomach to subside. It wasn't going to help the situation.

Putting her mobile back in her pocket, she placed both hands on the spot the water was spraying from, pushing against it in the vain hope that... What? It would stop? She had no idea, but what else was she supposed to do?

Tentatively, she lifted her hands. The spray had turned into a gush. She must have made the crack in the pipe worse and the pressure at which the water was escaping had only increased.

Slamming her palms back on the wall to stem the flow, Laura laid her forehead against the wall and opened her mouth, a deep guttural cry of hopelessness escaping her lips. She couldn't do this. What had she been thinking? She'd trained in admin, not hospitality, and however much research she'd crammed in before moving to Pennycress didn't make her an expert, it didn't make her capable of running this place, of fixing all the issues which came with it.

Although she hadn't planned on taking on any DIY tasks. Yes, eventually she'd kind of thought she'd learn how to maintain the place just to save money, but not now, not straight away. Pennycress was supposed to have been ready to reopen. That's why the contents had been sold along with the building, so the new owners could just move in and manage the place.

Broken guttering, loose tiles, woodworm, crumbling plaster and broken pipes weren't part of the deal. She'd thought she'd been buying an inn ready to open and start earning money, not somewhere which needed practically rebuilding.

Without thinking, she lifted one hand to wipe the tears springing from her eyes with the back of her hand, only to get a face full of water.

Slumping her shoulders and resting her head in the crook of her elbows, she tried to think. She *did* need to ring someone to help, she couldn't stay like this, in this position, forever. But who? She had no idea how far out the villagers had made a pact with traders not to do any work for her. She could be ringing round all evening and still get nowhere. She couldn't ask Richie or her dad. They lived too far away and by the time they'd arrived the place would likely be flooded. So that left only one person.

Jackson.

Who she hadn't spoken to since that weird moment in the garden. Who she'd heard sticking up for her in the pub. Who she had so many questions for, but all to which she didn't want the answers.

She had no choice, though. She knew that.

Bracing herself, she took one hand off the wall and ducked out of the way of the oncoming water before pulling her phone out and ringing him.

'Laura, hi. How are things? I was—'

'Jackson. I need your help. Right away.' She swallowed, her voice hoarse. 'Please.'

'Oh, okay. I'll pop round now.' And then he was gone. The phone silent.

Letting her mobile drop onto the mounds of wallpaper covering the floor, Laura began to cry.

17

The feeble tune of the doorbell pierced the silence in the hallway and Laura looked towards the front door. 'Jackson, is that you? Come on in, it's open.'

'Yes, it's me,' he called.

Laura watched as the front door inched open and Jackson stepped through, his jaw dropping as the door swung to a close behind him. She tried to wipe her face on the top of her arms. She'd prefer him to see her covered in plaster rather than spot the tears of self-pity drying on her cheeks. 'Surprise,' she muttered weakly.

'Jeez, Laura. What's happened here? It looks as though a herd of rabid goats have been let loose.'

'Or sheep.' Her voice was quiet, defeated, the joke a lame way to cover up how she was feeling. She watched as he waded through the wallpaper and plaster covering the floor until he was beside her.

'And I'm guessing from the way you're holding your hands and the fact you're completely drenched, that you've hit a pipe?'

She narrowed her eyes. Was he trying to be funny? At least

their moment from yesterday had well and truly passed. 'No, I'm installing a hallway shower. I'm surprised you've not heard of them, what with all the renovating you do. It's all the craze, apparently. Decontaminate the guests before they enter.'

'Okay, okay.' Jackson held his hands up, palms forward, a sheepish expression on his face. 'I asked for that. Let's take a look.'

'My pleasure.' Stepping back, she removed her hands, watching the water spurt out before jumping back into place and stemming the flow again. 'Believe me now?'

Frowning, Jackson shook his head slightly, obviously thinking better of cracking another joke. 'Give me a moment and I'll turn the water off at the stopcock.'

Laura watched him disappear through to the kitchen and listened as he rummaged through the cupboard under the sink before appearing back by her side.

'It's not working. It seems to be stuck. I'll run next door and grab my tools but will see if I can find the outside one on my way. Hold tight.'

Laura breathed heavily out through her nose. 'I'm not going anywhere.'

'No, of course not. Two minutes.' Turning on his heels, Jackson rushed outside, leaving the front door slightly ajar behind him.

Sniffing, Laura surveyed the hallway. She couldn't blame him for making a joke. It did rather look as though a herd of goats had made themselves at home. Still, it hadn't been the right time and she certainly wouldn't be in the mood to joke about the situation anytime soon. This – the pipe, the plaster, the wallpaper – was going to push her opening date back and drain the remaining few pounds in her savings account. And that was if she could find a tradesperson who was willing to step across the threshold.

She heard the clink of the gate shut, and then Jackson reappeared. Relief flooded through her at the thought of having him to help, and once again she was thankful her plan to have a completely fresh start had been flawed. 'Did you find the outside stopcock? Can I step away?' Laura shifted, ready to remove her hands.

'No!' Jackson shouted and held up a hand. 'I couldn't find it. It's probably long hidden under the grass or flowerbeds or somewhere.'

'Okay,' Laura answered. 'What now? Am I just going to have to stay like this for eternity?'

'Hey, I've got you. We'll fix it.' Jackson laid his hand gently on her shoulder.

And she believed him. Right there, right then, she believed that he had her back, that he would be able to undo the damage that she'd done.

'Right, let's see what we need.' Hefting his large toolbox onto the reception desk, Jackson filled his pockets with a handful of tools before coming to stand next to her. 'Okay, let's do this slowly to limit the amount of water which escapes.'

After toing and froing for a few minutes, Jackson had full control of the pipe and Laura was finally free.

'Ouch.' She rolled her shoulders back, trying to relieve some of the pain travelling from her fingertips to her neck.

'You okay?' With one hand blocking the pipe, he looked across at her and frowned.

'I will be. I just ache after standing in the same position for so long.' She rubbed her hands up and down her arms. She was cold too and the wet clothes weren't helping. 'Thank you for coming to the rescue.'

'No problem at all. Happy to help.' Jackson looked around the room again before pulling a rag from his back pocket. 'I've got to ask, what happened here?'

'Everything.' Laura slumped against the reception desk,

suddenly unable to hold her emotions in check any longer. 'There were a couple of patches of crumbling plaster, so I stupidly decided that I could patch it up.'

'That's not stupid.'

'Oh, it is.' She kicked at the pile of used tubes of ready-mixed wall filler. 'I kept finding more and more patches and before I knew it, the wallpaper was ruined and the easiest thing was to rip the rest of it down so I could see where the wall needed filling.'

'That makes sense.'

'Does it? Does it really? Because from where I'm standing, nothing does anymore. I bought the damn place in the hope I could freshen it up a little and open it up straight away, start earning money, and now... now even if I had enough in my savings, I can't even get any tradespeople in to help me, anyway.' She sank to the floor. She was covered in plaster debris, pieces of sticky wallpaper and water from the pipe anyway. What would a little more do?

'You'll sort it.'

'No, no, I won't. Have you seen the end of the banister?' She glanced behind her at the once intricately carved banister, now ruined. 'And if there's woodworm in that, well, it's probably everywhere.'

'It might not be woodworm. I'll take a look at it after this. We'll figure it out.' Jackson gave a small smile.

Laura shook her head slowly and spoke quietly as the realisation sank in. 'They were right.'

'Who was? About what?'

'My parents, Richie, Jenny...' she nodded fiercely towards the front door, 'the villagers. I'm not cut out for this, and I was pathetic for even thinking I could be.'

'Laura, you *are* cut out for this. You'd be perfect at running an inn. You're just the sort of owner that Pennycress needs.'

'Uh-uh. I'm not. It's embarrassing really. That I thought I could. I told my old work colleagues my plans before I left; my friends...' She wiped her cheeks with the pads of her thumbs. 'They'll all know what a failure I am when I return and beg for my old job back.'

'You won't...'

'And my family... well, everyone knows what they think of me already, and this will just be the confirmation they need. They knew I couldn't cope. They've been trying to talk me out of it ever since I began talking about buying an inn to run. I've failed.' She was on a roll now, all of her emotions pouring out of her. She remembered their reaction the first time she told them her plans. She'd been mulling the idea over in her mind for some time, gathering information before bringing it up in conversation during one of her mum's roast dinners.

She shook her head at the memory. Her mum had actually been speechless for a whole three minutes – her mum! And then it had been her dad who had uttered the first words – 'Are you sure, Laura? Are you certain you want to take on that amount of responsibility?' He hadn't needed to say anything else, that one question had spoken volumes to her: they didn't think she was capable. And they were right.

'Your family love you and support you. They always have. And you certainly are not a failure.'

'That's where you're wrong.' She stabbed her finger at him. 'They've never believed in me. I've always been the one who had to rely on people, first my parents, then Harry, then my parents again. And now you.'

'You're not relying on me. I happen to live next door. It's just fate.'

'No.' She began pulling little pieces of wallpaper from her T-shirt. 'They know me better than I know myself.'

With his shoulders sinking, Jackson looked across at her again. 'Nobody knows you better than you know yourself.'

Covering her face with her hands, she closed her eyes as she felt the big fat tears rolling down her cheeks. 'They do.'

'No, they don't.' Dropping the rag he held in his hand, Jackson muttered 'drat' under his breath before fixing his eyes on her. 'Look at me, Laura. Look at me.'

She slowly drew her hands back to her lap and met his gaze, their eyes locking. She didn't care that she looked a mess; she didn't care that her face was puffy and red. This was it. She couldn't go on pretending anymore that she had everything together because in that moment that illusion was so far from the truth, she'd laugh if she didn't feel so empty.

'You've got this. Pennycress Inn is a stunning building that just needs some love and attention. All the things you can give it.'

She shook her head. She didn't know why he was even pretending any longer. She'd accepted it.

Taking his hands away from the pipe, he turned to walk over to her before getting an earful of water and hurriedly turning his attention back to the wall. 'Damn.'

'Sorry,' Laura mumbled. Now look at what she'd done, she'd dragged him into this sorry mess and he'd given up his evening to help her, to get what in return? Ruined clothes and her crying at him, that's what.

'Ha, don't you apologise for that!' Jackson began to chuckle.

'I really don't see what's funny about this situation.' Laura sniffed. 'My life is falling apart around me. I mean, my property is literally falling apart around me. How is that funny?'

'It's not. It's not funny. It's just...' His expression becoming serious again, he shook his head. 'I wish you could see yourself the way I see you, the way the world sees you.'

'Like an awkwardly made Halloween costume of a snowman

having encountered a massacre with a wallpaper decorator?' She looked down at herself.

'Don't forget the pool party.' Jackson chuckled again.

'Oh yes, the pool party.' Pulling the sodden fabric of her T-shirt from her belly, she wrung it in her hands, watching the water dribbling to her lap, and slowly her tears turned to laughter as her shoulders shook and she surveyed the room, which up until a few hours earlier had been beautiful and upmarket and now looked like somewhere that had been abandoned for years and the local wildlife had made it their home.

'There, done.' Jackson stepped back cautiously, eyeing the pipe until he was sure the danger of being covered with water again had indeed been averted. Walking across to where she still sat curled up on the floor by the reception desk, Jackson lowered himself to the floor next to her.

'Thank you.'

'No problem. Nothing a little plumbers' putty won't fix.' He grinned as he ran his hands down his top, leaving a trail of grime on the once clean navy wool of his jumper. At least she could offer to wash it now the washing machine had been fixed.

'I wasn't thanking you for fixing the pipe, but thank you for that, too. I was thanking you for making me laugh.'

'Oh, well, all part of the service.' He grinned, his dimple appearing. 'Seriously though, please stop thinking and talking about yourself like that. You're one of the most capable people I know.'

'Ha, now I know you're still intent on joking.'

'I'm not joking.' He spoke quietly, each one of his words clearly spoken.

'Hmm. I know you're just trying to make me feel better, but I think we both know that's a lie.' She shivered.

'You're cold. Here, have my jumper.' Jackson pulled his jumper over his head and held it out for her.

'Don't worry, I'm disgusting.' She looked down at her T-shirt. 'I'd only get it dirty.'

'It doesn't matter. You're cold. Take it.'

'Thanks.' Pulling it on, she smiled a small sad smile. She had a wardrobe of clothes upstairs, but even fetching a jumper felt like too much for her at this moment. 'Why does everybody hate me?'

Jackson pulled a face as he leaned back against the reception desk. 'Nobody hates you.'

She rolled her eyes. 'Now there's no excuse for lying. I was there. I heard what they said in the pub earlier.'

Jackson took a deep breath in before sighing equally loudly. 'Oh.'

'Oh? That's all you've got to say?'

Rubbing his hand over his face, Jackson twisted his body so he was facing her. 'They don't hate you. They just don't like you living here.'

'They don't want me in Meadowfield?' She frowned.

'Not in Meadowfield. The fact you've moved to the village isn't the problem.'

'So it's the inn, then? They don't like the fact I bought Penny-cress.' She scratched at the cuticle on her thumb, her stomach churning. They'd seen through her already. 'They know how incompetent I am. I must just have one of those faces.'

'You're not incompetent.' Jackson shook his head. 'It's not you. They'd have a problem with anyone who had bought this place.'

'What? Why? What do they want? For it to stand derelict? To go to ruin?' She set her jaw. That wasn't fair on Pennycress. It was too beautiful for that, even with all of its problems. A flash of anger replaced the self-pity.

'It's a bit more complicated than that.'

'I'm listening.'

'Vivienne Fields was the previous tenant of Pennycress. The actual building was owned by a chap called George Yates, I believe. He moved out of Meadowfield about thirty years ago now and Vivienne had been running Pennycress ever since.'

Laura shook her head. What did Vivienne have to do with the way people were acting towards her?

'She's a very, very well-respected and liked woman in Meadowfield and the surrounding area. The inn attracted a lot of tourism, money, to the village and they were thankful to her for that.'

She looked up from her now raw cuticle. 'I don't understand. If they want Pennycress back up and running, then why won't anyone help me? Why can't I employ anyone to help with any of the tasks? Why won't anyone talk to me?'

'From what I can understand – and it's only what I've picked up here and there, so there may well be chunks of information missing...' He shrugged. 'But George Yates basically evicted Vivienne so he could put the inn up for sale.'

'And she didn't want to leave?'

'I don't think so, no. I don't think she was ready to retire. But she didn't have the money to buy at the price George was asking.'

'Oh.'

'It's still no reason for people to treat you the way they have.' A deep crimson crept up Jackson's neck from beneath the collar of his T-shirt.

'I didn't know any of this. Ms Taunton—'

'Evie.'

'Yeah, her. She didn't tell me any of this. In fact, the inn was a relatively good bargain compared to some of the other places I looked round. Especially as the sale included everything I would need to get it running again.' She looked around the hallway. 'Or I thought it was a good bargain, anyway.'

'I don't really understand why people can't see that you have nothing to do with Vivienne being evicted.' He shook his head.

She shifted position, trying to alleviate the cramping spreading up her calf. 'I guess it's a good job I'm selling up then.'

Jackson took her hands into his and met her gaze again. 'Don't do that. Please.'

'Huh, we can both see the damage I've done in just over a week. Imagine what I'll do to the place if I stay. I mean, look at that wall.' Taking in the bumpy blobs of filler covering the wall, she let out a short laugh and looked down at his hands. Her own were warm inside his. She felt safe.

'No. This needed to happen.' Jackson looked around them. 'And besides, I quite like the patchwork effect. It adds to the charm and character.'

She smiled and looked back at him. He'd made no move to pull his hands away and there was that look again. That intense look from last night when she'd been convinced they'd had 'a moment'. Or, more truthfully, convinced herself they hadn't.

'You can get it back to its former glory.' Jackson leaned forward a little. 'I can help you.'

'I'm supposed to be doing this on my own, remember?' She felt the pull too, a magnetic force as she herself inched forward. She could feel his breath against her skin, could sense the tingle between them as he paused a mere centimetre from her.

'Do you want this?' His voice was husky, nervous.

'Uh-huh.' Did she? She shouldn't. She closed her eyes as their lips met and she felt his fingers run up the nape of her neck, drawing her closer. It was... Kissing him was everything she'd ever imagined it would be: gentle, strong, wonderful. As she felt him pull away, she leaned back and searched his eyes. 'I've imagined how that would feel for a long time now.'

'Me too.' He grinned, his lips still so close to hers.

'You have?'

Drawing her towards him again, he leaned down and kissed her once more, harder this time, more passionately, before leaning back and running his hand across his face. 'Does that answer your question?'

'Umm, let me see...' It was her turn this time to run her fingers through his hair, to pull him towards her and kiss him. 'Yes, yes, I think it does.'

18

Reaching her arms above her head, Laura yawned. She hadn't slept as well as she had last night for a long time. Yes, she ached – so much – from all the work she'd done in the hallway yesterday, but she'd slept like a log. Maybe it had been because she'd been physically exhausted when Jackson had left, or maybe it had been because of the kiss, or kisses, they'd shared.

She rolled over and smiled. Today was going to be a good day. She could feel it. And she couldn't wait to see Jackson again.

The weak chime of the doorbell pulled her from her thoughts, and she threw the covers back before grabbing the jumper Jackson had lent her last night and holding it against her nose, breathing in the spicy, earthy aroma of his aftershave still distinguishable from the chalky smell of the wall filler smeared across the front.

There it was again. The doorbell. Of course. Pulling the jumper over her head, not caring that it was filthy – it still smelt of Jackson – she jumped out of bed and ran down the stairs, pausing for a few moments on the bottom step as she looked at the mess from yesterday. Shaking her head, she tiptoed through the debris and pulled the front door open. 'Jackson!' She felt a rush of pleasure seeing him standing in front of her.

'Morning! I hope I didn't wake you. I just wanted to bring you breakfast before I head to the pub for my shift.'

'Breakfast? You made me breakfast?' She took a deep breath in and grinned. 'Is it French toast?'

Jackson grinned too as he walked inside and stepped around the wallpaper and plaster covering the floor, following Laura through to the kitchen. 'A promise is a promise.'

'Yum, well, I am glad you keep your promises.' She opened the kitchen drawer and picked up two forks before sitting at the kitchen table opposite him.

Jackson took the metal lid off his serving plate and set it down before looking at her and pausing. 'About what happened yesterday...'

Laura felt her stomach drop. Not Jackson. *Please don't be like all the others, the men who promise the world and deliver very little. Don't be like Harry. Please don't.* 'I... You think it was a mistake?'

'What? No! Not at all.' Jackson widened his eyes as he looked at her. When he spoke again, his voice was quiet, unsure. 'Do you?'

She shook her head. 'I don't. I just assumed that's what you were going to say.'

'Not in a million years.' Shaking his head, he chuckled. 'I've been waiting a long time for that kiss, believe me.'

Laura grinned as relief swept over her. He was one of the good guys. She'd known he was. 'So, what did you want to say to me about it?'

Taking the fork she offered him, Jackson placed it on the table in front of him before meeting her gaze. 'Well, this is awkward, so

I'm just going to come out and ask you. Do you want to spend some time with me?'

'Spend some time with you?' What was he trying to ask her?

'Uh, would you like to date? Give a relationship a go? Start seeing each other?' There was that blush again, pinking his ears.

She swallowed. Was this really happening? Jackson, her teenage crush, was actually asking her out? Holding her hands in her lap, she pinched herself. Yep, that had hurt. She wasn't still dreaming. 'I would very much like that.'

'Well, I'm glad that's over.' Jackson chuckled before standing up and leaning across the table towards her.

Pushing the bench back, Laura stood up too and leaned forward. She could smell cinnamon on his breath.

The shrill tone of her mobile broke the moment, and she rolled her eyes as she picked it up. 'Oh, it's Dad. Sorry, I should answer. He never rings this early.'

'I'll wait.' He grinned, his dimple making an appearance.

'Thanks,' she mouthed before sitting back down and answering the call. 'Hi, Dad. Is everything okay?'

'Fine, sweetheart. Absolutely fine. I'm just ringing to let you know that Richie managed to get a last-minute day off from work and we're on our way to visit.'

Laura froze and looked across the table at Jackson. She could feel the blood seeping from her face. 'You're what?'

'Everything okay?' Jackson mouthed, his forehead creased, his expression concerned.

Shaking her head, Laura pulled a face. 'Dad, you can't do that. Richie deserves a proper day off, a break.'

'Don't worry, sweetheart. It will be a break. He's looking forward to it. Aren't you, Richie, lad?'

Laura listened to Richie's enthusiastic answer in the background. They were together already? She closed her eyes, knowing she needed to ask but dreading the answer she'd be given. 'Dad, where are you? You're not on your way already, are you?'

'We're about half an hour away. Can't wait to see you and your beautiful inn.'

Laura sat down with a plonk, the air escaping her lungs.

'See you in a few minutes, sweetheart.'

'No, I—' She was met with a deafening silence from the other end.

'Your dad and Richie are on their way here? Now?' Jackson grimaced.

Picking up the plate of French toast, Laura placed it on the work surface. She'd have to try it later, right now she had to focus on getting the inn into a state of some sort of normality. 'I don't actually know what to do. If they see the state of the hallway, they'll know they've been proven right.'

'Then we won't let them.' Jackson stood up and walked across to the kitchen cupboards. 'Where do you keep your bin bags?'

She pointed to the cupboard beneath the sink. 'In there.'

'Right, let's get this place cleaned up.' Jackson strode out into the hallway and began shovelling wallpaper and bits of plaster into the bin bag.

Standing in the doorway, Laura rubbed her eyes. 'They're still going to see the damage I've done to the wall.'

Walking across to her, Jackson stood in front of her, letting the bin bag drop to the floor before he cupped her elbows. 'They'll see the work of a very determined woman who has begun to fix this place up.'

'It's messy. The wall is bumpier than it was before I started.'

Jackson shrugged. 'It just needs sanding down, that's all. And the wall filler has to dry before it's sanded down.'

She searched his eyes. She wasn't sure if he was telling her the truth or just trying to prevent her from panicking, but he was right about one thing. If they cleared the rubbish, it would look a hundred times better. She nodded as they set to work again.

19
___

With the last piece of wallpaper in the bag and the floorboards swept of the worst of the plaster dust, Laura straightened her back and looked at Jackson. 'Thank you so much for helping with this.'

'No problem.' He picked up the bin bag and tied the end. 'We were just in the nick of time, by the looks of it.'

Grimacing, Laura followed Jackson's gaze to the front door and, sure enough, she could make out two figures coming up the garden path.

'I'll slip out the back and take this with me.' He lifted the bin bag.

'Are you sure?' She glanced between Jackson and the front door.

'I am. I don't think we should mention anything about last night's kiss or us dating to Richie before we know what's going on, do you?'

'Umm, you're probably right.' Laura followed him through to the kitchen and the back door. Richie hadn't exactly taken to any of her exes, instead letting his protective big brother side shine through. Apart from Harry, that was. He'd approved of Harry of all people.

The weak tone of the doorbell reached them, and she looked behind her.

Jackson pulled the back door open and took a step outside before turning to her. 'One thing before I go, though.'

'What?' She smiled as she realised what he was referring to and sank into his arms as he drew her close to him, meeting her lips.

The doorbell rang again, and Jackson stepped away, holding his hand up in a wave before he disappeared around the side of the inn.

Retracing her steps back to the front door, Laura touched her lips before swinging it open. 'Morning!'

'Hello, little sis. We didn't wake you when Dad phoned, did we? I know you're not usually a morning person.' Richie drew her in for a hug.

'That was in the past, Richie, lad. Isn't that right, Laura? You'll be up at the crack of dawn cooking breakfast from now on, won't you, sweetheart?' It was her dad's turn for a hug.

'Uh-huh. That's right. Come on in.' Laura held the door open as her brother and dad stepped inside.

'Oh.' Her dad spoke first as he turned slowly in the middle of the hallway.

'I know, I know. But I've not finished it yet, it still needs sanding and repapering, and it wasn't particularly planned. I found a patch of crumbling plaster, filled that in and then one thing led to another...' She spoke quickly, waving her hands around to indicate the patchwork wall.

'You did this?' Richie asked.

'Yep,' she answered quietly, and braced herself. As the silence dragged on, she looked from Richie to her dad and back again.

'Like I said, there's a long way to go and I hadn't quite realised there'd be this much to fix...'

'I'm impressed.' Her dad stepped forward and ran his hand over a patch of dried wall filler. 'For a first-timer, it's not a bad job.'

'You're impressed?' She let her jaw drop open.

Her dad nodded. 'I am. I don't think even your brother would have taken on a job this size on his own and definitely not Jenny.'

Richie held his hands out, palms outward. 'Too right, I wouldn't have. You've done a good job.'

'You wouldn't?' Were they being serious? They were actually praising her for the patchwork wall? She pointed to the part of the banister lying on the floor. 'I think it's got woodworm too.'

'Ah, now that's a shame.' Her dad walked across to the banister and knelt down on the floor to examine it, before breathing a sigh of relief. 'It's not woodworm, sweetheart. Do you see the way it's splintered? If it was woodworm, it wouldn't have done that. It's likely just old age and, judging by the looks of it, someone was quite rough with it.'

'The twins came round...' Laura shrugged.

'Enough said. I bet little Toby was trying to slide down it then. He tried that stunt when me and your mum took the twins to the museum last week.' Her dad tutted. 'Nah, that'll be an easy fix, I should think. It'll take some work to get it as fancily carved as the rest of it, but a true pro will be able to do it.'

Laura smiled. The two people who she'd thought would criticise her the most had given her nothing but praise since walking through the door. 'Thank you.'

'What for?'

She shook her head slightly. She couldn't very well admit to them that she'd been dreading them coming. Instead, she indicated the door through to the kitchen. 'Do you want to grab a coffee before I give you a tour?'

'Yes, please. Dad refused to stop at the service station.' Richie licked his lips.

'It's a waste of time and a waste of money stopping at those places. There's no chance I'm paying a fiver for a coffee I could make at home for a few pence.' Her dad shook his head.

Laura laughed. That had always been his excuse for not stopping on the way to holiday when they'd been growing up. Nothing had changed.

'Haven't I taught you anything?' Her dad looked pointedly at Richie. 'Look after the pennies and the pounds...'

'Will look after themselves,' Laura and Richie chorused.

'You did learn a thing or two from me, then?'

'Yes, we did, but it's also nice to treat yourself to an admittedly expensive coffee every once in a while, especially when travelling.' Richie walked across to the kitchen work surface and crossed his arms whilst his dad sat down at the table.

'Not to worry, I have lots of coffee.' Laura held up the jar. Maybe this surprise visit wasn't going to be as bad as she'd thought after all. Everything both Richie and her dad had mentioned so far had been positive.

'Ooh, is that French toast?' Richie turned around and picked up the fork lying next to the plate Jackson had brought over for her. Leaning down, he prodded it with the fork before taking a mouthful. 'Yum, that's good. Jackson used to make a mean French toast too.'

Nodding, Laura turned to face the window and filled the kettle with water, hoping Richie hadn't noticed the fierce blush flushing across her cheeks at the mention of Jackson's name.

'Do you mind if I have it?'

'Yep, that's fine. Go ahead.' She flicked the kettle on and leaned against the work surface. There went her chance to taste it, but she couldn't very well tell him that, no, he couldn't have any because his best mate had cooked it for her. There would be too many questions. Still, it was the thought that counted and the fact Jackson had thought about her was better than any dish anyone could ever make.

'I'm sure your mum said something about him living in this village.' Her dad slipped his glasses off and began cleaning them with the bottom of his top.

'Umm... that's right.' There was that heat again.

'You said he was next door, didn't you?' Richie stabbed another bit of French toast with the fork. 'I did tell you, Dad. On the way here.'

She looked from the breakfast Jackson had cooked for her to Richie, desperately trying to figure a way out of this line of conversation. Neither she nor Jackson were ready to come clean to Richie yet. Especially as all they'd shared so far was a kiss or three. It wasn't even as though they'd been on a date. 'How's work going?'

'Work? Oh, you know. It's going okay.' Richie tapped the fork against his chin. 'In fact, I think I might be in line for a promotion.'

'Another promotion? Didn't you just get one a couple of months ago?' Grateful for the change in topic, Laura poured the water, filing up three mugs.

'Yep.' Richie grinned before indicating the plate again. 'But his, this is good. Are you going to offer it on your breakfast menu? Because if you are I think me and Jane might have to pay a visit.'

Laura shrugged. She couldn't lie to him, but he hadn't asked if he'd cooked it herself, just whether she was going to serve it. 'I've not got as far as thinking about the breakfast menu yet.'

'Well, you should. This right here will put you on the map on its own.' He shovelled another forkful into his mouth.

Placing the steaming mugs of coffee on the table, Laura sat on the bench opposite her dad. Richie had a point, not that she'd actually had the chance to taste it, but if it was as good as it smelt, then she should ask Jackson for the recipe.

'Lovely, thank you.' Replacing his glasses on the end of his nose, her dad took a sip before looking over the rim of his mug. 'Young Harry visited us for tea yesterday.'

Spluttering, Laura wiped the coffee from her chin with the back of her hand. Harry had been round her parents' house? They'd invited her ex over for tea? And her dad had mentioned it so casually, as if telling her about a neighbour's cat strolling along the fence or her mum having a hair appointment. 'You invited my ex-husband round for tea?'

'Goodness, no. He popped round. Was in the area he said, and your mum felt sorry for him so asked him to stay.'

'Right, that makes all the difference then.' Laura raised her eyebrow at him. 'Why? Just why would Mum invite him in for tea – and what was he doing in the area? He lives on the other side of town.'

'He's not living there anymore. He's in some place in the centre of town now.' Her dad placed his mug casually down on the table.

'Oh.' Laura frowned. What did that information have to do with her? She'd heard from Jenny that he and Dina had split up so maybe he'd moved out.

'He was asking after you. He was.' Her dad took his glasses from his nose again and pointed them at her.

She wasn't going to ask. She didn't care what he'd been saying about her or what her parents had told him about what she was up to. He was her past and... hopefully, Jackson might be her future. Although it would be good to know what Harry's reaction had been. She'd always spoken about opening an inn or a café, her own business, and she'd always got the distinct impression he hadn't believed she was capable or that she'd really take such leap of faith. Not that he'd ever said that, but he'd always suggested it could be something they could look into in the future. Never now and never just her. She picked up her mug again, pointedly taking a slow sip of coffee.

'Your mother told him about your grand plans for this place.' Her dad began wiping his glasses again, obviously a stubborn mark giving him some trouble.

Despite all of her best intentions, Laura held her breath, willing him to continue. It wasn't that Harry's opinion was important to her, more that she was curious as to what he'd said about her buying Pennycress – something which would have been so out of character had she still been with him.

Her dad replaced his glasses once more and picked up his mug, oblivious to his daughter watching his every move.

Laura squirmed on the bench. Ah, she'd just have to ask him. Clearing her throat, she tried to ask in an off-hand, disinterested manner. 'So, er, what did he say?'

'When your mother told him?'

'Yes.' She nodded. Was he doing this on purpose?

'He was very surprised. Shocked, I think, was the word your mother used. Apparently, he stuttered.'

'You weren't there? You weren't part of this conversation?'

'No, I was in the garage at the time and when I came in for tea, they were chatting about the weather and the price of beetroot.'

'Beetroot?'

'Oh yes. It's all these price wars which are happening between the big supermarkets. One reduces the price of something – beetroot in this instance – and so does the other one and the cycle continues until they're practically giving it away.'

Laura breathed out slowly through her mouth, telling herself to remain calm. 'Harry was just shocked then. Mum didn't tell you what he actually said, just that he hadn't expected me to buy an inn?'

'Nope. Nothing else to report, I'm afraid.'

'Okay.' Laura turned her mug so the words 'Good Morning!' which were emblazoned upon the white ceramic in bright green and yellow writing, were facing her. Trying to get that slither of information from her dad had been hard work. And definitely not worth it either.

'She gave him one of my garibaldis though.' Her dad frowned. 'I wish she wouldn't do that, give them away to any Tom, Dick or Harry.'

'Good one, Dad.' Richie chuckled as he pointed the fork at his dad.

Laura rolled her eyes. Her dad always had been fiercely protective of his favourite biscuits. To the point he'd hide them if he knew Jenny was bringing the twins – or the human dust-bins as he'd nicknamed them – round. 'Well, I wish she wouldn't invite my ex-husband in for tea in the first place. And I wish Jenny wouldn't spend an eternity talking to him down the supermarket aisles. It's weird. We're divorced. We split up two whole years ago and yet I feel as though he's still part of this family.'

'I'm sorry you feel that way, but the fact of the matter is he was in our lives for a long time, all our lives, and it's not as though you split up because he was an awful person or anything. It's going to take a while for people to adjust.'

Taking a deep breath, Laura reminded herself it wasn't her dad's fault. It wasn't even him who had chosen to spend time with Harry. All the same, she wished he'd stay in her past. She drained the rest of her coffee and stood up. 'Anyway, that's enough talk of Harry for the day, thanks. Who wants to come and look around my *future*?'

* * *

Laura waved as her dad and Richie drove past, the car headlights illuminating the trees lining the street in the dim evening light, Richie sticking his hand out of the window to wave back at her as the car disappeared around the corner. Closing the gate, she walked back up the garden path and rolled her shoulders back as she breathed out a sigh of relief.

'That bad, hey?' Jackson's voice sounded behind her.

'Where did you spring from?' Turning, Laura grinned as she waited for Jackson to click the gate shut.

'I spotted Phil's car driving past.' He wrapped his arms around her waist before bringing her in for a kiss.

Sinking into his bear hug, Laura kissed him back before resting her cheek against his shoulder and simply enjoying the feeling of his arms holding her.

'What did they think of Pennycress?'

Stepping back, she began walking down the path again. 'They liked it. Or they said they did. They were even impressed with the appalling plastering I'd done in the hallway.'

'That's a good thing, surely?'

Laura looked down as she stepped over a wayward lavender stem. 'Yes, it is. They surprised me, to be honest, with how positive they were. Especially after Toby's fall, I'd expected Jenny to go back and tell everyone the inn was a dangerous building site.'

'I'm sensing a "but" here...' After following her through the front door, Jackson closed it quietly behind them.

'Yes, a big but.' She leaned against the reception desk and looked at him. 'They kept bringing up Harry.'

'That eejit? Why?' Jackson stood in front of her and took her hands in his.

'Well, apparently he stopped by my parents' house because he was "in the area"...' She curled her fingers around the words 'in the area', emphasising how ridiculous an excuse it was. 'And Mum only went and invited him in for tea!'

Jackson tilted his head. 'I suppose he's been in the family for a good number of years. I guess it's not that easy to just cut someone off completely.'

'Yes, it is. His family has! I've not heard a jot from any of them, didn't even get a Christmas card. Not that I care, mind you. I just don't understand why my own family seem to be on his side, that's all.'

'They're not on his side. They support you.' He rubbed his thumbs against the back of her hands.

'I'm not so sure. First, Jenny spends ages chatting to him in the supermarket and now this. Mum invited him in for tea. I mean, really?' She rolled her eyes before meeting his again, her tone becoming sarcastic. 'Maybe they secretly hope I'll get back with him – that way they can have him over for tea every night of the week, listen to him droning on about the price of beetroot.'

'Beetroot?'

'Long story.' Laura laughed. 'Of course they think I'm single too. If they knew—'

'If they knew, I think Richie would probably kneecap me.' Jackson grimaced.

'Haha, now you're just being overdramatic.' Pushing herself away from where she was leaning against the desk, she inched closer to him. 'I think they'd be pretty pleased. I mean, if they loved Harry, then imagine how they'd feel about me dating you.'

'I'm definitely not Harry.' He chuckled.

'No, definitely not.' She leaned in, their lips mere millimetres apart.

'Still, let's not say anything quite yet. I'd like to enjoy the full use of my legs for a while longer.'

Laura shook her head slightly before their lips touched.

Drawing back, Jackson tucked her hair behind her ears. 'I was going to ask you if you're free tomorrow?'

'Well, I may have to rearrange my diary. You know, what with all the commitments I have with my numerous friends in the village.'

'Haha. I'll take that as a yes then. I'm going to The Great Home Show in London and I've managed to get my hands on another ticket. I'm hoping to get some inspiration for the home renovations and thought you might enjoy it too?'

'Ooh yes, I'd love to.' She looked around her. 'I might even get some ideas on how to redecorate this hallway.'

'Great.' Jackson glanced behind him towards the door. 'Right, I hate to do this, but as much as I want to spend the evening with you, I need to run over to Billy's house and take a look at his boiler for him. They've got no heating or hot water at all.'

'If you ever have enough of renovating houses, you could always become a plumber. What with your heroic efforts here last night and now rescuing your brother?'

'Haha, maybe.' Jackson gave her a kiss before leaving.

Following him to the front door, Laura watched as he walked down the garden path and smiled as he turned and blew her a kiss before pulling the gate open.

She shut the door and leaned against it, surveying the hallway, a slow grin spreading across her face. Pennycress had had the seal of approval from both her dad and Richie. She wasn't imagining it, was she?

Pushing herself away from the door, she yawned as she headed into the kitchen and flicked the kettle on. The day had been emotionally and physically exhausting. After coffee and a tour of Pennycress, the three of them had spent the rest of the morning sanding down the bumpy patches of wall filler and in the afternoon they'd helped her tackle the back garden – well, as much as they could anyway before the evening had closed in.

She heaped spoonfuls of hot chocolate powder into her mug before hitting the power button on the old-fashioned radio she'd found at the back of a cupboard in the utility room. As nostalgic music from the nineties filled the room, Laura began to dance, throwing her arms above her head and shimmying around the tables. Her dad had liked the inn. He'd said he was impressed with what she doing here at Pennycress! Maybe everything would turn out all right after all.

20

Sliding their cardboard cups and plates to the edge of the table, Laura pulled out the wallpaper samples she'd collected from a handful of stalls displaying their wares in the vast hall at The Great Home Show. Spreading them out on the table, she looked at them before glancing around her. Twenty or so tables and chairs were positioned in a group at the far end of the exhibition, a variety of food and drink stalls surrounding them. The rest of the hall was crammed full with stalls and demonstration areas covering every aspect of home ownership and refurbishing anyone could ever dream of, from paint to panelling, bathroom fixtures to garden furniture, pipes to nails.

Laura watched as Jackson carried two more drinks back from one of the stalls and smiled. She'd really enjoyed spending the day with him, as well as gathering ideas on what to do with Pennycress.

'Here we go. I got you a chai latte. I remember you used to love them.' He placed the cups carefully on the table. 'If you don't anymore, I'm happy to swap.'

'No, I still love them. Thank you.' She picked up the cup and took a sip, letting the warm cinnamon taste linger in her mouth before swallowing.

'Are you trying to choose what to have in the hallway?' Jackson nodded towards the wallpaper samples.

'Yes, I just can't decide what direction to go in.' Placing the cup back down, she began moving the samples around on the table-top. 'Do I go for modern, classic or floral?'

'What do you like?'

'I like them all. If I go for modern, I'll have to slowly redo the whole inn, but then I probably will eventually, anyway.' She tapped her fingers against a pink and purple floral design on a deep green background. 'I do like this one though and it will be in keeping with the rest of the inn and the petals might even match the lavender purple of the front door.'

'That one is rather lovely.' Jackson smiled.

'It is, isn't it?'

'Yes, it's very you.'

'Huh, do you think?' Laura frowned. For the last umpteen years, she hadn't felt as though she'd had much of a style or any strong opinions about anything. Harry had always made the decisions about how they decorated the house, which restaurant they visited, her clothes even. Not in an overly controlling way, more that he suggested she chose the sharp-cut top rather than the flowy one she'd have chosen, or that the painting with the peppers was more in keeping with their kitchen decor than the whimsical one she'd found. She'd let him. Not because she'd been wary of his reaction, just that she'd valued his opinion and mistrusted her own. But here was Jackson, who she hadn't spoken to or seen in a good few years, sitting opposite her and recognising which wallpaper was 'her'.

'Yes I do, but it doesn't matter what I think, you'll make the perfect decision for Pennycress.'

Keeping her eyes down, she slid the wallpaper samples around the table again.

'Have I said something wrong?' He reached out and touched her hand lightly.

Looking up at him, she shook her head. 'Not at all. It's just, I guess I've become so used to letting Harry make all the decisions that... I don't know, it's refreshing to hear someone say something like that. "This one is very you." As if you know me better than Harry ever did.'

'Is that so bad?'

She knitted her eyebrows together. 'I was married to Harry. He was supposed to be the one person who knew me better than anyone else. The one person who respected me and what I wanted and liked over anyone else's opinion and yet... he didn't.'

Jackson looked at her, his brow furrowed.

'I think I'm just starting to see that now.' She shifted in her chair. 'I guess I did towards the end of our marriage, and it was probably part of why I felt I had to walk away, but this is the first time I've really put those feelings into words, really begun to understand it. I think he watered me down... That doesn't make sense, does it?'

Jackson nodded slowly. 'It does. It makes perfect sense.'

'You could see it, couldn't you? That's why you don't like him.' It was more of a statement than a question. 'But why can't anyone else see it? My family still talk as though they think I made the wrong decision to walk away.'

'He's a charmer. And he knows how to make people think as he wants them to.' He ground his jaw.

'Like he did with me.' She nodded. It was true. At the beginning of their relationship, in the honeymoon period, he'd always been more than lovely towards her. It had only been the last three or four years when he'd begun to show her nothing but uninterest, indifference even. He'd never wanted to go out for a drink or for dinner, or anything for just the two of them, and yet if any of his mates asked him, he'd jumped at the chance, leaving her at home alone to watch TV and do very little else. On the rare occasions he'd asked her to go out with him, usually when all of his friends were bringing their wives and girlfriends along, then he'd pretend to be the perfect husband for a few minutes before leaving her to twiddle her thumbs and wait until he'd had enough of chatting to his mates before they went home.

In the end, she'd declined his offers, knowing full well that whether she spent the evening in some pub or restaurant surrounded by people or at home by herself, she'd feel equally lonely. But that didn't have anything to do with her lack of self. Or did it? Had merely the fact he'd so easily pass her company up for someone else's indicated to her that she wasn't interesting enough, or fun enough, or anything enough? Had that added to the reason she'd stopped trying to impress him, to be interesting, that she'd simply withdrawn?

'Are you okay?' Jackson ran his forefinger across her cheek.

Blinking, she nodded. 'Sorry, I was miles away. I think you're right. He's a charmer who likes everyone to admire him, and left me struggling for any space or support to be my own person. I can't go back there.'

'Why would you?'

'I don't mean getting back with him. I mean, back to my parents. However lame it sounds, this is my chance to rediscover myself again. To learn to, I don't know, like myself, for who I am again.' Yes, Jackson's one simple comment had fuelled the drive in her to succeed, stoked her determination.

'You should love yourself, not just like.'

She grimaced. 'Let's start with like, shall we? I think it'd be a far stretch to think I could love myself.'

'Laura—' Cupping her cheek, Jackson stared into her eyes. If she were to read anything into the way he looked at her, it would be that he thought she was enough, that she was worthy, but it was herself who needed to be convinced, not him.

'No. Don't.' Reaching across the table, she traced the tip of her forefinger across his soft lips. She knew he only meant well, but it actually felt good to be able to vocalise how she was feeling, to put how Harry had made her feel into words. 'I'm fine. I just wish there was something I could do to get people to give me a chance back in Meadowfield.'

This made Jackson's expression lighten. 'You may just be in luck. I've been doing some thinking and a little digging too.'

'Ooh yes? Do you actually think there might be a way to encourage people to be a little more welcoming?' What was he going to suggest? That she join the local Women's Institute? Learn how to play pool down at the pub? Or bake cakes and go door to door? Apart from the final possible suggestion, which would likely give her neighbours a touch of food poisoning and make them hate her even more, she'd be willing to give anything a go.

'I do, yes.' Laying his hands on the table, he met her eyes. 'I think you should go and visit Vivienne Fields.'

With her mouth suddenly turning dry, Laura swallowed before answering, 'You think I should go and visit the previous tenant who was kicked out so that I could buy Pennycress?'

'She wasn't technically evicted so you personally could buy the inn, she was evicted months before you even put an offer in, but, yes, I think you should.'

'Why? What would I say? How would it achieve anything?' She searched his eyes, trying to work out what he was thinking and how he thought this would pan out.

'I think just introducing yourself and explaining what your

intentions for Pennycress are will be enough for her to see that you want the best for the inn she so loved.'

'But it's not her who has been the problem. It's everyone else. It's the rest of the village who hate me, I've never even met Vivienne.'

'No, but if people are willing to do everything in their power to discourage anyone who tries to run Pennycress from staying because they respect her so much, then she'd likely be able to influence them not to as well.'

She looked down at the wallpaper samples and moved them into a pile, carefully lining up the edges of the short stack. 'I don't know. I don't know if I'm brave enough to turn up on a stranger's doorstep and beg them to get their friends to give me a chance. So much could go wrong.'

'And so much could go right, too. Besides, by all accounts, I think she's probably a really nice person.'

Laura raised an eyebrow. 'And how do you figure that one out?'

'Because she has the support of everyone in the village. I just don't think someone awful would get that. The local residents would be happy to see the back of her if she wasn't a nice person.'

'Hmm, I suppose there's some sense in that.' She slipped the samples into her bag and leaned back in her chair. 'I still don't think I'm brave enough, though.'

'Think about it for a few days, but it can hardly make things much worse for you.'

'True, no one speaks to me, anyway.' She nodded. He was right, it was just so far out of her comfort zone to rock up at someone's house, who she'd never met, that she wasn't sure if she was ready to. But she'd think about it.

21

'And you're sure you don't want me to come in with you? Or just to the door, even?' Jackson switched the engine off and turned in his seat.

Laura glanced out of the car window towards the small bungalow. The pale yellow front door had a beautifully made winter wreath hanging from the door knocker and a small concrete gnome standing beside the shallow step below. As welcoming as it looked, she still felt butterflies in her stomach. 'No, I need to do this on my own.'

'Okay.'

'Thank you, though.' She reached across and touched his forearm. 'I really appreciate the offer.'

'I'll wait here for you then. Take as long as you need.'

'Thanks.' She pulled down the sun visor and peered in the small mirror. 'Do I look okay? Professional enough to run an inn, but friendly enough to show her I care about it?'

Jackson leaned over and cupped her cheek. 'You look beautiful. Perfect.'

Scrunching up her nose, she shook his compliment off and took a deep breath. 'Okay, here goes nothing. Wish me luck.'

'Good luck. Not that you'll need it.'

'I hope not.' Pushing open the car door, Laura stepped outside before she could talk herself out of the idea of visiting Vivienne Fields. She could do this. She was doing this. It would be fine. Or as she'd told herself umpteen times in the few days since Jackson had first voiced his suggestion, it couldn't make things much worse than they already were. Especially since yesterday, when she'd popped into the village centre for the first time since overhearing the conversation in the pub and she'd been completely blanked in the grocery store – to the point that she'd had to check herself in the small mirror on the carousel displaying reading glasses to reassure herself she hadn't in fact turned invisible. Yes, things couldn't really get much worse.

Laura crossed the tarmac path and walked through the small garden towards the front door, where she stood and stared at the small sign sellotaped to the letter box – 'No salespersons, no canvassing, no leaflets. Thank you!'

She shifted from one foot to the other and glanced behind her towards Jackson, waiting in his car. Was she really going to do this? Try to plead her case with the previous tenant of Pennycress after knocking on her door completely out of the blue?

No, it was a bad idea. She couldn't. Not today.

Turning on the spot, she stepped down from the shallow step. Just because she'd chickened out this time, it didn't mean she couldn't try again, tomorrow perhaps, or the next day. Or next week even. She froze as she heard the front door open behind her.

'Hello, can I help you, dear?' The voice was calm, friendly maybe.

Laura turned slowly and saw a slight woman, with her white

hair neatly curled, wearing a yellow cardigan almost as pale as her front door. 'Hi.'

'What can I do for you?' The woman smiled, laughter lines deepening around her eyes as she did so.

'I...' She'd got this far. She might as well come out and tell her who she was. 'Are you Vivienne Fields?'

'Last time I checked, I am.' The woman's smile broadened.

Laura nodded. She needed to introduce herself now or the whole visit would be a waste. Opening her mouth, she blurted it out, 'My name's Laura Price and I've bought Pennycress Inn.'

Vivienne staggered back and held the palms of her hands against her cheeks.

'Sorry, I shouldn't have come. I knew it was a bad idea. I just didn't know what else to do.' The last thing she'd wanted was to give the villagers any more ammunition to hold against her. And she clearly had by upsetting the very person they felt they were sticking up for. She should have followed her first instinct to stay away. Stepping back, Laura went to turn around again.

'Why don't you come in, dear?'

'Come in?' Twisting around again, Laura watched as Vivienne pulled the door open further, standing back to usher her inside. Laura searched Vivienne's face and instead of seeing the anger she'd expected to find, her shocked expression had quickly transformed to one of warmth.

'Yes, I've only just poured water in the teapot. The tea should be ready about now.'

'Umm, I don't want to impose.' Laura looked down at the ground.

'Oh, you won't be imposing. It would be my pleasure.'

Laura looked at her. Vivienne didn't look as though she was about to wield a baseball bat or hit her over the head with a frying pan. But who knew? It wasn't something that the perpetrator would give a warning about. What did she have to lose, though? Apart from her life, perhaps? 'Okay.'

'Good, good. I'll get us both a piece of the fruit cake I baked yesterday too.' As soon as Laura had stepped through the door, Vivienne closed it quietly behind her and pointed to the door to the right. 'Go on in, dear, and make yourself at home. I'll fetch the tea and cake.'

Laura followed the instructions and entered the room. The walls were painted pale yellow, almost an exact match to the front door, apart from a feature wall behind the fireplace in dark florals, much like the wallpaper Laura herself had picked out for the hall-way. Two small two-seater sofas sat in the middle of the room facing each other, a large glass coffee table between them, a cream vase of roses centred on the coffee table, a TV guide lying open next to it.

Laura perched on the edge of the sofa nearest the door. She could hear Vivienne humming above the clatter of crockery across the hallway. This wasn't the welcome she'd expected. After all she'd been put through at the hands of the Meadowfield community, she'd convinced herself Vivienne must be this formidable person, instead here she was making tea for Laura and bringing her cake. She certainly didn't appear displeased or annoyed to see her.

After what felt like at least half an hour but was likely just a few minutes, Vivienne walked into the room holding a tray with a teapot, two cups and saucers, a milk jug and two plates of cake.

'Here we go.' Setting the tray down on the coffee table with a clatter, Vivienne sat on the sofa before standing up again. 'Oh, I've forgotten the sugar. I knew there was something. Silly me, it's because I don't take it. I forget that I should offer it.'

'I don't take sugar in my tea either. Thank you, though.'

Sitting back down, Vivienne smiled. 'That saves me a trip then.'

Laura reached out to help set out the cups and saucers as Vivienne picked up the teapot. She couldn't remember the last time she'd had tea from a teapot, probably when she'd been younger and had visited her grandma.

'Milk?' Vivienne held up the small milk jug.

'Yes, please.' She watched as Vivienne poured the milk, the white swirling on the top of the dark liquid. Despite the reason she'd come, she felt strangely at ease sitting here opposite the woman who had run Pennycress before her. 'Thank you.'

'Remember your cake too, dear.' Vivienne passed her a plate, a slice of fruit cake sitting proudly in its centre.

'Thanks.' Taking the plate, Laura took a bite of cake, bracing herself for the too-rich-for-her taste, but it was lovely. Light and fruity rather than heavy. Beginning to feel a little calmer, she took another bite. 'This is delicious.'

'Thank you. I used to make it all the time for the guests at Pennycress.' She smiled proudly. 'It was always the first of the cakes to disappear.'

'I can see why.' Laura spoke between mouthfuls.

'At the door, you mentioned that you're the new owner of the inn?' Holding her cup and saucer, Vivienne shuffled back on the sofa, getting comfortable.

'Yes, that's right. I moved in a couple of weeks ago now.' Biting down on her bottom lip, Laura felt the nerves come flooding back as the change in conversation reminded her why she was here.

'You have actually bought it? Or are you renting it from Mr Yates?'

'I bought it.' Laura nodded.

'Right. That's interesting.' Vivienne suddenly looked deep in thought.

'It is?' Laura frowned. Didn't she look like someone who would buy an inn? She supposed she probably didn't. After all, even though she'd dreamt of doing so for so long, she'd never really thought it would ever be possible, ever be a reality. It had just been a pipe dream and pipe dreams didn't often come true.

'Yes, yes.' Vivienne sat up straighter. 'Sorry, dear. It's just a little surprise, that's all.'

'I don't look as though I should be running an inn, do I? You can tell I don't have any experience?' Laura placed the rest of the cake back on the plate and lowered it to her lap. Vivienne didn't trust her. That was it.

'It's not that. It's just, Evie told me it had been rented out again.'

'Evie Taunton?'

'Yes. You know her? Did she sell you Pennycress?'

'That's right, she was the estate agent in charge of the sale.' Laura nodded. Why would she have told Vivienne it had been rented out again rather than sold?

'Umm... that's a little strange. I'd say she got her word muddled up, but we had a couple of conversations on the matter.'

'Oh, I definitely bought it. I'm recently divorced and used the money from the sale of my marital home to put down a deposit for the mortgage.'

'That's okay, dear. I believe you.' Vivienne shook her head sadly. 'Evie sometimes likes to stir the pot, so to speak.'

'You think she misled you on purpose?' Something about it didn't really surprise Laura all that much. She'd never felt a good vibe from Evie Taunton since the day they'd met. In fact, if she hadn't fallen so much in love with Pennycress, then the estate agent herself may have put her off the purchase altogether. She'd been a little difficult and slow getting back to her for the entirety of the sales process.

'Possibly, possibly not. Who can tell?' Vivienne took a sip of her tea before continuing. 'Anyway, it's lovely to meet you and wonderful to be having tea with the new owner. I so loved my time running Pennycress and hold those special years close to my heart.'

'Thank you for the tea and cake. It's nice to meet you too.' Laura smiled. She was glad she'd come. She could sense a genuine warmth from Vivienne. She wasn't the woman who Laura had thought she would be, she was just someone who had loved Pennycress as much as Laura herself did.

'Well, I'm pleased she wasn't sold off to one of those hotel chains who would make her a carbon copy of a hundred other hotels they own.'

'No, I definitely want to keep her as unique and special as she is now. That's what I loved about Pennycress when I first viewed the inn. I admit, I only went to have a look at a few other places before I came here, but Pennycress had the most character out of all of them. And I guess I just got a feeling that this was the path I was supposed to take. That sounds silly, doesn't it?' She looked down at the plate on her lap. Had she said too much?

'Not at all. It sounds as though you felt just as I did when I first stepped inside. I knew she'd make a difference to my life – a positive difference – and she did. All the people I met who came to stay, all the functions I organised there...' Vivienne smiled.

'Functions?'

'Yes, little tea parties for local children, knitting clubs, family dinner parties. I rather enjoyed those the most, watching how people interacted with each other.'

'Oh, that's a good idea. I didn't realise Pennycress had been used like that.' Now that Vivienne had said that though, she could just imagine Pennycress being filled with the chatter and laughter of families coming together.

'No? Didn't Evie tell you?'

Laura shook her head. Ms Taunton hadn't been very helpful. She'd let her glance at the books for a few minutes, but that had been about it. She hadn't told her much about Pennycress at all.

'Ah, that's a shame. Still, you're here now and hopefully we can meet again and discuss it all. I'd love to help you with anything, any questions, or anything I can do practically to help.'

'That would be lovely, thank you.' Laura nodded eagerly. It would be great to learn more about how Pennycress fitted in with village life and to have Vivienne's experience and expertise on hand, of course.

'And how are things over at the old place? I hope she's treating you well?'

Laura smiled. She could tell how much Pennycress had meant to Vivienne by the way she referred to 'her'. 'Good thanks. Well, I've had a few little disasters, if I'm honest, but okay in the main.'

'Oh, I hope it wasn't that darn banister. I've been pleading with Mr Yates for a good couple of years to fix it, I have.' Vivienne shook her head. 'I do hope the old girl was left in a decent state when you moved in? I hope he'd fixed things?'

Laura squirmed on the sofa. 'The banister broke.'

Vivienne took a deep breath and sighed. 'As much as I absolutely adored looking after Pennycress, I relied on Mr Yates as the landlord to do any of the big repair works. I was only renting, you see, and it was in the agreement that he was to take care of any structural repairs that needed attending to. The banister was one of the things I raised with him and he assured me he'd get round to fixing it one day. Of course, weeks turned into months and months turned into years and, still, he didn't visit or send anyone over to repair anything.' She picked up a spoon and stirred her tea, a look of disappointment clouding her face.

'That's terrible.'

'It is. I did my best, of course, but I was giving him a fair share of the profits and the little I had left I reinvested. I learned quite a lot over the years about how to fix this and that. It was just the big works I didn't like to carry out myself. Scared, I suppose, in case I did something wrong and made it worse.'

Unsure of how to answer, Laura took a sip of her tea.

'I complain, but he wasn't so bad, not as landlords go. He kept himself to himself and let me get on with it without any interference from his part. And I so enjoyed my time there. I really did.' Vivienne leaned forward and placed her cup and saucer down. 'I'm so glad she's now been passed on to you. You talk about her like I do.'

'I do?' Did she? She'd felt an almost instant connection to Pennycress from the very first viewing, but she didn't think she spoke as passionately as Vivienne. Maybe Vivienne could tell she meant well.

Vivienne nodded, her tight curls dancing on top of her head as she did so.

Laura sniffed. She'd been so worried about coming, but Vivienne had been nothing but kind to her since she'd arrived, which actually thinking about it didn't make sense at all.

'Are you all right, dear?' Vivienne frowned.

'Yes, sorry, I just don't understand. You're being so lovely to me and yet...' Should she say anything? If she did, she'd be badmouthing Vivienne's friends, her neighbours.

'And yet?'

'Sorry, I shouldn't have said anything.' Why had she? She should have just accepted Vivienne's kindness and left out the real reason she'd come here.

'Don't give me that, dear. Tell me if something is bothering you. We might just be able to figure out a solution together. Is there something wrong besides the banister in the inn?'

'It's not that, it's just... I've struggled to fit in with the local community, I guess.'

'Ah.' Vivienne sank back against the sofa cushions. 'In other words, people are being quite rude, but you're too polite to tell it how it is.'

Laura shrugged. 'A little.'

'Hmm. I was afraid this would happen. Leave it with me. I'll sort the lot of them out.'

'You will?' Laura could feel the tension which had been building since she'd arrived in Meadowfield begin to dissolve. 'I don't understand. Why haven't they given me the opportunity to show them who I am? I've hardly spoken to anyone since I moved here.'

'I think what's going on is a little displaced rebellion. You see, it wasn't a particularly pleasant experience when Mr Yates decided to evict me. People get used to things. They like their stability and so it was a big adjustment for them. Remember, they used to come to the inn for all sorts of reasons. It wasn't just the guests from outside our area Pennycress provided a haven for, it was those clubs, those meet-ups, those family events just as I mentioned. Well, people lost all of that when I was forced out.'

'I understand. But no one mentioned any of that to me. I'm more than happy to start offering some of those things again.' And she was. It sounded as though Pennycress had been a big part of the village, possibly as much as Vivienne herself. Yes, it would take a little more effort and planning on her part, but on the plus side, she'd also bring in more money too.

'Yes, but I'm wondering: if Evie told me that Mr Yates rented Pennycress out again despite sending me packing, then she may well have said the exact same thing to others – or at least suggested it or omitted the truth.'

'And therefore people wouldn't like the fact that I was seemingly renting it and you'd been evicted for no apparent reason?'

'That's it. Plus, of course, they'd think that if you were to leave, then that would mean Mr Yates wouldn't receive his rent. So, you see, it really has nothing to do with you, it's between the people of the village and Mr Yates. Unfortunately you're caught in the crossfire.'

'I've done nothing wrong, then?'

'You've done a wonderful thing taking on Pennycress, a wonderful thing, and I for one am very glad it's you who has taken the reins.'

'Oh, thank you.' Laura could feel herself welling up.

'You seem like a kind person who has the best interests of the old girl close to your heart. I'm the one who should be thanking you, not the other way around.'

Laura finished her tea. She had so much to think about that her mind was whirring. After replacing her cup and saucer on the tray, she stood up. 'Thank you again for the tea and cake and a huge thank you for clearing everything up for me. I was so worried I'd done something wrong.'

'You're very welcome, dear.' Vivienne stood up and led her to the front door.

After saying goodbye once again, Laura walked back along the garden path, feeling a lot lighter than she had been on the walk up.

Jackson held his hand up enquiringly, first showing the thumbs down signal and then the thumbs up. She replied by giving him the thumbs up.

As she neared the car, Jackson leaned across the passenger seat and opened the door for her. 'How did it go?'

'Great. Really good, actually! I'm glad you suggested me visiting. It's cleared up a lot of questions for me and I've learned a lot about Pennycress as well.'

'That sounds positive.' Jackson started the ignition.

'Yes, it was.' She grinned. She needed to process everything Vivienne had told her, about the extra functions being offered at Pennycress through to the way Evie Taunton had behaved. She didn't really understand why Evie would do what she had, but she was determined to find out.

'Did Vivienne shine any light on the reason why people are treating you as they are?' Jackson glanced at her as he drew away from the kerb.

'Yes, and no. The people in the village love her and respect her just as you'd said, and she said some of it could be the fact that the local residents just don't like change. But she also mentioned that Evie Taunton had told her that I was renting the inn from the previous landlord.'

'Renting it?'

'Yes. And so, Vivienne suspects that people probably figure that if they can encourage me to leave, then Mr Yates will have to start the process of finding a tenant again and lose out on the rent money in the meantime. I guess they want to prove a point to him.'

'Okay... that makes sense about people wanting Mr Yates to lose money. From a few things I've heard in the pub, I don't think he had many fans here when he moved out himself decades ago and then fewer fans when he failed again and again to help Vivienne with the upkeep of the property, so I can kind of see the logic in that, although it still seems harsh to behave the way they have to a complete stranger.'

'Yes, I guess it does.'

'But Evie? I can't imagine her telling people you were renting from Mr Yates on purpose. What would she stand to gain from it?'

Laura shrugged. 'I really don't have a clue. Not much makes sense to me at the moment. I mean, it makes more sense than when I walked in there to see Vivienne, but I still don't feel I understand all of what's going on.'

'No.'

Laura looked out of the window as they drove back to Wisteria Lane. She could do with an early night. She felt so emotionally drained after her conversation with Vivienne.

22

Stretching her arms above her head, Laura tried to inch her back taller. It hadn't done her any good to move the furniture around in the owners' suite by herself, but she'd been too impatient to wait until Jackson finished work to ask him. Still, it looked better now after her reshuffle. And it felt more like hers. As though she was putting her stamp on the place a little.

Her mobile phone rang, and she picked it up. 'Hi.'

'Hey, Laura.' Jackson's voice wafted through the phone, filling the room. He sounded cheerful. 'What are you up to?'

'Right now?' She looked around at the pile of clothes she had taken out of the drawers to make the furniture lighter to shift, at the clumps of dust on the floor from where she'd pushed the wardrobe along and the cobwebs she'd unearthed from behind the curtains. All the stuff that could wait if it meant she could spend some more time with Jackson. 'Nothing.'

'Great. I was hoping you'd say that. I have a favour to ask you.'

'Go on.'

'Will you come down to the pub for a bit, please?'

Laura sank onto the edge of the bed, disturbing the pile of

clothes. Leaning down, she plucked a T-shirt from the floor and replaced it in the now untidy heap on the bed. 'I don't think that's such a good idea.' Yes, Vivienne had explained why people might be treating her the way they had been but Laura hadn't yet had the opportunity, or mustered up the courage to do anything, to speak to anyone, in an attempt to dispel the myths Evie had been spreading.

'Please? I have a new menu I'm testing and I'm in need of an impartial opinion.'

'I'm not sure. I don't know how impartial I can be, anyway.' She wasn't impartial at all, not when it came to anything to do with Jackson. She was falling for him, and fast. Maybe it was because of their history, because they knew each other so well, or maybe it was because she'd always harboured feelings for him ever since that teenage crush. She wasn't sure, but one thing she did know was that she was completely incapable of being impartial.

'Please? Just for a bit?' Jackson pleaded down the line.

How could she say no to that voice, to him? She exhaled heavily. 'Okay, okay, but I'm legging it right out of there the moment anyone gives me a dirty look.'

'Deal.'

'All right, but you know that means I'll literally only be there a few milliseconds at the most. Probably less than that. What's smaller than a millisecond? A billisecond?'

'Ha, I've no idea.' Jackson chuckled. 'See you soon.'

'Umm, bye.' Laura ended the call and then stared at the screen. She really didn't want to venture back into the pub. She hadn't stepped foot inside the place since she'd heard Evie and the other group of people talking ill of her. In fact, she hadn't ventured into the village centre since then at all, apart from that one time she'd run to the grocery store and been completely ignored. She'd been using her car and travelling to buy supplies and food. It was annoying, but it was just the way it had to be for now. Still, a second in the pub to taste a meal Jackson had created wasn't too much of him to ask her.

Pulling her hood down and rolling her shoulders back, Laura paused outside the pub door. She could do this. She could. It wouldn't be for long, and she'd told Jackson she'd be escaping the moment someone looked askance at her, so in reality she probably wouldn't even make it to the bar. She just needed to show her face and then she could get the heck out of there.

She reached for the handle and pushed, the warmth of the pub escaping into the street carrying the aroma of beer laced with food. Yum, it did smell good. She took a step inside and paused, looking around before continuing towards the bar, where she could see Jackson waiting for her.

Something was wrong. She paused again and turned, briefly taking in the scene. The pub was busy, tables were taken and people were standing huddled in groups by the bar. She blinked. That was it, that was what was different. People were talking, continuing their conversations. No one was looking at her, nobody was openly shunning her. So unless all the people were talking about her, then it seemed everyone was just getting on with their evening despite the fact she'd just walked in. What was going on?

She took the few short steps towards the bar and slipped onto the bar stool nearest Jackson, who was deep in conversation with a customer.

'Evening, what can I get you today? We've had a new delivery of some local wines if you'd like to sample some?' The bartender, who on her previous visit had ignored her, smiled at her.

'Umm... yes, that would be lovely, thanks.'

'Coming right up.' The bartender picked up a glass and began to pour. 'On the house to welcome you to the village.'

'Really?' Laura cleared her throat and tried again, keeping her tone light. She was being welcomed into the village? Why had his attitude towards her changed? And why had everyone else's? 'That's great. Thank you.'

'No problem. I'm Darren, by the way.' Walking away, the bartender began taking someone else's order.

Looking towards her, Jackson caught her eye and sidled across to her, leaning his elbows on the bar between them. 'Hey, glad you could make it.'

'Hi. What's going on?' She nodded towards the bartender. 'I was just given a free drink as a welcome to the village.'

Jackson grinned and pointed across the pub towards a table in front of the roaring open fire. 'It has nothing to do with me.'

Following his gaze, she twisted round on her stool and smiled. Vivienne Fields was sitting at the head of the table, surrounded by people Laura recognised from the awkward village meeting – Miss Cooke the mayoress and Mrs Pierce the owner of the bakery among them. 'But how? Why?'

'I guess she set the record straight.' Jackson shrugged.

'Really? So you're not actually testing out a new menu? That was just a ruse to get me to agree to come down here?'

'Oh no, I am trialling some new dishes and really would love your input, but, yes, I did use that to get you to agree to coming. I knew you'd make up some excuse not to if I didn't make it obvious that I needed your help.' Jackson laid his hand on hers.

'Ha, you're right, I would have. I didn't think I'd ever step foot in this place again.'

Tapping her hand, Jackson winked at her before turning away. 'I'll catch you later.'

'Hello, you must be Laura, the new owner of Pennycress Inn, is that right?'

A voice to her right caught her attention and Laura turned to see Jill, the woman who had been asking for volunteers for the craft fair. 'Hi, yes, that's me. I'm Laura and you're Jill, right? I remember you with your toddler from the village meeting.'

Jill broke into a grin. 'Yes, that was me. I've left little Kasey at home today. This evening is adults only.' She held up a glass of wine before taking a sip and lowering her voice. 'I'm ever so sorry I treated you the way I did. I so wanted to say hi and welcome you to Meadowfield, but...' She glanced behind her.

Laura tried to see who she was referring to but was met with a blanket of people. Still, whatever the reason, Jill had at least smiled at her and begun to speak when Laura had said hello to her on the way out of the hall. That was more than anyone else had. 'Don't worry. What's in the past is in the past and I'm sure you had your reasons, as did everyone else.'

'That's just the thing...' She did it again, looked over her shoulder. 'Anyway, are you still happy to volunteer on the day of the craft fair?'

'Absolutely. Count me in.' Laura nodded enthusiastically. She still couldn't tell who Jill kept looking at, or indeed if she was. She might have just been trying to search someone out in the sea of faces in the pub.

'Fantastic to hear. We're so grateful to everyone who helps. It makes it possible to run these events.' Placing her handbag on the bar, Jill rummaged through it before taking out her notebook and flicking through the pages. 'I'll pop your name on the list now.'

'Thank you. Do you run other events, then?'

'Oh yes, a few craft fairs dotted throughout the year, obviously a massive one in the summer and another big one at Christmas. We then run events in the village for May Day and a huge carnival in the summer holidays. That's usually a busy one. The tourists flock to our carnival and the floats are amazing! Mrs Pierce from the bakery goes all out and wins almost every year.'

'Wow, that does sound good. I've not been to a carnival since my hometown stopped having them when I was in my teens. I never understood why they stopped, to be honest. They were always the highlight of the summer.' One year Laura, Jenny, Richie and Jackson had been involved in transforming Farmer Gilkes' trailer into a sea of flowers for the local dance company, who danced, or attempted to, whilst Farmer Gilkes pulled the trailer through the town centre with his tractor. All had been going well until the tractor had taken the corner at St Hughes Street a little too fast and the dancing children had all toppled into the wooden flowers they'd all spent weeks painstakingly painting. Still, until then, their trailer had looked the best.

'It's a lot of organising – and I mean a lot – but all the local groups and clubs get involved.' Jill replaced her notebook and perched on the stool next to Laura's. 'Just think, Pennycress Inn will be booked out that week.'

'Oh, I do hope so.' Laura frowned into her glass. That would be if she were able to get all the work completed before she ran out of savings. She looked across at Jill. Was she someone she could trust? 'Can I ask... why the change of heart?'

'About the volunteering?'

'About you coming to speak to me at all.'

Jill took a slow sip of her wine before looking at Laura. 'Vivienne seems to like you. She says you only want the best for the inn.'

'Oh, is that why?' Laura frowned as she watched Vivienne standing up and refilling the glasses around the table. She'd just told people she liked her? And now she was suddenly accepted into the Meadowfield community? That's what she'd wanted and she should feel happy, relieved, she knew she should but on the other hand, these people still didn't know her, they were only acting the way they were because they'd been told to.

'Well, that and the fact that she said you'd bought the inn. Is that right? And you're going to keep it as the Pennycress Inn we all know and adore? You're not part of some big hotel chain who's going to transform it into some grey box before moving on to the next one?' Jill looked earnestly at her, obviously seeking some sense of reassurance.

'What? No, of course not. I love the style and the feel of Penny-cress. It was what drew me to put in an offer in the first place. I love it as it is.' Laura shifted on the stool. 'Of course, there is some remedial work I need to do to the place, but everything I do will be in keeping with the age and style of the building. And there one hundred per cent won't be any grey.'

'Or any moving on to find the next hotel?'

'Nope. I'm here to stay. Whether people accept me or not.'

'That's a relief to hear.' Jill shook her head and looked down into her glass. 'There are just so many rumours going around about you and Pennycress. We were caught off guard and believed them, believed that you were some high-and-mighty business tycoon just after a good deal which led to Mr Yates evicting Vivienne.'

Laura laughed. Had people really imagined her as a business tycoon? She needed to remember that phrase to tell Jenny and Richie. They'd never believe her. 'That is so far from who I am. All of this is new to me, and I probably shouldn't say this, but I'm kind of learning on the job. I haven't owned an inn before. Heck, I haven't even owned a business or got anywhere in my previous career either.'

'Really? How are you coping then? I can imagine running an inn would be quite a big task?' Jill questioned, her voice full of curiosity.

Maybe she shouldn't have admitted she was a complete novice. Just when people had seemingly decided to give her a chance, she'd given Jill all the ammunition she'd need for people to plot against her again. If they didn't think she was up to the job, then they'd shun her once more. 'It's a learning curve, that's for sure, but I'm so determined to do my best for Pennycress and to make it a success that I'll do all I can in order to do it justice.'

'I'll drink to learning new things and taking on new adventures then.' Jill held up her glass to Laura.

Raising her glass, she clinked it against Jill's before taking a sip. 'To new adventures.'

'I'm taking on a new adventure soon myself, too.' Jill leaned in towards her.

'You are? What are you doing?'

'I'm starting my own gardening business. You know, upkeep, landscaping, things like that. It's super early days, but I'm excited to finally start using my knowledge of horticulture.' Something clouded Jill's face for a moment. 'Not that I've done anything remotely to do with horticulture since I left uni eight years ago, that is. I seem to have been popping out babies, raising them and organising events for Meadowfield.'

'I'm sure it's not something you forget. Besides, if you're passionate about it, I think you'll be able to make anything work. By the sounds of things, you're brilliant at organising and I've only known you for like...' Laura glanced at the clock behind the bar. 'Half an hour.'

'I like you.' The smile returned to Jill's face.

'Thanks.' Laura tilted her head, thinking. 'When are you starting your business?'

'In a couple of months, probably. I need to get little Kasey settled into nursery first. Why? You're not looking for a gardener, are you?' Jill clamped her hand over her mouth. 'Oh, excuse me, I shouldn't have asked that. It was so rude of me.'

Laura laughed. 'Please don't apologise, but yes, I might be. I mean, yes, I definitely will be. I know nothing about flowers, plants or gardening at all. I can work a lawnmower, but that's about it, and with the size of the inn's back garden, it would be safer if I entrusted its upkeep into the hands of an expert.'

'Wow, seriously?' Jill's face lit up. 'I'd absolutely love love love to work on the inn's garden! Vivienne always did such a lovely job on it. It was one of the reasons I studied horticulture at university, actually, her garden. She had a knack of making that place look magical and she inspired me. Sounds silly, doesn't it? Choosing a whole life path because of one person's garden?'

'Not at all.' Despite her spending hours alongside her dad and Richie trying to clear the back garden, they'd hardly made a dent in the amount of work which needed to be done. But if Jill really could work some magic, then it would be a huge asset to the inn. 'Pop round when you start your business. It sounds as though you'd know exactly what to do with it.'

'Oh, I will. I'll start drawing up plans now from how I remember it...' She indicated her glass. 'Well, tomorrow anyway, and maybe I could visit to take a look sometime? See how different it is from what I remember and go from there?'

'Haha, yes, no rush. Just let me know when you're ready.'

'Oh, I'm ready. Now you've promised I can let my creativity loose on Vivienne's famous garden, I'd be thrilled to begin planning.' Jill grinned.

'In that case, that would be lovely.' Laura glanced up as Miss Cooke came and hovered between their stools.

'Jill, darling, why don't you go and tell Vivienne all about the new puppy you're getting? I think it's time Laura and I had a word.' Miss Cooke's voice was friendly but firm as Jill stood up and scurried away.

Laura glanced across at Jackson, who was serving a couple at the bar. Catching his eye, he gave her the thumbs up. She had a feeling she might need more than that. From what she'd witnessed at the village meeting, Miss Cooke, or Mayoress Cooke, ran the village.

'Laura— Can I call you that, or do you prefer Mrs, Miss or Ms Price?' Slipping onto the stool so shortly vacated by Jill, Miss Cooke clasped her hands together on the bar.

'Laura is fine, thanks.' Laura took a long sip of her drink, forcing herself not to glug the whole thing down. What did the mayoress want from her? Jill had told her that Vivienne had been singing Laura's praises, but she had a feeling Miss Cooke wouldn't be so easily influenced.

'Good, good. In that case, I want to offer the warmest welcome to the wonderful village of Meadowfield on behalf of myself and all the villagers.'

'You do?' Laura shut her mouth quickly. She hadn't meant to say that out loud, and definitely not in a tone laced with sarcasm. 'Sorry, I mean, thank you.'

Lifting her hands from the bar, Miss Cooke inspected her nails before looking back at Laura. 'I can imagine you've not had the best introduction to village life and I also want to offer you my sincerest apologies.'

'Oh, right, thank you.' Laura shuffled on her stool. 'Yes, things have been a little... difficult.'

'As I said, my apologies. You see, we were working on information given to us about you instead of passing our own judgement. That was wrong and I regret it. I hope you'll see this as a fresh start?'

A fresh start? Laura looked into her drink. It was almost empty, a centimetre of wine left at best. Could she really forgive the way people had treated her? Yes, they'd been misinformed about her intentions, but did that excuse their behaviour?

She looked around the pub. A group suddenly cheered raucously from the far end of the room and a table of people at the other end burst into singing 'Happy Birthday' as the bartender lowered a cake to the table. These were good people. Or they looked it. Jackson said so, too. Maybe she should just forgive them and put everything that had happened down to someone spreading rumours. After all, from what she'd gleaned from Vivienne, the villagers had only been sticking up for the elderly woman and wanting Pennycress to remain an independent inn rather than be taken over by some huge hotel company.

She nodded slowly.

'Good, good. Any problems or issues with anything, then please come to me and, as your mayoress, I will do my very best to resolve them.' Standing up, Miss Cooke held out her hand.

'Great. I will do, thanks.' Taking the proffered hand, she smiled as Miss Cooke shook hers firmly. After watching her retreat to Vivienne's table, Laura turned and stared into her wine glass. These were the same people who had been shunning her and yet, after a few words from Vivienne, they had made complete one-eighty. She couldn't quite believe how much things had changed in the space of one evening.

23

Jackson sidled up to Laura, his eyebrows raised as he nodded towards Miss Cooke's retreating back. 'High praise indeed if the mayoress was talking to you. Unless she was asking you to leave town of course?'

'Haha, no. She apologised for the way people have been ignoring me.' Laura looked behind her before meeting Jackson's eyes again. 'I don't really know what to make of all this. It's great that people are now being nice to me, or seem to be being nice to me, but that doesn't really excuse the way they behaved towards me, does it? I'm supposed to suddenly forgive and forget because Vivienne has put a good word in for me?'

'People were misinformed...'

'Yes, I know that, but they still shouldn't have made me feel as unwelcome as they did. They didn't know me then and they don't suddenly know me today.' She picked up her glass, bringing it to her lips before realising it was empty.

Holding out his hand, Jackson took the glass and poured in some more wine before placing it back in her hand.

'Thank you.' Taking a long sip, Laura shook her head. 'I would never treat someone like that. And then to expect me to just pretend it never happened?'

Leaning his elbows on the bar, Jackson placed his chin in his hands. 'It's a tricky one, yes, but they thought you were working for Mr Yates and had evicted Vivienne for no reason other than to turn their beloved inn into a chain hotel or whatever. How they treated you was wrong, but perhaps they thought they were doing the right thing. Making a stand to support a local villager?'

Laura twisted the stem of her glass with her fingers. 'Umm... I don't know. Jill seemed nice, genuinely nice, and she actually tried to say hello to me the other evening.'

'There you go then?' Jackson nodded.

'One person. Jill is just one person out of the whole village.'

'Do you know what my advice would be?'

She reached out and took his hand. 'What would you do? Would you forgive them all or, I don't know, bar them from forever setting foot inside Pennycress Inn?'

Jackson chuckled. 'One thing's for certain, I definitely wouldn't advise you to refuse their money.'

'Yes, you're right there. Okay, would you forgive, or would you jack up the price of tea and cake whenever they walked through the door?'

'I think I'd probably forgive, take it at face value that their hearts were in the right place and see how things panned out.'

Laura rolled her eyes. 'Of course you would. You're the worst at holding grudges.'

'You got me.' Holding his hands up, Jackson grinned before taking her hand again. 'Give people a chance. Meadowfield and the people who live here have a lot to offer.'

'I...' Laura stopped short as her mobile rang. Pulling it from her back pocket, she held it up. 'Sorry, it's Mum. I should take it.'

Nodding, Jackson waited while she answered.

'Hi, Mum, is everything all right?'

'Perfectly fine, thanks, sweetheart. How are things at your new inn?'

'Good, thanks. All good.'

'Super. Now, I know you're busy with everything your end and that this is short notice, but are you able to pop round for a spot of early dinner to celebrate your dad's birthday tomorrow?'

Laura slapped her forehead. It was Dad's birthday tomorrow? Of course it was. She'd clean forgotten, what with everything which had been going on recently. 'I'd love to.'

'Fantastic. We'll see you about one, say? That should give you plenty of time to travel back before it gets too dark.'

'Yes, yes, one is good.'

'See you tomorrow then. Love you.'

'Love you too.' Ending the call, Laura lowered her forehead against the bar.

'Everything okay?' Jackson's voice was full of concern.

Pushing herself up, Laura sighed. 'I forgot it was Dad's birthday tomorrow and I've not got him anything and Mum has invited me over for dinner. What am I supposed to get at this time of night?'

'Ah, how about picking something up in the morning, before you go?'

'As much as I love Meadowfield, I don't think there'll be anything in the few shops for him and it'll be Sunday so not everywhere will be open.' She scrunched up her nose. There had to be something she could lay her hands on easily that her dad would love.

'How about...' Now it was Jackson's mobile whose tune filled the bar area. Glancing at the screen, he frowned. 'It's your mum.'

'Oh, that's weird. I wonder what she wants?' She nodded towards the mobile in his hand. 'Answer it then.'

Jackson answered the call and held the phone against his ear.

Looking down at her own mobile, she texted the message group she had with Jenny and Richie:

LAURA

Forgot it's Dad's birthday tomorrow! Help! What can I get him? xxx

Tapping the mobile against her palm, she waited until it pinged.

RICHIE

Haha, I almost forgot too but Jenny has bought something from all of us! X

LAURA

Really? That's amazing – THANK YOU! What is it? xxx

JENNY

Hey, no worries. Knew you'd be run off your feet at your new place and, Richie, I knew you'd forget! Got him and Mum tickets to a theatre in London xxx

LAURA

Ooh sounds good. Thanks again. Let me know how much I owe you xxx

RICHIE

Me? Forget? Oh you have so little faith in me!!!! X

JENNY

Nah, just know you too well xxx

'I think we may have a problem.' Jackson's voice drew Laura back to reality, and she put down her mobile. She'd answer them again later.

'Oh, how come?'

'Because your mum has invited me to your dad's birthday meal, too.' Jackson took a deep breath.

'Ooooh,' Laura groaned and hid her face with her hands. 'How's that going to work? We'll have to turn up at different times. Just like they do in films when two people are trying to pretend they're not together when they really are.'

Jackson chuckled. 'Not possible, I'm afraid. Your mum suggested I travel down with you.'

'How did they...? Ah, they don't know we're together, do they? They just know we live next to each other.'

'Exactly.' Jackson leaned across the bar towards her before tucking his finger beneath her chin and kissing her. 'I'd be more than happy to tell them about us. It's just Richie who I'd worry about knowing.'

'Me too.' Laura nodded. There was every chance that Richie would be happy for them, but if he wasn't, it could ruin everything. 'Okay, well, tomorrow's going to be fun then.'

'Yep.' Jackson nodded.

'But we can pull it off.' Laura drank the rest of her wine before grinning. 'Maybe we can pretend to be mad at each other, so they'd never even twig we were together?'

'Haha, maybe. Although they might wonder why we drove up together.'

'True. Okay, we'll just be friends in front of them.' Laura shrugged. 'It can't be too hard. We've been friends long enough.'

'Exactly. It'll be fine.' Jackson nodded behind her. 'Evening, Vivienne. What can I get you?'

'I'm on my way out, thank you. I've just come to speak to Laura here.' Vivienne indicated the stool. 'May I?'

'Hi. Yes, of course.' Laura smiled. 'I think I owe you a thank you. I would have come over myself and said so, but I didn't like to intrude.'

'You wouldn't have been intruding, dear. And you also do not owe me anything such as a thank you. I merely told your side of the story to the mayoress and the rest was taken care of.' Vivienne patted Laura's hand. 'You're a good person, I can see that and so does everyone else now.'

'Still, thank you for putting in a good word for me.'

'You're very welcome.' Vivienne stood up again. 'Now, I really must go. My bed is calling me, and my lovely daughter is outside ready to give me a lift. I'll pop by one day next week if the offer to come and take a look at the old place is still open?'

'Yes, of course. That would be lovely.' Laura nodded.

'Thank you.' Vivienne held her hand up to Jackson, who was busy serving. 'Thank you, Jackson. And thank you for the lovely dinner. Superb, as always.'

''Night, Vivienne.' Jackson waved back before disappearing into the kitchen.

Laura turned her attention to her mobile. By the looks of the text conversation, Richie was still defending himself against Jenny's claim that she knew he'd have forgotten their dad's birthday. She smiled. It would be good to spend the day at home tomorrow.

'And voilà! A selection off the new menu.' Returning to the bar, Jackson began offloading plates from the tray he was carrying.

Laura took a deep breath in, the aroma of freshly cooked food reminding her that she hadn't yet eaten. 'Yum, they smell delicious.'

'Help yourself. Just let me know what you think.' Jackson held up a plate. 'Goats' cheese and onion chutney bites.'

'Ooh well, you know what I'm going to be saying about those.' Taking one, Laura let the tasty combination of flavours fill her mouth. 'They are absolutely the most delicious thing I have ever ever eaten.'

Jackson grinned. 'I thought you'd like them. Goats' cheese and onion chutney toasties were always your favourite growing up.'

'You remember?' She took another bite.

'Of course I do. I was usually the one making them.'

Laura laughed. Of course he had been. Throughout the months before her exams, she'd hardly left her spot at the dining table, surrounding herself with textbooks, notebooks and revision cards. 'Do you know something? I probably wouldn't have eaten anything if you hadn't made me those.'

'I know and I couldn't very well let Richie's little sis starve, could I? All those hours of revision would have been wasted.'

'Haha, they would have.'

'Why don't you go and join them at the darts board? Show them how it's done?' Jackson indicated the group of people playing darts at the far end of the pub.

'Oh, I don't think so. I can't just go and barge in on their game.' Laura shook her head before taking a mozzarella stick covered in breadcrumbs.

'Sure, you can. They're a good group. Catherine, the captain, and her partner, Dan, started the club from scratch last year. They're decent people and really helped me feel at home here.'

'I don't know.' Laura shook her head. She loved playing darts, but she hadn't played in years. She'd probably forgotten how. 'I'm really rusty.'

'Catherine's coming over to the bar now. Here's your chance to talk to her.' Jackson smiled as a woman joined them.

'Hi, Jackson. Can we grab another round of drinks, please?' Catherine glanced at Laura. 'Hi, you must be Laura? From Penny-cress Inn?'

'Hi, yes, that's right.' Maybe Jackson was right, a game of darts would be a nice way to get to know more people.

24

'Yes!' Raising her hands above her head, Laura jumped up and down. She was the first to get to zero! She hadn't played darts for years and now she'd won the whole game!

'Woohoo! We need you on the pub's team.' Dan laid his arm over her shoulder.

Laura grinned at him. She may have only met this small group an hour ago but already they were treating her as one of the locals.

'Yes! You're on fire, girl!' Catherine held her hands out. 'And Dan is right. We need you on our side.'

Giving Catherine a double high-five, Laura grinned. Joining the team would be great. She hadn't had so much fun in ages, years even. 'I'd gladly join you.'

'Fantastic.' Catherine gave a little dance before collecting the darts from the board. 'Another game?'

'I'll grab another round if we're playing again.' Dan headed to the bar.

'Ooh, here comes Jackson's stalker.' Terry, who Laura had learned also played in the pub's darts team, stroked his beard.

'Jackson has a stalker? Who?' Laura frowned.

'Evie Taunton. The same woman who spread the lies about you.' Terry pointed across the pub.

Turning, Laura watched as Evie sauntered to the bar on her high heels. What did Terry mean by calling her Jackson's stalker? Jackson had said they'd dated for a while and it was fairly obvious that she still harboured feelings for him despite them both supposedly ending the relationship amicably, but surely calling her a stalker was a little harsh?

'Well, I don't think she'll be getting much of a reception tonight somehow.' Catherine handed out the darts. 'Not if the way you and Jackson have been acting together is anything to go by?' The other woman looked at Laura over her glasses, a slow grin spreading across her face.

Feeling herself blush, Laura drank the dregs from her wine glass. After not touching a drop of alcohol in months, she felt decidedly tipsy.

'I noticed the same. You and Jackson there seem to have hit it right off.' Terry nodded towards her.

'We've known each other for years. He's my brother's best mate and, believe it or not, I hadn't realised he'd moved here,' Laura offered as a way of explanation.

'Uh-huh, and the rest. My brother's best mate doesn't look at me the way Jackson looks at you, and he certainly doesn't kiss me.' Catherine raised her eyebrows.

'I can imagine Dan would give him a bruised lip if he tried.' Terry chuckled.

'Who am I supposed to be fighting?' Arriving back, Dan lowered the tray to the closest table and handed out the drinks.

'No one. We were just teasing Laura, that's all.' Catherine held her glass up. 'Here's to our new team buddy and best weapon, Laura.'

'Oh thanks.' Glad the interrogation about Jackson had ended, Laura clinked glasses with her new teammates before grabbing a used napkin from the table and drying up the dribble of wine making its way down the stem of her glass. Leaning against the table, she watched as Dan, Terry and Catherine began the game.

'Ha, beat that start!' Catherine held her hand up for a high-five from her opponents, Terry and Dan, who sighed and looked away. 'Ooh, now you two are going to be sore losers this time around.'

'Who said we're going to be the ones who lose?' Dan picked up his dart, kissed the back of his hand and drew his hand back, ready to release his dart.

Laura looked across at the bar. Jackson was still speaking to Evie Taunton. What were they talking about? She watched as Evie glanced her way, catching her eye. That answered that question then. They were talking about her.

'Hey, Laura. Your turn. Come and show Dan here how it's done.' Catherine poked her tongue out at her partner.

'Umm, I'll pass on this game, thanks. Just need to pop to the bar.'

'It's closed. That's why I went to get the drinks,' Dan called across.

'Nah, I don't need another drink.' Laura dismissed him with a wave of her hand. No, she'd drunk enough for one night. What she did need, though, were answers.

As she made her way towards the bar, she smiled as people greeted her, a complete contrast to the last time she'd ventured into the pub. Maybe, now she had the villagers' approval, she'd finally begin to feel a part of the community.

'I'm afraid the bar's closed for the night.' Darren paused in his cleaning and folded the cloth he was using to wipe the bar down. 'I can grab you a water though, if you like?'

Placing her wine glass on the bar, Laura laid her forearms next to it, the sticky residue of an evening's worth of spilt alcohol sticking to the sleeves of her jumper. 'Nope, I'm happy with my wine.'

Darren nodded before picking up his cloth again. 'Fair enough.'

Turning her head, she watched Jackson and Evie, deep in conversation. She couldn't hear what they were saying – their voices were too low for that – but by the way Jackson had his arms crossed and that look on his face, she was pretty sure she didn't need to worry that they were arranging a date or anything.

Laura picked up her glass and brought it to her lips. What was she actually doing here at the bar? If she wasn't going to interrupt their conversation, then what did she hope to achieve?

She took another sip as she watched Jackson hold his hand up, palm forward towards Evie, before turning on his heels and disappearing into the kitchen.

Before she could question her actions, she picked up her glass and walked across to where the other woman was sitting. 'Hello.'

Jerking her head to look at Laura, confusion washed across Evie's face before realisation dawned and she recognised her. 'Laura Price.'

Laura pulled herself up onto the bar stool next to her and twisted her wine glass by the stem. Now here, she wasn't quite sure what to say, how to begin the conversation. She cleared her throat. 'Why?'

'Why? Why what? Why am I here? I should think the same reason as you.' Evie looked pointedly at Laura's glass. 'Although perhaps not, as some of us have more class than to drink ourselves under the table.'

There was no point in trying to have a conversation with her. Evie's defensiveness and cattiness had just proven Laura would get nowhere if she tried to ask her what her motivations were. Heck, she'd probably never find out, but suddenly Laura wasn't sure it mattered anymore. Vivienne had seemingly set everyone straight, and certainly the atmosphere in the pub tonight had been a million times better than how Laura had been greeted, or more accurately, not greeted, before. Maybe she should just be happy with that.

'Nice talking to you.' Evie slipped off her stool.

'I...' Laura stopped herself. She'd drunk far too much to say anything particularly coherent, and besides, what would she say. Whatever she said would make her sound like a child at the hands of the school bully pleading for mercy and she wasn't about to give Evie the satisfaction. No, she'd rather not know. There might not even have been a reason. Hadn't Vivienne herself said that the estate agent liked to 'stir the pot' sometimes? Maybe it was just her thing?

She watched the pub door close behind Evie before turning back to her glass. Picking it up, she looked at the pale liquid inside, suddenly no longer in the mood to drink. Lifting her head, she watched as the door to the kitchen behind the bar opened and Jackson appeared, carrying a bowl of chips.

Pausing, he frowned. 'Everything okay?'

Laura nodded. 'Yep.'

'Where's Evie got to?' He looked down at the bowl.

Laura shrugged. Had those chips been for Evie? Had he cooked her them despite the kitchen having closed over an hour ago? 'She left.'

'Oh, right.' Jackson shrugged and placed the bowl on the bar in front of Laura. 'Here, help yourself.'

They had been for Evie. They must have been, or else why would they suddenly be going spare? Laura picked up a chip turning it over in her fingers before replacing it in the bowl and slipping off her stool. 'I'm going to head home actually.'

'You are?'

'Yes, it's been a weird evening and I'm tired.' She pulled her coat on before walking towards the door.

'Hey, Laura! Are you off home now?' Catherine ran up to her, standing between Laura and the door.

'Sorry, I should have come over and said bye.' Laura shrugged. 'Too much wine.'

'Haha, no worries. You'll be on our darts team, though, won't you?'

'I'd love to be.' That was one thing she was certain about. She enjoyed playing darts, and Catherine, Dan and Terry had been nothing but nice to her. Besides, apart from tonight, she hadn't seen them around Meadowfield, so even though they probably wouldn't have spoken to her before Vivienne's intervention, they hadn't actively shunned her.

'Fab!' Catherine turned and walked the rest of the way to the door with Laura. 'We have formal practice on Wednesday evenings, although quite often if we happen to spot each other in the pub or around the village, then we'll throw together a quick game, too.'

'Okay, great. Well, I'll see you Wednesday then.' Laura pulled open the pub door.

'See you.' Waving, Catherine turned and headed back towards the darts board and Dan and Terry.

25

Stepping outside, Laura let the heavy door close behind her, shutting in the murmur of chatting and the chink of glasses. As she walked through the small courtyard of outside seating, she pulled her scarf from her pocket and wrapped it around her neck. The evening had been odd – lovely, but odd all the same and she'd be glad to get home and have the time to process everything.

'Hey, Laura. Hold up.'

Turning, she watched as Jackson jogged towards her, his coat in his arms. 'You didn't need to leave now, too.'

'I know, but it's not every night Darren offers to finish clearing the kitchen. Besides, I help him out behind the bar enough, he owes me.' He chuckled as he shrugged into his coat before holding his hand out towards her.

Looking down at his hand, she took it, glad of the warmth from his skin.

'Did they ask you to join their team? Catherine, Dan and Terry, I mean.'

'They did. How did you know?' She looked across at him.

'Dan was singing your praises when he came up to the bar. Said he was looking forward to taking down the Red Lions.'

'The Red Lions?'

'The team from the next village along. They're decent, really decent, but with you on our team now, they won't stand a chance.'

'Ha, I'd better get some practice in then. I'm still more than a bit rusty.' She smiled. It would be good to a part of something, belong to a group.

'I don't think Dan thought you were rusty.' Jackson lifted her hand to his lips and kissed it.

'Well, I was.' She shrugged.

'Are you okay? You seem a bit... deflated?'

'I'm fine.' She swallowed. How could she say how she was feeling without coming across as ungrateful? 'It's just weird. Yesterday, heck, even this morning, I was the talk of the village for all the wrong reasons, either ignored or the receiver of so many dirty looks and now... now suddenly people like me.'

Jackson squeezed her hand, giving her the space to continue.

'I know that sounds ungrateful to Vivienne and I don't mean to be, I really don't but...' She looked up at the sky. It was clear, the newly crescent-shaped moon surrounded by stars. Meadowfield would be the perfect place for stargazing.

'You don't sound ungrateful.'

'Oh, I do. I hear myself and I cringe.' She let out a hollow laugh. 'But I also can't help the way I feel. I guess it will just take a bit of time to get used to what's happened and forgive people for treating me as they did.'

'That's only natural.'

'I mean, I know they were only ignoring me because they thought I was working for Mr Yates, and they didn't agree with how he'd behaved towards Vivienne. I understand that.

Completely.' She sighed. It would just take time, but time she had. She wasn't going anywhere and after having the chance to speak to Vivienne, it had only confirmed what Laura had already known deep down, that she loved Pennycress and all the opportunities it could bring. There was another question whirring in her mind, though. One which she wasn't sure if she wanted to know the answer to. 'What were you and Evie Taunton speaking about?'

She looked down at the kerb as they crossed the road before glancing at him again. 'Sorry, maybe I shouldn't have asked.'

'I don't mind you asking.' He ran a palm across his face.

'Okay...' He clearly did or he wouldn't be stalling, would he? 'Look, forget it. You've got history with her and we've only just started...' she held up their hands, '...this.'

'We may have only just started dating, but we've known each other for years, so please never feel as though you can't ask me something.' He smiled a short, tight smile. 'I was actually asking her what she'd hoped to achieve by ostracising you and spreading those rumours.'

'Oh. And what did she say?'

'She didn't really give an answer.' He shrugged. 'I don't think she particularly understands the damage she's caused.'

'You don't think she did it on purpose, then? You don't think she knew exactly what she was doing by telling people I was renting, by suggesting I was going to turn Pennycress into some huge commercial chain hotel?' Evie must have known. She must have.

Jackson was quiet, and it was only when they reached Wisteria Lane that he cleared his throat and spoke again. 'I don't know.'

Laura nodded. For whatever reason, Jackson clearly didn't want to think Evie was capable of lying to the extent she had. That was fine. That was up to him.

Jackson paused outside his gate. 'Do you fancy coming in for a coffee or hot chocolate?'

Did she? Her bed was calling her, the aftermath of the wine surfacing, but she didn't want to leave things with Jackson like this. It felt awkward, and that was the last thing she'd wanted when she'd asked him about Evie. 'One of your hot chocolates sounds good. Have you got cream?'

A grin spread across his face as he opened the gate and ushered her through. 'Do you even need to ask?'

'Haha, no I don't suppose you'd have offered me a hot chocolate if you hadn't.' She smiled. Whatever Evie Taunton's game had been, it wasn't worth jeopardising what she and Jackson had found together.

She waited as he unlocked the front door before stepping into the hallway. As she'd assumed, his house was a lot smaller than Pennycress, but the original features were equally beautiful. She slipped her boots off onto the black and white tiled floor of the small porch before stepping through to the long narrow hallway. Looking up, she took in the stunning beams.

'It's gorgeous.'

'Thanks. It's taken a fair amount of work and I still have two bedrooms to finish off, but I'm content with how it's coming long.'

'Content? You should be over the moon. It's stunning.' She walked into the living room and ran her fingers across the wooden mantelpiece.

He grinned. 'It's amazing what you can pick up at the reclamation yard.' He nodded towards the fireplace.

'Is that where this is from?'

'It sure is. That was a lucky find. It only needed sanding down and bringing back to its natural state. You should have seen the one I found for the master bedroom. It had at least ten layers of black paint on.'

She looked again at the mantelpiece. 'It looks as though it's always been here.'

'Thanks. I'll go and make the drinks. Make yourself at home.'

She waited until he'd left before turning on the spot. The room really was beautiful. He'd always been creative, but she'd never realised he'd be so good at something like this.

She lowered herself onto the sofa, leaning her back against the soft cushions and smiled as she listened to Jackson making their hot chocolates: the clatter of mugs being placed on the work surface, the click of the switch as the kettle finished boiling.

Rubbing her eyes as wine-induced sleep threatened, she pushed herself to standing and walked across to the small leaded window sunken into the yellow Cotswold stone of the cottage overlooking the garden and looked down at the photo frames displayed there.

Picking one of them up, she laughed. It was a photo of Jackson with her, Richie and Jenny. Taken on the beach at Whitby Bay, if she wasn't mistaken. They were all smiling and holding ice creams. She and Jenny had their hair in bunches despite being in their early twenties, and Richie and Jackson had spiked theirs up with gel.

'Oh, you found that pic.' Jackson chuckled as he held out mug towards her.

'Ha, I did.' Carefully replacing the photo frame, she took the mug. 'I think I remember that day.'

He grinned as he looked at it. 'About ten years ago we'd gone down to Whitby Bay on a day trip. Is that what you were thinking of?'

'Yes, we tried to recreate a photo taken when we'd been younger.'

'That's right. Hence the Mr Whippy ice creams and the shocking hairstyles.'

She shook her head. 'Harry asked me to move in with him that day.'

'He did? I didn't know.'

She nodded. She'd felt confused even back then. 'I almost said no. I think if it hadn't been for the fact we were by the beach and everything else was perfect, I might have told him we should wait.'

'Seriously?' Jackson sat down on the large blue sofa.

'Yep. Jenny and Richie had been talking about how super happy they were with Rob and Jane, and I felt left out.' She shrugged. It had felt right when Harry had asked. The timing had anyway. She just hadn't been so sure about the man. 'And you'd just got with that girl. What was her name? Tania? And you were so in love.'

'Tasmin.'

'That was it.' Sitting beside him, she ran her finger through the cream on her hot chocolate before licking it off.

'And just for the record, I wasn't "so in love".' He curled his free forefinger around the words.

'You weren't?'

'Nope. It was you I wanted, but you were with Harry, and I had to let the idea of you and me ever getting together go.'

'Ha, now I know you're joking.' She pointed her finger at him. It had been her who had had the crush on him, not the other way around, despite what he'd previously hinted at. She'd have known if he'd felt anything more than friendship towards her.

Jackson reached around the back of her and drew her towards him for a hug. 'Think what you like, but it's true.'

'Well, *if* you are being honest...' She shifted against the cushions so she was looking at him. 'And that's a big if. Then we've wasted so many years trying to be happy with other people and being in rubbish relationships which we've tried so desperately to make work. And for what?'

'For nothing.'

'Exactly. For literally nothing.' She drank some hot chocolate, its sweet flavour just perfect after the wine. 'Are you being really honest though? Or just saying what you think I want to hear?'

'Have I ever lied to you?' His expression was serious.

'Umm, no.' She laughed. 'Actually, how am I supposed to answer that? If you have, then I wouldn't know anyway, unless you're a super rubbish liar and I found out after.'

Jackson chuckled as she leaned back against him. 'True. Well, I'll promise you that I haven't then.'

'Uh-huh.' She nodded and balanced her half-full mug on her lap before closing her eyes. It just felt so right with him. All the feelings she'd spent years trying to squash down inside her, trying to bury and tell herself they weren't real, were surfacing and she'd never felt so happy, so sure of being with someone before.

'Penny for them.' Jackson's breath tickled her hair as he spoke.

'I was just thinking how perfect this was, that we've met again like this, and how much I love you.' She clamped her hand over her mouth and sat up, her hot chocolate dribbling down the side of the mug and forming a puddle on her jeans as she did so. What had she said? She stood up, her face hot with fierce embarrassment. 'I'm so sorry. I've drunk too much wine.'

'No need to apologise.'

'Oh, there is, there really is.' She looked around for a coaster, somewhere to place her mug before spying an envelope standing behind a picture frame on the mantelpiece and placing it on there. 'I shouldn't have had so much to drink. I've not had a sip of alcohol in months and it's gone straight to my head. I'll let myself out.'

'Please don't go.' Jackson stood up and placed his own mug on the coffee table to his right.

'I need to.' She pointed to the door, backing away as he approached her. How could she have been so stupid? How could she have let the 'l' word slip? How could she stay now after she'd made such a huge idiot of herself? 'I really need to. I'm so sorry.'

Taking her hand in his, Jackson rubbed his thumb along the back of her hand. 'Did you mean what you said?'

Could this get any worse? 'Of course not. We've only just started seeing each other. Like I said, I'm drunk. I've had too much wine. There, you can feed back to Darren that the local wines he's sampling are too strong...' Her voice quietened, the excuses tailing off. All she could focus on was the gentle caressing of Jackson's thumb against the back of her hand and his eyes, dark blue and brooding, meeting hers.

'I love you too.' His voice was soft, suddenly unsure and lacking in confidence. His statement almost a question.

She blinked, her throat dry. 'You do?'

'It is early, too early, to be feeling like this about one another if we'd only just met, but we've known each other so long and I think we both felt something beforehand, so...' He shrugged.

Tucking her hair behind her ear, she looked down at the floor. Had he actually said it? Had he really told her he loved her too? She needed to get home, back to the inn, and make sense of it all. Suddenly she needed to be alone. She needed to think. Looking back up at him, she smiled. 'I'm still going to go now.'

'You are?' Dropping her hand, confusion swept across his face.

'Yes, but not because we've told each other how we feel, just because so much has happened in the past few hours and I need to make sense of it all.'

'Right. Okay.' Jackson nodded.

She searched his face – his forehead was creased with confusion – and felt a pang of regret that she'd spoilt the moment. She hadn't meant to hurt him, to make him second-guess himself, second-guess her intentions. She literally just needed to take some time for herself. Taking both his hands in hers, she leaned forward, their lips millimetres apart. 'I can't believe you feel the same way.'

Jackson relaxed, his grin returning. 'I'll walk you to your door.'

26

Home sweet home.' Laura pulled the car up next to the path in front of her parents' house, the reality of what they were about to do suddenly resurfacing. Throughout the journey, they'd spoken about anything but pretending to just be friends in front of her family. She'd so desperately wanted to avoid thinking about how they were about to deceive her parents and her siblings that she'd waffled on about whatever she could think of, and she'd sensed Jackson felt the same. Now that they were here though, now that the house was right in front of them, neither of them could ignore it any longer.

'This is going to be fun.' Jackson turned in the passenger seat to face her. 'A whole afternoon of pretending to be nothing but friends.'

'Ha, yes. Especially after last night's conversation.' Laura could feel her cheeks heat at the memory. She'd hardly slept at all after going back to the inn from Jackson's house. His words had just kept going round and round in her head, all jumbled up with the night at the pub. She still couldn't believe that he felt the same way towards her as she did towards him.

'Exactly.' Jackson groaned and covered his face with his hands. 'How are we going to survive?'

'Umm, well, we could go down the route you suggested and pretend to be mad at each other.' Laura prised his hands from his face and met his eyes.

'Oh, we could, but I'm not sure how much of a performance I can put on. I'm still trying to come to terms with the fact that you told me you loved me.' He grinned, his dimple showing.

She raised her eyebrows at him. 'Oi, you said the same to me.'

'I did, and I meant it. It still feels surreal though, doesn't it?'

'Oh yes, it certainly does. Honestly, if you hadn't told me again this morning how you felt, I may just have notched up last night's conversation to me being slightly tipsy and confusing things.' She laughed. Slightly tipsy was probably an understatement. After not drinking for months, she'd forgotten how quickly wine got her drunk. Still, at least she seemed to have avoided the dreaded hangover, apart from the slight headache tugging at her temple anyway. That's what living with her parents and avoiding the local pubs in case she ran into Harry had done to her. And she still blamed the wine for the fact she'd been so open with Jackson last night; she certainly couldn't think of a single situation when she'd told her very new boyfriend that she'd loved them so soon. But the gamble had paid off. Thankfully.

'Okay, let's do this.' Jackson straightened his back and held his hand out towards her. 'Thank you for the lift, my friend and neighbour, Laura Price. It was very kind of you.'

Giggling, she took his hand before pulling him towards her and wrapping her arms around him. She could feel his shoulder move beneath her arms as he chuckled.

'Let's just enjoy one moment before we go in.' Leaning back, Jackson cupped her cheeks with his hands and leaned in.

Meeting his lips, she closed her eyes. This was really happen ing. She and Jackson were really together after all these years of knowing one another, being friends but also both feeling there was a deeper connection between them. A connection which they'd both tried so very hard to suppress, but which now they'd shared, they wouldn't be able to bury again.

Pulling away, Jackson ran the pad of his thumb across her lips. 'I really do love you.'

'Quick!' Jerking back, Laura nudged Jackson as the twins came running out of the house and down the garden path towards the car. 'Poker faces on.'

Jackson nodded seriously. 'Poker faces on.'

Opening the car door, Laura stepped out just as Tammy threw her arms around her waist.

'Auntie Laura! Nana said you were coming.' Tammy looked up at her, her arms still wrapped tightly round her aunt's middle.

'Hi, Tammy.' Laura laughed as Toby joined the hug. 'Hiya, Toby. How's your ankle?'

'It's okay. All better now.' Toby grinned.

'Oh, that's good news.' Untangling herself, Laura walked around to join Jackson on the path.

Covering her mouth with one hand, Tammy stage-whispered to Laura, 'Apart from on PE days. He tells the teacher it hurts again then and gets to sit out on the bench.'

'Oi! You promised you wouldn't tell anyone!' Toby crossed his arms and pouted.

'It's okay, Toby. Auntie Laura won't tell Mummy or Daddy, will you?' Tammy skipped through the garden before calling over her shoulder. 'It's our little secret, isn't it, Auntie Laura?'

'Umm...' Laura pulled a face, unsure of what to say.

'What's this about secrets?' Jenny appeared in the open doorway and drew Laura in for a hug.

'She's going to bring us some chocolate next time she visits.'

Tammy spoke quickly before running past her mum and inside, shortly followed by Toby.

'Chocolate? Huh? I hope you remember to bring me some too.' Jenny stepped back and turned to Jackson, her arms outstretched. 'You did bring him! Jackson! Long time no see. How many years has it been now?'

'Lovely to see you, Jenny.' Jackson stepped into her embrace. 'Too many, that's for sure.'

'Too right. Come on through, both of you. Rob's got the kettle on already.' Jenny closed the door behind them.

'Thanks. I'm parched.' Laura shrugged out of her coat.

'That'll be all the wine last night.' Jackson chuckled.

'What's this? You've got Laura to go out again? Mingle with people her own age?' Jenny glanced behind her towards the kitchen door. 'Don't tell Mum or Dad I said that, but that's good if you're getting out and about again. You spent too much time holed up in here after you and Harry finished.'

Laura swallowed. She could feel the red of self-consciousness crawling across her cheeks. 'It was just a night at the local pub.'

'And I was working, so, unfortunately, I wasn't able to join in the merriment.' Jackson grinned, seemingly oblivious to how embarrassed Laura felt due to Jenny's comment. Either that or he wasn't fazed. Laura couldn't tell. 'Is Richie here?'

'Yep, he's...' Jenny turned as Richie walked into the hallway. 'Here.'

'Jackson, mate! It's so good to see you.' Richie drew Jackson in towards him and patted him on the back before he turned to Laura. 'And you too, little sis.'

'Hey.' Laura hugged Richie back.

'Laura, Jackson, come on through and stop loitering in the hallway.' Her mum ushered everyone through into the living room. 'Rob's just making coffees, unless you want anything stronger, Jackson?'

'No, I'm good with coffee, thanks.' Jackson sat down on one of two large cream sofas.

'And I'm taking it you're driving, Laura, so coffee for you.' Her mum smiled as she walked back into the kitchen.

Laura perched on the other sofa away from Jackson, as Richie sat down next to him. She could hear her parents back in the kitchen, pots and pans clattering as they finished off the roast dinner. An empty bouncy chair sat in front of the sofa and an array of toys were strewn across the carpet.

'Where've Tammy and Toby got to?' Jenny appeared in the doorway, her hands full of cutlery.

'I think they ran out into the garden.' Richie shrugged before continuing the conversation he was having with Jackson.

'You're kidding? In this weather? They'll just bring all the mud inside.' Jenny shook her head before stepping over the toys and making her way to the glass patio doors at the back of the room. Sliding one open, she called out, 'Toby, Tammy, come on in. I've a job for you both.'

'Me job.' Ava, Richie's toddler, poked her head around the corner of the sofa.

'Oh, Ava, sweetie, there you are.' After closing the patio door once the twins had run inside, Jenny bent down and held her hand out towards Ava. 'Yes, a job for you, too.'

'What's the job, Mummy, and how much pocket money will you give me?' Tammy kicked her wellies to the side of the doormat.

'Tammy? Really? We're at Nana and Grandad's. You can do a job for them out of the goodness of your heart, understood?'

Tammy nodded sullenly. 'Okay.'

'Good. Right, you two can lay the table and let Ava put the

napkins out, okay?' Jenny turned and walked out of the room, the three children following behind her.

'She's grown!' Jackson nodded towards Ava as she gripped Tammy's hand on her way out of the room. 'I think the last time I saw little Ava was when she was a newborn.'

'That's right, it was.' Richie grinned. 'You wait until you see Jasper, he's four now.'

'Four? Wow, when did that happen?' Jackson shook his head.

'When you were MIA, that's when.' Richie stood up. 'And let me locate little Lucas. You've not even met him.'

Jackson watched Richie walk out of the room before leaning across and taking Laura's hand in his. 'This is nice.'

'It is.' Laura squeezed his hand. 'Strange though. Just a few weeks ago, I was living here and now I'm visiting again. Surreal.'

'Ha, I bet. And of course...' Jackson nodded towards their hands. 'Something else is different, too.'

'Yes.' Laura laughed and pulled her hand away just as Richie walked back into the room with baby Lucas in his arms.

'Aw, now you are a cutie, aren't you?' Standing up, Jackson peered at him. 'How old is he?'

'Twelve weeks.'

'So small.'

'Small but fierce and with the lungs of a forty-year-old on a night out at the football. Here, do you want a hold?' Before Jackson could answer, Richie had passed baby Lucas across to him.

'Hello, little one. Nice to meet you.' Jackson swayed slightly as Lucas stretched in his arms before closing his eyes again and nuzzling his head against Jackson's jumper.

'You're a natural at this.' Richie fluffed Jackson's cushion before his friend sat back down.

'Says the dad of three.' Jackson chuckled.

'Yes, well, it's not easy having three under four, but it's Jane who bears the brunt of it whilst I'm at work.' Richie looked behind him as Jane walked through the door, their four-year-old Jasper on her hip.

'Is that my name I hear?' She paused and shifted Jasper further up. 'Jackson, you're here. So lovely to see you again. I see Richie's already got you babysitting?'

'Oh, I don't mind.' Jackson gently pulled Lucas's pale blue blanket down a little from his face. 'Great to see you again too.'

'Hello, Laura. How's the inn?'

Standing up, Laura hugged Jane. 'It's getting there, thanks. You'll have to come and visit.'

'Oh, I intend to. Looking forward to it.'

Smiling, Laura sat back down, her eyes automatically drawn to Jackson as he held Lucas. Richie was right, he really was a natural.

'Jackson, you and Richie should get together more often.' Jane came and sat next to Laura, sliding Jasper down onto the floor and watching as he began playing with the bricks. 'Richie's always saying that, aren't you, love?'

'I am.' Richie patted Jackson's knee. 'I could do with a lads' night out.'

'Hey, you know where I am.' Jackson shifted position and leaned baby Lucas over his shoulder, rubbing his back. 'I think this one might have a little wind.'

'Oh, watch out, he has a habit of—' Richie covered his mouth and laughed. 'Throwing up down your back. Sorry, Jackson. Too low.'

'Haha, better out than in, isn't it, Lucas?' Jackson smiled as he brought the baby back into his arms again.

'Here, catch. Wipe him up, love.' Jane threw Richie a cloth, who began wiping Jackson's back.

Laura grinned. She couldn't take her eyes off Jackson. He was so good with the kids. With his niece, Eden, with all of them. Maybe if their relationship continued to go from strength to strength, Harry wouldn't have been her last chance to have children after all. Maybe...

'What do you say, Laura?' Richie's voice rose.

'Huh? Sorry, I was miles away.' She shook her head, bringing herself back to reality.

'Yes, we noticed. Getting all broody over Lucas, were you? I'm sure Jackson will share him.' Grinning, Richie shook his head. ' was asking if you'd be Lucas's godmother with Jackson.'

'With Jackson?' She widened her eyes. Had they guessed their secret? Was it really that obvious?

'Yes, you as the godmother and Jackson as the godfather. Richie frowned.

'Right, yes. Yes, I'd be honoured.'

'Good, that's settled then.' Richie turned on the sofa. 'Now where's Rob with those coffees?'

'Dinner time. Nana said everyone's got to come to the table now.' Tammy skipped into the room, a fork in her hand.

'Careful with that, Tammy.' Standing up, Jane took the fork from her niece before following her through to the dining room.

'Here, I'll lay him down.' Standing up, Richie held his arm out for baby Lucas before whispering, 'No one breathe.'

Obediently holding her breath, Laura smiled as she watched her brother lay his son in a Moses basket set up by the bookcase.

Straightening his back, the baby successfully still asleep Richie held his palm up first to Jackson and then to Laura to high five quietly.

27

In the dining room, Laura sat down next to Jenny as Rob balanced a tray of mugs on the edge of the table and began passing them around.

'Sorry, got a little distracted, but better late than never. Even if it does mean having a coffee with your roast.'

'Thanks.' Taking her mug, Laura sipped it before grimacing. He'd forgotten the sugar.

'Oh yuck. Did you put sugar in this, Rob?' Jenny pulled a face too.

'Oops. Umm, sorry, that one's Jenny's and that one's yours, Laura.' Rob swapped the mugs over.

'Thanks, much better.' Laura grinned as she took another sip of coffee. Yep, this one was hers.

'Here, Jackson. No need to be polite. Come and take a seat.' Richie pointed to the empty chair next to Laura.

'Thanks, mate.' Sitting down, Jackson smiled at Laura before accepting his own mug from Rob.

As her parents brought in the serving dishes, Laura looked around the table. It felt like such a long time since all of them had managed to get together for one of her parents' roasts. Of course, with the exception of Jackson, it had actually only been a few weeks. The last one had been the week before she'd moved into Pennycress, but as she wasn't seeing them every day now that she lived so far away, it felt like longer.

'To Laura and her move to Pennycress Inn.' Her dad stood up and held his coffee cup aloft, waiting until everyone else had copied him. 'And to Jackson. Good to have you back with us.'

'To Laura and Jackson.' The chorus of voices filled the room and Laura stifled a laugh. If they only knew.

'To Auntie Laura and Jackson.' Tammy stood up from the small plastic children's table her parents had set up next to the dining table to make room for everyone. 'Can we eat now?'

'Yes, yes. Dig in, everyone.' Her mum laughed as Tammy plonked herself back down and picked up a roast potato.

'How are you settling into village life, Laura?' Jane smiled as she poured the gravy.

'Good, thanks. I guess there's been a few hiccups here and there and some people are quite close-knit...' She glanced at her mum, who gave her a worried look. 'But I've joined the local darts team at the pub Jackson works at.'

'That didn't take you long, sis. Good for you.' Richie picked up a Yorkshire pudding and tore a piece off before shoving it into his mouth.

'Use your fork, Richie,' their mum reprimanded him.

'Sorry, I forgot I was here.' Richie chuckled before catching Jane's eye. 'Not that I eat like that at home. Nothing of the sort.'

'And you, Jackson? Richie tells us you're a property developer now?' Her dad reached for the salt shaker.

'Oh, I wouldn't say that, but I've bought a few properties to renovate, yes. I'm onto my fourth one now, but I still work as a chef at the local pub alongside.'

Her dad nodded. 'I'm impressed. Well done, lad.'

'Thank you.' Jackson nodded towards Laura. 'Laura is doing an amazing job with Pennycress.'

Laura kicked him under the table, unable to utter the words, 'thanks very much.'

Much to Laura's dismay, her dad turned his attention to her. 'Yes, yes. Richie and I visited last week. You seem to be taking to life as an innkeeper, Laura.'

'I'm enjoying it.' Laura nodded. The less she could say about the stack of disasters she'd encountered at Pennycress, the better, but hopefully things were finally turning a corner. 'I've arranged for a gardener to start soon too.'

'That's a bit premature, isn't it, sweetheart? Shouldn't you open up first and start bringing in some money before you employ people?' Her mum frowned.

'She's not starting for another couple of months yet. It's perfect timing actually; she has to wait until her son settles into nursery, which will be after I open.'

'Well, as long as you've explored all the costings and know you can afford it.' Her dad looked at her over his glasses.

'Yep, all costed out.' Laura nodded. She hated lying to her parents, but it would be fine. Besides, she and Jill hadn't even discussed payment yet.

'Is it someone local to you?' Jenny asked.

'Yes, her name's Jill and she seems really nice. She was telling me that she's always loved Vivienne's garden and used to think it was magical as a child, so she's really excited to make a start.'

'Vivienne's garden? I thought you said she'd be working on yours?' Her dad frowned.

'Sorry, yes. Vivienne used to run Pennycress before me.'

'Ah, so you've met the previous owner then? I hope you managed to get some good tips from her.' Her mum stood up and picked up a water jug from the middle of the table. 'Anyone for water?'

'Yes, I did. She's been really helpful, actually.' Laura held up her empty glass for her mum to fill, trying desperately not to catch Jackson's eye. She really didn't want to get into any details about just how helpful Vivienne had been and she was worried that if she met Jackson's gaze, she'd end up telling the whole sorry story. 'You'll all have to come down for the opening.'

28

'That was delicious, as always. Thank you, Ruth and Phil.' Jackson placed his knife and fork together on his empty plate and leaned back in his chair.

'Maybe you'll bless us with your presence a little more often now then.' Richie chuckled as he stood up and began collecting the plates.

'I'll help you.' Pushing her chair back, Laura piled Jenny's plate onto hers.

'I certainly will.' Standing, Jackson nodded to Richie. 'Sit down, mate. I'll help Laura. You've probably been up all night with the little ones.'

'Now this I could get used to. Someone who appreciates how difficult it can be raising kids.' Richie slumped back in his chair.

'Oi! We're not difficult!' Tammy shouted across the room at her uncle.

'He means babies. Not children your age.' Rob lowered his voice. 'Although I can assure you, Richie, mate, just because they get older it doesn't mean they automatically start to sleep through the night.'

'Aw, she's not that bad. She just had a bad dream last night, that's all.' Jenny passed Laura the empty gravy jug.

'Thanks.' With her hands full, Laura retreated to the kitchen, leaving the baby talk behind her.

'Hey, you.' After placing the crockery down on the work surface, Jackson went back and closed the door quietly behind them.

'Hey.' She began unloading the plates and gravy jug onto the counter before opening the dishwasher.

'I think we'll be safe for a few moments.' Jackson glanced behind him in the direction of the dining room before walking across to her.

Letting the dishwasher quietly close again, she allowed him to pull her into his arms before resting her cheek against his chest. 'Yes, we should have a couple of minutes.'

Jackson tucked his finger beneath her chin and gently tilted her head to face him. 'Time for this?'

As he leaned down, she felt his lips against hers, soft and firm and kissed him back before looking up at him. 'Maybe we should just come out and tell them about us? What's the worst that could happen?'

'I was just thinking the same thing. Even if it's a shock to them at first, I'm sure they'd come round to the idea.'

'Exactly. I mean, they love you and so they'd trust you. What could be better than two people they love getting together?' Laura grinned. Although, admittedly, sneaking around behind her family's backs had been fun to begin with, now, with each passing minute, she just wanted to be able to reach out and take Jackson's hand in hers or lean against him on the sofa. Plus, she hated keeping secrets from her parents. It had been bad enough omitting to tell them about the troubles she'd been having with the local residents in Meadowfield, but she'd known that convers

tion wouldn't be worth the hassle and interrogation that followed. But her and Jackson? That was different.

'Are we going to do this, then? Come clean?' Jackson looked at the closed door.

Laura nodded. 'Yes, after pudding though?'

'Okay, let's do it.' Jackson kissed her on the forehead before turning and clearing the dishes away.

The kitchen door swung open and Richie peered round. 'Wow, you two were quick at tidying. You make a good team.'

'We do indeed.' Jackson caught Laura's eye.

'Mum's sent me to help bring pudding through to the living room. The kids are getting restless.' Richie pulled open the fridge door and took out a large cheesecake.

Opening the cupboard, Laura picked up a stack of bowls.

'Here, let me.' Taking them from her, Jackson brushed hands with her and nodded.

She nodded back. They were really going to do this. They were going to come clean. She followed Richie and Jackson through to the living room and, with the sofas being full, she lowered herself to the rug next to where the children were playing.

The loud and cheerful tone of her parents' doorbell cut through the sound of her nieces and nephews playing and the chatter of her family.

Her mum looked across to Laura, a knife in hand as she began to cut the cheesecake sitting on the coffee table. 'Are you all right getting that, sweetheart?'

'Yes, of course.' Laura stood up again and headed towards the door.

'If it's the window cleaner, the cash is on top of the shoe cabinet,' her dad called out.

'Okay,' Laura shouted back before pulling the door open. With her fingers gripping the door handle tightly, she felt her stomach knot. 'Harry.'

'Laura, hi. Fancy seeing you here.' Harry smiled at her, his self-confidence etched into every pore.

Laura narrowed her eyes. It was her dad's birthday, of course she'd be here. 'What are you doing here?'

'Who is it, sweetheart?' Her mum's cheery voice filtered through to the hallway.

Harry turned to look in the direction her voice had come from and raised his voice. 'Afternoon, Ruth! It's just me, Harry. I'm returning your salad spinner.'

'Salad spinner?' Laura widened her eyes. He'd borrowed a salad spinner from her parents? She hadn't even realised they'd owned one.

'That's right. We hosted a dinner party yesterday evening and only realised we couldn't find ours at the last moment.' Harry picked up a plastic bag from the step and held it up before taking a step forward.

Without thinking, Laura moved to block the doorway. 'We?'

'Yes, me and Dina.' Harry jerked his head behind him, indicating his car. 'You remember her? From the pub?'

Looking from Harry to his familiar blue Peugeot, she swallowed. He *was* back with Dina then. And he'd brought her to Laura's parents' house. When he'd no doubt had a pretty good idea she would be there. What was he playing at? 'You're back with her then.'

'Yes, we had a break, but...' He shrugged as he tried to step around her. 'I guess when two people are meant to be, nothing can stand in the way.'

Moving into his path again, Laura held her hand out. What did he mean by that? And by reminding her that Dina had frequented the same pub as them? Was he admitting he'd had feelings for her when he'd been with Laura? The suspicion had niggled away at her for some time now, but she'd never had any evidence and she doubted she ever would. Always needing to be the good guy, Harry was too careful for that. 'I can take that for you.'

'Oh, I'd rather give it to Ruth myself. Thank her properly.'

'I think...' Her voice tailed off as she heard footsteps behind her.

'Harry, sweetheart. Lovely to see you.' Her mum appeared by Laura's side, forcing her to step out of the way.

'I just wanted to return your salad spinner. Thank you for lending it to me.' Harry held out the bag. 'There's a card and a little something in there for Phil too.'

'Why don't you come on in, give it to him yourself?' her mum smiled warmly.

'I'd like that. Only for a moment, mind.' Harry's self-assured smile returned as he walked past Laura, his arm brushing her sleeve.

Left alone in the hallway, Laura slowly closed the front door and shifted from foot to foot as she listened to her mum fussing over Harry. How often had he really been popping round since she'd moved out? She'd only been gone a couple of weeks and she knew for a fact that her mum had already invited him in for tea and now she was lending him kitchen paraphernalia? Why was he still hanging around? Because he knew it would annoy her? Or simply because he missed being part of the family? And Jackson? What would he think, seeing Harry just turning up like this?

She peered through the glass of the front door; she could just about make out someone sitting in the passenger seat. Dina. The woman Harry had been seeing shortly before he and Laura had met. The woman Harry had returned to. She pressed her fingers against her temples and massaged them, the headache returning.

A few moments later, Harry reappeared in the hallway and made his way back to the front door. 'Bye, Laura.'

'Bye,' she muttered as she held the door open for him, watching her ex-husband make his way down her parents' path to his car, to his new partner. His ex *and* present partner should she say? She walked back to the living room as she tried to make sense of the situation. As she made her way through the toys scattered across the carpet again, she glanced quickly in Jackson's direction. She couldn't read his expression. Was he okay after seeing Harry? He didn't think there was anything going on between them, did he?

'That was nice of him to pop round like that, wasn't it? And he knew just what to get you for your birthday, didn't he?' Her mum nodded towards the bottle of whisky sitting on the carpet next to her dad's feet before leaning forward and continuing to cut and dish out the cheesecake, seemingly oblivious to how uncomfortable her own daughter was feeling.

Sitting down on the rug again, Laura closed her eyes briefly. This wasn't exactly what she'd envisaged happening before she told her parents and siblings that she and Jackson were now an item.

'And it seems he's back with Dina again, sweetheart.' Her mum passed her a bowl.

'Yes.' Taking the bowl, Laura scraped some cream from the edge of the cheesecake. 'That's nice for him.'

'No need for that tone, sweetheart. I had the poor lad crying in my kitchen when he broke up with her the week you moved out of here.' Her mum passed Jackson a bowl too.

Shifting her position on the floor, Laura bit down on her bottom lip. She took a deep breath before speaking, trying desperately to keep her voice steady. 'You do know that he was seeing her before me and him got together, don't you? And that there's a strong possibility he at least had feelings for her before our marriage ended.'

Her mum snapped her head up and looked at her. 'No, he wouldn't have done that to you. Not Harry.'

Gripping her bowl in her hands, Laura clenched her jaw. What was she supposed to say to that? How was she supposed to respond to the fact that her own mum was adamant that she knew Laura's ex-husband better than she did herself? 'Okay...'

'Are you crying, Auntie Laura?' Tammy looked up from where she was helping Jasper make a tower with the brightly coloured plastic bricks.

'No, sorry. I'm not.' Swiping the back of her hand across her face, Laura placed her bowl on the rug in front of her and stood up before making her way to the kitchen. As she walked past the sofa, she quickly glanced at Jackson, trying and failing once again to decipher from his expression what he was feeling.

'Sis, wait up.'

Once in the sanctuary of the kitchen, Laura held the door open until Richie had stepped through before turning away from him.

'Are you all right?'

'Well, I didn't expect my ex to gatecrash my dad's birthday celebrations, and even less expected my family to welcome him with open arms.' She took the tissue he held out towards her and turned to face him. 'It almost feels as though everyone's on his side. Not that there should be sides, but... did you hear Mum when I dared to suggest Harry might have been unfaithful?' She tried to keep her voice steady and low as she felt a flash of anger.

'I—'

'And you're just as bad. Well, not as bad as Mum, but you still don't understand my decision to end things with him. What with you saying you wouldn't have to worry about me if I was still with him. You said that on the phone when I first moved into the inn.' She took a deep breath before carrying on. 'Why can't you see that he has faults too? And why can't you all understand that I'm happier now that I'm not married to Harry? I wasn't happy with him. I was lonely, so lonely, and I know how stupid that sounds because I was with him and now, I'm living on my own but—'

'Laura.' Stepping forward, Richie drew her in for a hug. 'I'm sorry if I've said anything to make you feel like you've made the wrong decision. That was never my intention. I just want you to be happy.'

'You do?'

'Yes, of course I do. I admit I liked Harry. I thought he was a good guy, and I had absolutely no idea that you felt so alone when you were with him. I also didn't have a clue that you thought there was anything going on between him and Dina. If I'd known, I'd have told you to leave him before you did.'

'Really? Even though you and him always got on so well?'

'Hey, we didn't get on that well. Not enough to see you unhappy. You're my sister, remember, and it's you I care about. Harry can do one.' Richie squeezed her before releasing her. 'Ready to go back in and face the music?'

'I guess so.' Just as they reached the door, Jackson peered inside.

'Everything okay? Are you all right, Laura?' Holding the door open, his face was full of concern.

Sniffing, Laura nodded. 'Yes, thanks. I'm fine. I just...' She shrugged.

'Good, as long as you're okay.' With his hand on the door, Jackson stepped back, letting her and Richie through.

'Oh, there you are, sweetheart. I'm sorry, we didn't mean to upset you. It was just a shock, you making accusations like that hadn't thought you suspected him of any wrongdoing.' Her mum looked across at her.

'That's it now. No more talk of Harry and no more letting him in the house and feeding him.' Her dad looked pointedly at his wife.

'Point taken.' Her mum nodded.

'Sorry, I shouldn't have overreacted.' Laura picked up her bowl again and lowered herself to the floor.

'No, we shouldn't have made him feel so welcome here. From now on, this is a Harry-free family.' Richie spoke firmly.

'Harry who?' Jenny laughed.

'Exactly. And besides, now the fun can really begin. We can start setting you up on dates!' Richie rubbed his hands together.

'Ooh, yes. One of my clients is recently divorced and super hot,' Jenny joined in.

'Hot, is he?' Rob raised an eyebrow.

'For Laura, I mean.' Jenny rubbed his arm and grinned. 'He's definitely not my type, all muscly and brooding...'

Rob crossed his arms and huffed before chuckling.

'But what do you think? Shall I set you two up? I'm sure he'd love to meet you.' Jenny pulled out her phone. 'I think he has a photo on his business page.'

'Wait. I don't want to be set up with anyone.' Laura grimaced. Even if she and Jackson hadn't been together, the last thing she'd have wanted was to have her siblings arrange blind dates for her. 'Besides—'

'There's Dave who I play squash with.' Richie looked at his wife. 'I think he'd be your type, don't you think, Jane?'

'Umm, yes, I think so. He seems a really nice guy.'

'Stop. Please stop.' Laura held her hand up and laughed despite how exasperated she felt. Though the fact that Richie was talking about trying to set her up with a friend was a good sign that he'd be more accepting of her and Jackson than they'd first thought. Maybe they'd been worrying about nothing.

'I've got an idea.' Tammy stood up and pointed to Laura with one hand and Jackson with the other. 'I think Auntie Laura and Jackson should marry.'

Leaning forward, Richie burst out laughing. 'Oh, Tammy, we do love you, but you have some funny ideas.'

'Well, I think it's a good idea. Auntie Laura is sad because she doesn't have a Harry anymore and Jackson is lonely, so I think they should kiss and marry.' Tammy crossed her arms as a plastic brick fell to the floor from her grasp.

Coughing, Laura felt the slither of cheesecake she'd just put into her mouth go down the wrong way. Managing to swallow, she calmed herself as she felt the heat of a blush flush across her face. Tammy's words may have been uttered innocently but she couldn't have read the situation better if she'd tried.

'I don't think Auntie Laura and Jackson will get together, Tammy, sweetie.' Jenny leaned forward and rubbed her daughter's shoulder. 'It's a good idea, but they're too much like friends for that.'

'Oh, friends can marry. I'm friends with Jenson at school and he told me he wants to marry me,' Tammy said matter-of-factly.

'They can, but not Auntie Laura and Jackson.' Jenny glanced across at Laura with a grin as Tammy sat down with a plop. 'Kids!'

'Don't laugh at me.' Tammy pouted and threw a brick, which landed on Jenny's foot.

'Come on now. No throwing. Why don't you come and help me see if we've got any after-dinner chocolates anywhere?' Laura's dad stood up and held out his hand towards Tammy.

As Laura watched her dad and niece leave the room, she wished she could tag along with them. Instead, she was stuck here, listening to all the reasons why she and Jackson could never be together. She cleared her throat, trying her best to keep her voice light. 'And yet you've literally just tried to get me to agree to go on a date with your mate Dave, Richie.'

'That's completely different.' Her brother chuckled.

'He's your friend and so is Jackson.' She spooned a lump of cheesecake into her mouth and tried not to choke as the biscuit base stuck to the roof of her mouth.

'Jackson is Jackson. He's been about forever. You've never met Dave.' Richie looked from her to Jackson and back again. 'Why? Please tell me there isn't anything going on between you both?'

'Of course not, mate. What do you take me for? I know your little sis is off limits.' Jackson slapped Richie on the back.

Laura felt her stomach plummet. Before Harry had turned up, they'd been going to tell everyone they were dating and now... this? What had changed? Had she put him off by accusing Harry of cheating? Or was he just wary of Richie now he'd said what he had? Forcing herself, she joined in with the laughter despite just wanting to cry.

'Phew.' Richie wiped his hand across his forehead and sighed dramatically. 'You almost had me going then. Almost!'

'Please don't go setting me up on any dates, though, any of you.' Laura looked around the room, trying to keep the wobble from her voice. 'I'm happy being single for the time being.'

'Can't I just bring you up in conversation with the guy I was telling you about? Just a little?' Jenny held her thumb and forefinger slightly apart.

'Not at all.' Standing up, Laura placed her bowl in the pile of used ones on the coffee table. 'Right, I'm going to head off now. I need to be up early tomorrow. You don't mind, do you, Jackson?'

'Of course not.' Following her lead, Jackson stood up too.

'Oh really?' Jenny pushed herself to standing and drew her in for a hug. 'Can't you stay a bit longer?'

'Nope. It's a fair drive back, remember?' And she really wanted to be in the dark and safety of her car before the tears began to fall.

She walked out of the living room, averting eye contact with Jackson.

After giving and receiving what felt like a million hugs and having a Tupperware dish of leftovers shoved into her hands, Laura pulled open the front door and looked on as it was Jackson's turn for the hugs and goodbyes. 'I'll meet you out in the car, Jackson. I have a quick call to make.'

'Drive carefully, sweetheart.' Her mum rubbed her on the forearm. 'And we're okay? Me and you? I didn't realise that you felt that uncomfortable about Harry coming here, and I certainly didn't even have an inkling that you were questioning his faithfulness to you when you were married.'

'I will. Thanks again for dinner. And, yes, we're fine.'

Stepping outside, the cold air hit her as she hurried down the garden path, frantically clicking her key until the lights blinked to inform her the car was unlocked. Slipping behind the steering wheel, she pushed the key into the ignition. How could he? How could Jackson have spoken about her like that? So easily dismissing the mere notion that they could ever be a couple? He hadn't even attempted to stand up to Richie. Hadn't even tried to tell her brother he was being ridiculous by telling Laura who she could and couldn't date.

She turned the key as soon as she heard the passenger door open, barely waiting for Jackson to sit down and click his seatbelt on before she pulled away.

'That was a bit intense, wasn't it?' Jackson finally spoke.

'Uh-huh.' She kept her eyes on the road ahead. She couldn't even bear to look at him. How little must he think of her? Of what she thought they had together?

'You're annoyed with me, aren't you?' Jackson reached out and touched her forearm.

Shaking his hand off, Laura swallowed. 'Yesterday you told me you loved me and then today you're agreeing with my brother over what a ridiculous idea you and I are as a couple. Which one is it? How do you really feel?'

'You know how I feel.'

'That's the thing, I don't. Because in one of those conversations you were telling the truth and the other one was just a really good performance.' And if he could lie so easily to Richie, then what else was he lying about? How he felt about Evie Taunton? Harry had gone back to his ex, what was there to say Jackson wouldn't do the same? That the feelings Evie Taunton so overtly had for him weren't reciprocated? How could she trust him now?

'Laura...'

'Don't. Just don't. Just let me drive.' She reached over and turned the stereo on, turning the volume up until she couldn't hear him anymore. She just needed to get home, back to Penny-cress. That's all she wanted right now.

29

Ignoring the dainty tune of the doorbell, Laura folded over the sandpaper in her hand and scrubbed at the floorboards, trying to rid them of the sticky residue of wallpaper. She'd lost count of the number of times Jackson had come to the door today and how many times she'd ignored the doorbell, the knocking and him pleading through the letter box to open up. How many more times would it take until he got the hint that she didn't want to talk to him? Hadn't the car journey home told him all he needed to know?

She scrubbed a little harder against the floorboards. That had been the longest two hours of her life. After a few minutes of having the music up eardrum-piercingly loud, he'd stopped trying to defend his actions and had let her drive in peace, so why couldn't he let her live in peace too?

Laura wiped the back of her hand across her cheeks as more tears sprung. She should have known it was all too good to be true. She should have realised that if they had been meant to be together, then they would have got together years ago. She'd been stupid, so stupid, to tell him she'd loved him. What had she been thinking?

She hadn't. It had been the wine that had been doing the talking. Well, never again. She sniffed. Not that she'd be going into the pub again anyway, so at least the chance of her getting tipsy any time soon was limited. She slapped her forehead. The darts team. What was she supposed to do about that? She'd just have to drop out, that's what.

The doorbell rang again, and she took a deep breath, ready to tell Jackson to leave her alone.

'Laura, are you there, dear? It's Vivienne and my daughter, Nicola.'

It was Vivienne! She'd been ignoring Vivienne. Hurrying to the front door, she pulled it open. 'Hi, Vivienne. I'm so sorry. I thought you were someone else.' Why had she said that?

'Ah, don't worry, dear. I've been having a few people call round to try to get me to let them redo my driveway.' She reached out and laid her hand on Laura's forearm. 'I don't even have a driveway. I don't blame you for ignoring the doorbell.'

Laura smiled. 'You would have thought that would be the first thing they'd notice.'

'You would think so, wouldn't you? Seemingly not.' Vivienne indicated the woman standing next to her. 'This is my daughter, Nicola. Nicola, this is the lovely Laura I was telling you about, the new owner of the wonderful Pennycress.'

'Hi, nice to meet you.' Nicola pushed her glasses further up her nose before holding her hand up in greeting. Her warm smile was the spitting image of her mum's and her eyes the same deep hazel, which complimented her dark hair beautifully.

'Great to meet you too.' Laura smiled.

'I'm sorry. I hope you don't mind us popping round now? If

you're busy, we can come back another day. You just mentioned about me visiting and...'

'Of course. Come on in. Thank you for coming round.' Standing back, Laura held the door open. Maybe the distraction of Vivienne and her daughter visiting would help keep her mind off Jackson and the hurt he'd caused her.

Stepping inside, Vivienne paused and looked around. 'You're busy. We can come back another time.'

'No, it's fine. Please excuse the mess. This DIY malarky is all new to me.' She grimaced as she indicated the banister still lying in pieces on the floor against the wall, embarrassed that she hadn't tidied it better. 'And I have someone coming in a couple of days to take a look at the banister.'

'It looks as though you're doing a fine job. Better than I ever could.' Vivienne ran the palm of her hand over the wall. 'I told Mr Yates that this wall needed replastering years ago. I'm sorry he didn't repair it before you bought the place.'

'It's not your fault. I should have noticed that things needed fixing.' Laura placed the cloth on the reception desk and stood next to Vivienne and Nicola as they surveyed the wall. 'I wasn't really sure what I was supposed to be looking out for and, well, I fell in love with the inn regardless.'

Vivienne chuckled and looked across at her daughter. 'What did I tell you, Nicola? I told you the old girl was in good hands.'

Laura grinned. 'Thanks. Sorry, I've forgotten my manners. Would you both like a drink?'

'I'd love a tea if you have one, please?' Vivienne smiled as she made her way through to the kitchen.

'Would you like one too, Nicola?' Laura stood aside, letting them both go through before her.

'Have you got any coffee, please? I've been up all night packing.'

'Oh, I have coffee.' Laura grinned. 'Are you moving?'

'Not quite. I've been packing up my ex-partner's clothes and belongings.' Nicola sat down on the bench at the kitchen table.

'Sorry to hear that.' Laura filled the kettle up.

'Don't be. She's better off without him.' Vivienne sank onto the bench opposite her daughter. 'Sorry, love, but you are. He was never any good for you.'

Nicola sighed and picked up the salt shaker Laura had left in the middle of the table, turning it over in her hand.

'It's always difficult though, isn't it? When a relationship breaks down. Whether you know it was the right thing to happen or not.' Laura spooned coffee into two mugs before reaching for the teabags.

'That's the problem. I thought we were good together. It was only when I discovered he'd been cheating that I saw him for who he really was.' Nicola stifled a yawn.

'Ah, that's rubbish. I'm sorry.' Laura carried Vivienne and Nicola's mugs to the table before going back for hers. 'My husband and I split up two years ago now, so I can understand a little of what you're going through.'

'I still can't believe it's happening.' Nicola wrapped her hands around her mug. 'You never think it's going to happen to you, do you? We're all sold the fairy-tale happy ever after as young girls, then it's a shock when life doesn't turn out like that.'

'You can say that again.' Laura took a long sip of coffee and bit her lip. Nicola didn't need to know that life wasn't full of roses after a break-up either, that even when you thought you'd found The One the second time around, they still let you down. She shook her head. Vivienne and Nicola had come round to see their beloved inn and to tell her more about it, and the least she could do was to focus and stop brooding over Jackson.

'How did you cope? With your marriage breakdown? I

honestly don't know if I'm coming or going one day to the next and there's a tiny part of me which wonders whether I've done the right thing in kicking him out rather than forgiving him and trying to make it work.' Nicola replaced the salt shaker on the table and shook her head. 'I'm sorry, I've only just met you, I shouldn't be asking you questions like this.'

'Oh, I don't mind. It's refreshing to be able to talk to someone who understands. Umm, that's a tricky question though.' Laura shifted on the bench. 'I had to move in with my parents whilst our house was sold and then I bought this place.'

Nicola nodded.

'So I guess you could say that it was either the best thing that happened to me or else it pushed me to have a midlife crisis.' Laura laughed.

'Ah, this place is definitely the best thing and not a midlife crisis.' Vivienne tilted her head and smiled. 'Although, who knows? Maybe it was both, but it's definitely the best thing too.'

'I think so.' Laura turned back to Nicola. 'How long has it been? Since your relationship ended?'

'It's been three months, two weeks and four days since I found out about the affair.' She looked down into her mug. 'But only two weeks since I told him to leave.'

'So it's all still new to you, then. I'm sorry to hear you're going through all this.'

'Thank you, but as Mum here says, I'll survive.' Nicola smiled sadly.

'You will, love. You will.' Reaching across, Vivienne stroked her daughter's cheek.

'Yes, that's if I can find a job before I'm kicked out of my house for not paying the rent.'

'I've told you I can give you the money.'

Nicola frowned at her mum.

'Lend it you, then. You shouldn't be too proud to take help when it's offered.'

'Have you lost your job too?' Laura stirred another spoonful of sugar into her coffee.

'Unfortunately, yes. My ex was also my boss and, well, I just can't bring myself to go into the office and see him day in, day out.' Nicola brought her mug to her lips.

'I don't blame you there.' Laura frowned. 'What did you do?'

'Events management. We were only a small team, but we were always busy and our business even won a few awards.' Nicola lowered her mug to the table, coffee splashing over the rim and pooling on the table. 'I'm sorry.'

'Don't worry.' Standing up, Laura grabbed a piece of kitchen roll and passed it to Nicola.

'Thanks.' She wiped up the spilt coffee before continuing. 'I enjoyed it and it's difficult to walk away from something I put so much into, but ultimately I know I just couldn't carry on working with him, not after the way he's treated me.'

'I'm sure something will come up. It sounds as though you've had a lot of experience.' Laura smiled kindly.

'I'm sure it will. I just need to think positively.' Nicola looked at Vivienne, who nodded.

Laura sipped her coffee. She wasn't the only one then. The only one left heartbroken, only she hadn't been left heartbroken by Harry, it had been the one person she thought would always have her back who had broken her trust – Jackson.

30

Keeping her head down, Laura tucked her empty canvas bag into her coat pocket and hurried past Jackson's house. He'd called round twice again since Vivienne and Nicola had left and the last thing she wanted was to run into him on her way into the centre of the village. She'd been tempted to drive to the nearest supermarket, but after spending the night tossing and turning and replaying the conversation Jackson and Richie had had, she didn't trust herself to drive that far.

But she needed more coffee and so here she was, almost running past Jackson's house and hoping he wouldn't spot her. The quicker she could get into the centre and back out again, the better. Coffee with Vivienne and Nicola had been just what she'd needed to distract her, but now they'd gone, the afternoon stretched ahead of her and all she really wanted to do was to hole up and go to sleep just to escape Jackson's words that kept repeating in her mind.

Her mobile rang, and she pulled it quickly from her pocket. The last thing she needed was to draw any attention to herself. She checked it wasn't Jackson before answering. 'Hi, Richie.'

'Hey, sis. How's things going?'

'Much like they were when I saw you yesterday.' Apart from the fact she no longer had a boyfriend.

'Good, good.' There was a pause.

'What's up?' Laura frowned. Richie was normally one to get straight to the point when he rang. He wasn't one to skirt around an issue.

'Now don't be mad with me, but I've invited my mate Dave over for dinner next weekend...'

Laura narrowed her eyes. 'At least you have the good grace to sound sheepish.' She paused and looked around. 'Which reminds me, I haven't seen any sheep recently.'

'Sheep? You say that as though you see them often.' Richie cleared his throat. 'Anyway, back to the topic. Are you free to come for dinner?'

'With you, Jane and this Dave bloke?'

'Yes.'

'No.'

'No?'

'That's right, no. I told you not to set me up with anyone and I meant it. I'm not going to come.' Laura pinched the bridge of her nose with her free hand.

'Aw, please? I've asked him now. I'll look a right idiot if you don't turn up.'

'Well, you should have thought about that before you invited him. Perhaps when we were at Mum and Dad's, *yesterday*, and I categorically told you and Jenny that I didn't want to be set up with anyone. Remember that?' She cringed as she heard herself. She was being unnecessarily harsh, but it was Richie's fault she and Jackson were over, and she still didn't quite understand why it was okay for Richie to set her up on a date with his mate from squash and yet Jackson was a complete no-go according to him. And to Jackson, it would now seem.

'Will you think about it at least? Pretty please?'

'The answer won't change.' She took a deep breath in as she crossed the road. She had to remind herself that he hadn't known about her and Jackson. It wasn't Richie's fault they were now over. Oh no, that had been all Jackson. It had been Jackson who had ended up agreeing with Richie about his stupid no-Jackson rule. 'Look, I know I sound like a brat and I know you're only trying to do me a favour, but I don't want to come to dinner as a set-up with your mate, I really don't, and I wish you'd respect my decision.'

'Point taken. I'm sorry. Consider Dave dumped.'

'Dumped? He wasn't even dated.' Laura shook her head. Richie was trying to make light of the situation, trying to make her laugh, and any other day it would have likely worked, but not today. 'Look, I've got to go.'

'Okay. I promise I won't try to set you up again. Bye.'

'Bye.' Pulling her phone away from her ear, Laura pressed the End Call button just as she walked smack bang into someone and she watched her phone skid across the path. Seriously? What else was going to go wrong?

'Laura Price.'

Jerking her head up, Laura sighed. That. That's what else was going to go wrong. She'd run straight into Evie Taunton, of all people. 'Evie.'

The estate agent looked down at the bunch of flowers she was carrying and plucked off a petal. 'You squashed my chrysan-themums.'

'And you've likely broken my mobile.' Laura scooped her phone from the path, surprised and relieved to see the screen intact.

'I think you'll find it was you who barged into me.'

Narrowing her eyes, Laura glared back at Evie, anger suddenly rising from the pit of her stomach. Did this woman have no compassion whatsoever? Had she ever heard of morals or kindness or any other thing which could make a person likeable or even passable? 'What is your problem with me?'

Evie blinked, seemingly processing the question Laura had posed. 'Excuse me?'

'I said, what is your problem? What have I ever done to you? I'd never met you until the day I viewed Pennycress Inn. That viewing, and the two minutes we spent together so you could pass over the keys, were the only times we met in person and yet you tried to ruin my life.'

'I think that's a little dramatic.' Evie plucked off another petal.

'Dramatic?' Laura stepped towards her, one hand gripping her mobile, the other holding on to the canvas bag that kept slipping from her pocket. She knew this wasn't the time or the place to be having this conversation. And she knew that the anger she was feeling towards Evie Taunton wasn't all deserved, but she couldn't help herself. It was Evie who was standing in front of her, not Jackson, and it was Evie who had lied about her, led people to believe her intentions weren't good. 'Your lies almost destroyed my chance at a new start in this village. Why? Why did you say the things you did?'

'A new start?' Evie glanced up briefly from her precious flowers. 'Usually people desire a new start away from everyone they know. They don't usually want to move next door to an old family friend.'

'What are you talking about?' Laura frowned. Evie wasn't making any sense.

'I'm referring to Jacks.'

'Jackson? What's he got to do with any of it?' What was she suggesting?

'You heard me.'

Laura shook her head before glancing around the village green. If they hadn't been the only ones standing there, she may have been tempted to ask someone to translate for her, to try to make sense of what the other woman was telling her, or trying to. 'You're going to have to be clearer than that.'

'Clearer, hmm.' Evie locked eyes with her. 'Is the fact that you, an old family friend of Jacks, swooped in to steal him from me clear enough?'

'I... I didn't even know Jackson lived here in Meadowfield when I bought Pennycress. Heck, I probably wouldn't have gone through with the sale if I'd known.' And now, if she had known what would have happened between them, then she certainly wouldn't have moved here. However much she loved Pennycress, she would have chosen to save her heart.

'I'm sure Jacks would believe you.' Sarcasm rolled off the woman's tongue as she looked back down at her flowers.

'Evie, I really don't understand what you're trying to say, but whatever it is, I don't think anything would warrant spreading lies about me.' It couldn't be because of Jackson and Evie splitting up – that had happened a couple of months before Laura had moved here.

'You do know what I'm saying. You understand perfectly. You and I both know Jacks was the reason you wanted to move here.'

Laura shoved her phone in her pocket, trying to compose herself. 'If that's what you thought, then why on earth did you accept my offer on Pennycress?'

'I didn't know who you were until Mr Yates had accepted it.'

Shaking her head, Laura still didn't understand, but whatever Evie Taunton thought had happened, she couldn't grasp why it would lead to the lies. 'I can't do this.' Spinning on the spot, Laura began walking back home, picking up her pace until she was certain Evie could no longer see her.

Once she'd reached Wisteria Lane, she slowed again before stopping by a large tree growing on a patch of grass by the road. Leaning her palm against it, she closed her eyes. Evie had said she'd known who she was. How? Jackson hadn't known she was moving in. He hadn't realised who had bought Pennycress until he'd brought his welcome basket round. How had Evie known before she or Jackson had? And why would she care, anyway?

Laura took a deep breath and pushed herself away from the tree again, forcing herself to continue her journey home. That part of the puzzle she guessed was easily solved. Terry had joked about Evie stalking Jackson. She obviously still liked him. Laura had picked up on that almost instantly too, before she'd known Evie and Jackson had been together.

But the other part... How had Evie known she and Jackson knew each other? She'd called them 'family friends'.

Laura crossed the road and made her way up the garden path.

'Laura?'

Looking up, Laura halted. Jackson was sitting on the steps up to the porch of the inn, holding a bunch of flowers. 'I really don't want to talk to you.'

'Please let me explain.' Standing up, he left the flowers on the step and began to make his way towards her.

Laura shook her head, desperately trying to locate her keyring in her pocket. 'You said enough yesterday at my parents' house.'

'No, no, I didn't. I should never have said what I did. I just panicked. Richie had been so close to guessing what was going on between us that I just said what I needed to to push him off course.' Reaching for her, he laid his hand on the sleeve of her coat.

Looking down, all Laura wanted to do was stretch out and take his hand, to hold him tight, but she couldn't. 'Would that have been such a bad thing? We had agreed to tell them anyway.'

'I know, I just...' He ran his fingers through his hair, his dark curls springing straight back up.

She didn't want to lie to her family, and after yesterday's performance, she knew Jackson wasn't going to be ready to tell her family, to tell Richie, about them any time soon. 'I can't do this, Jackson. You've made your thoughts about us perfectly clear. I know now that if we carry on seeing each other, it will be in secret, and I can't live like that. I can't live a lie.'

'No, it won't. I'll tell Richie. I should have told him yesterday. I should have set him straight instead of pretending.' He locked eyes with her.

Blinking, Laura looked away as she wrapped her finger around the teddy keyring. The words, 'And I don't know what else you've lied about,' were on the tip of her tongue but she couldn't say them – she had no proof he'd lied about how he felt about Evie Taunton or that he still liked her that way. Hadn't he been sticking up for Laura when he'd last spoken to her? 'I need to go.'

'But—'

She strode down the path and let herself in, shutting the door firmly behind her. Going through to the sitting room, she threw her keyring on the mantelpiece before slumping onto the sofa, her coat still on.

This was it; she and Jackson were over. She'd done the right thing. She knew she had. She didn't have a choice. She couldn't live a lie to her family and she couldn't be with Jackson without their blessing.

Holding on to the arm of the sofa, Laura pulled herself up and made her way across the room to the mantelpiece to pick up her keys. If she didn't put them on the reception desk as she had every day since she'd moved in, she'd forget where they were.

As she picked them up, she knocked the photo frame with the drawing of Pennycress in it. Bending down, she picked it up, holding it in her hand and staring at it as everything finally made some sort of sense.

Jackson had a photo in his living room of him with her family. Evie must have recognised Laura from the photo. That's how she'd found out that Laura and Jackson knew each other.

She replaced the photo frame, lining it up with the other one on the other side of the carriage clock. Even so, would that have been enough to make Evie jealous of Laura to the extent she wanted her run out of the village? Jackson had told her both he and Evie had agreed to end their relationship, but what if Evie hadn't really wanted it to end, what if she'd only agreed to save face and she thought if she could pressure Laura into selling up, she could win Jackson back? Just as soon as she'd answered one question, another one emerged.

Laura shook her head. She needed to go and lie down. She needed a break from thinking altogether. A break from trying to decipher what other people were thinking and the reasons behind their actions – Jackson, Evie Taunton, the villagers, her family. She had so much to think about, so many other things on her mind, the repairs to Pennycress, all the things she had to organise before she could even think about opening up. It was all too much. How was she supposed to wrap her head around it all?

Dropping the keys on the reception desk, she walked up the stairs, pressing against her temples with the pads of her fingers in a vain attempt to disperse the headache forming.

31

Walking out of the village grocery store, Laura glanced around quickly. She hadn't seen or heard from Jackson since running into him in her garden yesterday and although she was relieved he had listened to her and respected her wishes, she couldn't help feeling upset that he hadn't bothered to even attempt to talk to her again.

She gripped hold of the coffee jar she'd just bought as she shoved her purse into her pocket. She was being unfair. Jackson couldn't win. He'd badgered her to try to explain his actions, and she'd told him to leave her alone, and when he did stay away, she got upset. But did that indicate that she hadn't meant anything to him after all? If she was so easy to move on from, then surely he hadn't cared about her, let alone loved her as he'd claimed. If he had loved her, he would still be fighting for her, wouldn't he?

Pulling her mobile from her pocket, she checked it again. Nothing. No messages, no missed calls. She slipped her mobile back into her pocket and swallowed, fighting back the tears. She'd spent enough time crying over him. If he couldn't even make the effort to try to talk to her again, then so be it. He wasn't the person she thought he was.

'Laura, morning!'

Laura looked up and waved as Catherine from the darts team jogged towards her. 'Hi.'

'Been to stock up on the essentials, I see?' Catherine nodded towards the coffee jar.

'Oh yes.' Shoving the jar into her canvas bag, Laura nodded.

'Are you busy at the moment? For once, I've actually got a couple of hours to spare in the day today. Did you fancy going to get lunch at the pub and having a game of darts, maybe? Get a bit of practice in?'

Laura looked across the road towards the pub. The last thing she wanted was to venture in there and be stuck pretending everything was okay between her and Jackson. 'I'm really sorry, I can't today, but another day would be great.'

'No worries.' Catherine dismissed the idea with a wave of her hand. 'They probably aren't serving food anyway, not after what happened to Jackson.'

'Jackson? What do you mean? What's happened?' Had he walked out? Had culinary differences with the landlord, maybe?

'Well, after the accident, of course.'

'Accident? What accident?' Laura could feel her throat drying. Was he okay? What had happened?

'The car accident. Sorry, I assumed you knew.' Catherine laid her hand on Laura's arm. 'He was involved in a car crash last night. I'm pretty sure he's still at the hospital. Or that's what I heard from Mrs Pierce in the bakery.'

'A car crash.' Laura froze. That's why Jackson hadn't tried calling her again or popping round to talk to her. He was hurt. Or worse! 'I need to go there.'

'Yes, of course. I'm really sorry, I honestly thought you'd known. Give him our love.'

Laura picked up her pace until she was running through the

streets of Meadowfield, the coffee jar in her canvas bag banging against her leg as she did so, but she didn't care. She needed to get to Jackson. She needed to see if he was okay.

* * *

Her legs felt like jelly as Laura stumbled to the ward she'd been directed to. She'd had to plead her case with the woman on the reception desk and convince her that she was Jackson's fiancée just to find out where he was. The receptionist hadn't told her anything else. She hadn't told her what had happened, when he'd been brought in or if he was okay. Laura literally didn't know what to expect.

She paused and leaned her hand against the wall, waiting until the wave of nausea had passed. He hadn't tried to ring her again. That thought came to the forefront of her mind once more. What if it hadn't been because she'd told him not to? What if the reason he hadn't contacted her was because he couldn't? He could be in a coma for all she knew.

And, if he was, what if he didn't recover? The last time she'd seen him had been to have a go at him. The last words she'd uttered to him had been to tell him to leave her alone. She'd never forgive herself if the worst were to happen. If that was his last memory of her.

Why hadn't she let him explain? What harm would that have done? She'd felt so hurt, so disregarded and yet she'd disregarded him too. Despite his pleas to talk, she had ignored him. She'd behaved just as badly.

And now she might never get another chance to listen to him. She might not get another chance to hold him, for him to hold her, for them to be together. They'd both waited years for this moment and yet she'd allowed something as simple as him pretending to Richie that they weren't seeing each other to ruin it all, to jeopardise any future happiness they may have had.

Hearing that Jackson was in hospital had made her realise one thing, though. She didn't care that he wanted to keep their relationship secret. How she felt towards Jackson and how he felt towards her – that they loved one another – was the most important thing. More important than having the blessing of her family, even. And more important than the insecurities Harry had stirred in her. Jackson wasn't Harry and whatever Evie Taunton was playing at wouldn't be down to Jackson. She was sure it wouldn't.

Besides, Richie would come round. Even if he wasn't happy with the idea at first, given time, he'd come to realise that they were serious about each other and he'd surely grow to understand, to accept. At least she hoped so. That was all she could do – hope.

Nothing would be too difficult to overcome as long as they were together.

She checked the signs on the wall. Yes, she was going in the right direction and if she'd understood the receptionist correctly, Jackson's ward would be just around the corner. She took a deep breath, trying desperately to compose herself before she continued down the corridor and pushed open the door to the ward. The nurses' station stood to the right, a nurse in scrubs busy scribbling in a patient's folder. 'Excuse me, please?'

'Oh, hello. How can I help you?' Looking up from her work, the nurse smiled kindly at Laura.

'I've been told that Jackson Scott is here?' Clasping her hands on the counter circling the nurses' station, Laura tried to stop herself from shaking.

'Jackson Scott?' The nurse ran her finger down a clipboard.

'Ah, yes, Jackson. He's just down the corridor, the last room on the left. I believe he may have another visitor in with him at the moment, but as long as there're no more than two of you, it should be fine.'

'Thank you.' Laura left the nurse to get on with writing up her notes and headed down the corridor. Someone was with him already. That's what the nurse had said. Would Billy, Jackson's brother, have visited him? That would make sense, seeing as he was Jackson's only living relative – him and Billy's daughter, Eden, of course.

Pausing outside the door to his room, Laura braced herself for what she'd find inside. *Please be okay, Jackson. Please be okay.* She pushed the door open and stepped inside, ready to rush to his bedside. Halting on the spot, she took in the scene in front of her. Jackson was sitting up in bed, his back slumped against a mound of pillows, the blue sheets of hospital bedding covering his legs and lap.

'Jackson! Oh, Jackson, I've only just heard what happened about the car accident. Are you okay? Are you hurt?' Her words tumbled out of her mouth at a million miles per hour as she hurried towards his bedside. His skin was pale, broken only by a patch of white gauze above his eyebrow. Relief flooded through her as she realised he was conscious, alive.

'Laura.' Jackson's voice was croaky as he pushed himself forward, sitting up straighter. 'I'm so glad you came.'

'What happened? Are you okay? Your forehead!' Taking his hand in one of hers, she ran her finger along his forehead, careful not to touch the gauze. 'You're hurt.'

'I'm okay. I was lucky by all accounts. Not that I can remember much about it.'

'If I'd known, I'd have come right away.' She wiped the back of her free hand over her eyes, brushing away the tears. Why had he rung her? Had it been because of what she'd said? Because she'd told him she didn't want to speak to him?

'Don't worry. I survived.' Jackson gave a weak smile, his dimple barely visible. 'Unfortunately, my phone didn't.'

'Ah.' That explained the radio silence.

'I need to tell you something...' Jackson looked towards the door of his room as the sound of footsteps approached.

'Don't worry. I overreacted. I shouldn't have let what you said to Richie come between us.' None of it mattered now. It really didn't. The only thing that mattered was that he was okay. 'I should have realised why you were saying it.'

'It's not that, I need to—'

'I have your water, Jacks. All cool and fresh straight from the—'

Laura turned slowly and watched as the click-clack of footsteps stopped and the voice – that unmistakable voice – petered out. She looked from Evie Taunton to Jackson and back again.

'Oh, I'm sorry. I didn't realise Jacks had company.' Striding into the room, Evie placed a jug of water on the small bedside table with a clang. 'Hello, Laura.'

'Evie.' Dropping hold of Jackson's hand, Laura looked across at him, desperately trying to catch his eyes, wanting him to give her a logical explanation as to why Evie Taunton, his ex and the woman who had made her life miserable for the past few weeks, knew he was in hospital before she did, the person he supposedly loved.

'Laura.' Jackson's voice cracked. 'I can explain.'

'No, no.' She staggered away, the back of her knees hitting a chair positioned to the left of his bed. 'I think I understand now.'

'But...'

'Bye, Laura. Thanks for stopping by.' Evie's voice was laced with false friendliness.

Turning, Laura fled out of the room. How could he? After everything?

'All okay?' The nurse looked up from her paperwork as Laura hurried past.

She didn't have the will to answer. She couldn't. Picking up the pace, she half walked and half ran through the maze of corridors and back outside to her car. She'd been right. Evie held a torch for Jackson. The entire village had noticed that, but what she couldn't understand was why Jackson had pursued her, Laura, and told her he loved her, if he was still involved with Evie.

Unless... She dropped the car key and knelt to the ground, her knees against the cold tarmac of the hospital car park. Unless it had all been an extravagant game, unless Jackson was working with Evie in an attempt to run her out of the village?

Standing up, she clicked the keys, grateful to hear the lock release. Pulling the door open, she slipped inside.

But Jackson wouldn't do that. He wouldn't be so cruel, and he had genuinely seemed pleased she had moved in next door to him. And the time they'd spent together, the cuddles, the kisses, the 'I love you's. No, Jackson wouldn't want to hurt her. Not intentionally.

Turning the key, she ground the gears into reverse. There must be another explanation for why Evie was there, at the hospital with Jackson. Maybe she should have given him the chance to explain. Then again, whatever he said, how would she know she could believe him? But Jackson had seemed happy to see Laura.

She shook her head. Why would Jackson have been pleased to see her if he felt nothing for her, if he was with Evie?

Nope, nope, nope. She hit the steering wheel. She wouldn't believe it. She didn't want to, and she wouldn't. She knew Jackson and he would not have told her he was in love with her if he had Evie hovering in the wings. No.

Then again maybe she didn't know him as well as she thought she did? She just didn't know what to think anymore.

With her shoulders slumping, she let the tears fall. It was a good job they hadn't told her family, told Richie. It would have caused all that upset, for what? For nothing.

32

Gripping the arm of the sofa, Laura pushed herself to standing and dropped the empty cookie dough ice cream tub and spoon onto the coffee table before calling out to the incessant ring of the doorbell, 'Coming.'

For once, she was grateful for its weak tune. She'd spent the night curled up in bed, wide awake, and her head ached with the lack of sleep. And guilt. She'd planned to get on with some of the renovating this morning, her idea being that it might help take her mind off Jackson, but she just hadn't been able to face it. She'd got so far as to take the lid off the paint tin to begin the woodwork in the hallway and quickly decided it was ice cream she'd needed rather than a lungful of paint fumes.

She glanced towards the carriage clock on the mantelpiece and groaned. It was two in the afternoon already and her family was here. Looking around the vast sitting room, she shrugged. She should have been more organised and tidied, but she really didn't have an ounce of energy in her body to care. When her mum had rung last night and told Laura she'd arranged for the family to come and visit, she hadn't the energy or the space in her brain to protest. All she could think about was Jackson and all she could picture in her mind's eye every time she'd tried to go to sleep was Evie Taunton click-clacking her way into Jackson's hospital room.

Her parents could come, Jenny and Richie and their families could come, but nothing would change what had happened yesterday.

The doorbell sounded again, barely audible this time, and, taking one last redundant look around the sitting room, Laura walked through the hallway to the door, trying to plaster a fake smile on her face before pulling it open. 'Hi, welcome to Pennycress Inn.'

'Oh, Laura. I can see why you fell in love with the place now. It's a stunning building and Meadowfield is such a cute, quaint village.' Her mother bustled in, two huge picnic bags in her hands, and leaned over to land a kiss on Laura's cheek before pausing in the middle of the hallway.

Propping her foot against the door to hold it open, Laura greeted the rest of her family with a smile she hoped they didn't realise was false, before closing the door. 'Mum, you didn't have to bring food. I could have made something.'

'Don't be silly, sweetheart. I can't expect you to drop all your tasks for the morning and prepare lunch for us. Besides, it's just a little something – bread, olives, hummus, cheese, tomatoes, cucumber, a little sweet treat for the kids...'

'Thanks.'

'So, do we get the grand tour this time?' Jenny grinned as she pulled Tammy's trainers from her daughter's feet. 'I know we've been before, but, in a way, I feel this is our first time, as all we got to see was the kitchen and hallway.'

'Umm...' Laura looked longingly towards the kitchen. She

needed caffeine. 'Why don't you two, Tammy and Toby, show everyone round? You had the chance to explore the last time you came, didn't you?'

'Ooh, can we?' Tammy clapped her hands together.

'Yes, you'd be doing me a favour.' Laura smiled as her niece began ordering people to get into pairs and queue up at the bottom of the stairs. 'No sliding down the banister though, it's still not fixed, so you'll likely end up in hospital again, okay?'

'Okay.' Toby nodded solemnly before joining his sister at the head of the queue.

'What have you found there, Jasper?' Jane picked up her son as he ran from the sitting room into the hallway. 'Here, I'll have that, poppet.'

Reluctantly releasing the ice cream tub and spoon, Jasper rushed to join Tammy and Toby by the bottom of the stairs.

'Are you coming to help, Jasper?' Toby leaned down to his little cousin's height and took his hand.

'Here you go, Laura. Sorry, nothing's safe with Jasper around.' Jane laughed as she passed her the tub and spoon.

'I'll come and help you with this lot.' Richie picked up the picnic bags and grimaced. 'Jeez, Mum is stronger than she looks. I think she must have packed everything but the kitchen sink.'

Laura nodded and turned to the kitchen. Since her dad and Richie had visited and praised her work, she'd so been looking forward to showing her family around Pennycress. Yes, it was tatty in places and needed a lot of work, but it was hers and she at least felt as though she was accomplishing something on her own. But if she was honest, she could have done without it today. Yesterday's events with Jackson and Evie were too fresh, too sore.

She pinched the bridge of her nose as she made her way towards the kettle. And, despite all that had happened between them, she was worried about Jackson. Was he still in hospital? How long were they keeping him in?

She sighed. It wasn't any of her business, not now.

'Everything okay, sis? You look as though you've been up all night.' Richie placed a bottle of milk on the work surface.

'I will be.'

'What's happened?' He laid his arm around her shoulder and pulled her towards him before nodding at the ice cream tub she'd discarded next to the kettle. 'Problems of the heart?'

Laying her cheek on his jumper, she took a deep breath before straightening up again. She couldn't very well tell him why she was out of sorts, why she was worried. 'Is it that obvious?'

'It's cookie dough. It's always been your staple in any heart-break situation. Is it because you saw Harry the other day?'

'No.' She shook her head and sighed. She'd have to say something to Richie. He knew her too well to see through her excuses. 'Not him. Just someone I thought was something he wasn't.'

'Oh, sorry to hear that, sis. I'm always here if you need to talk.' He squeezed her shoulder and lowered his voice. 'Would it be easier if I made up an excuse to everyone and rescheduled today?'

'No, don't worry.'

'You sure? I'm happy to turf them all out for you.' Richie gave a quick grin.

She smiled. 'No, thank you though. I think this distraction might just be the very thing I need.'

* * *

'...And six!' Tammy moved her counter across the Snakes & Ladders board set up on the coffee table in the sitting room. 'Only three more spaces and I win!'

'Well done, Tammy, but make sure you watch out for that snake there.' Ruth patted her granddaughter on the shoulder and pointed to the board.

Shaking the dice, Toby released them onto the floor, watching as the plastic cubes chased each other across the carpet.

Before they had the chance to roll to a stop, Ava reached out and grabbed one in her podgy little hand.

'No, Ava, that's for big boys and girls, not babies.' Standing up, Tammy tried to prise the die from her cousin's hand, resulting in Ava screaming and running from the room with her treasure. 'No, Ava! Mummy, Ava has the dice. She might eat it and then we won't be able to finish our game.'

Laura watched from the sofa as Jenny, Jane and Richie jumped up from their seats and hurried out of the room, following the small thief.

'Oh, the joy of small children.' Ruth turned to Laura. 'Of course, the worry never stops, even when those children grow into adults.'

'I bet.'

'And it's inevitable that we worry, especially when one of them moves away.' Her mum patted Laura's knee. 'But I'm proud of you for taking this leap. This is a really nice place you've got here.'

'Thanks, Mum.' Laura turned as Tammy and Toby came tearing back into the room, the stolen die held victoriously above Tammy's head. She laughed. 'You got it then?'

'Yes. And now we can finish our game.' Skidding to a stop, Tammy threw herself down on the floor again and passed the die to her brother.

'I think this little one needs a distraction.' Richie returned, Ava giggling in his arms as he tickled her, Jenny and Jane following shortly behind.

'I'll make us another cuppa, shall I? And then maybe we can get the food ready?' Laura stood up.

Tilting her head, Jane looked behind her towards the hallway. 'Is that your doorbell, Laura?'

'Oh probably. I keep forgetting to buy new batteries for it.' Laura gathered as many mugs as she could in one hand before walking out. Placing the mugs on the reception desk, Laura walked across to the door and pulled it open, before freezing. 'Jackson!'

'Laura, please let me explain.' Standing on the doorstep, he still sported the gauze dressing above his eye, but he looked better, he had more colour in his cheeks.

'You're out of hospital.' Why had she said that? Of course he was. He wouldn't be standing in front of her if he wasn't.

Jackson nodded. 'Evie volunteers at the hospital. That's why she was there. That's how she knew I was there too.'

She let out a sharp laugh. 'Ha, Evie volunteering. Now I know you've got something to hide.'

'It's true. And I was on the way to see—'

She held her hand up as she heard Tammy's and Toby's voices coming closer. 'I have everyone round.'

'Jackson! I've just won Snakes & Ladders.' Tammy peered out from the sitting-room door.

'Oh wow. Well done.' Jackson looked back at Laura.

'Please leave. I can't get through another afternoon of pretending nothing has happened between us, especially after yesterday.' Looking down, she used the pads of her thumbs to dry her eyes.

'Laura, please?'

'I'm sorry.' Closing the door in his face, she turned her back to the twins.

'Come play with us, Auntie Laura.' Tammy slipped her hand inside Laura's and pulled her towards the sitting room.

Making sure to wipe her eyes with the back of her hand, Laura plastered a smile on her face again, trying desperately to bury the confused emotions inside her as Tammy pulled her through the doorway. Whatever Jackson had done, she still loved him and that was a feeling which wasn't going to disappear any time soon. And she so desperately wanted to believe him about Evie volunteering at the hospital, but she just couldn't think straight. Not with everyone here. Maybe once they'd left she'd be able to ring the hospital and find out if he was telling the truth. She sighed. If she had to do that – ask the hospital rather than believing Jackson – they wouldn't work as a couple anyway. What was a relationship without trust? She just didn't know what to think anymore.

'Who was it, sweetheart?' Her mum twisted on the sofa to look at her.

'No one.' Laura lowered herself to the floor next to the coffee table and the game of Snakes & Ladders.

'You can be the yellow one. Mummy says it's your favourite colour.'

'Thanks.' Laura blinked and tried to focus on the game board.

'Jackson! So pleased you could join us.' Her dad's voice boomed above the chatter and laughter in the room.

Toby bounded into the room, sporting a large grin. 'I'm a big boy now, I opened the door to Jackson.'

Jerking her head up, Laura's heart sank. She really didn't know how she was going to cope with him here, but what else was she supposed to do? Yell at him and tell him to leave? That would just result in questions she knew neither of them wanted to answer.

Hovering in the doorway, Jackson held his hand up in greeting.

'You're hurt! What happened, love?' Standing up, her mum hurried across to him.

'It's nothing. I'm fine.' Jackson dismissed her concern and looked towards Laura.

'Thanks for standing me up yesterday afternoon.' Richie jiggled Ava on his knee and indicated Jackson's dressing. 'I hope that wasn't the reason why?'

'Yes, it was, mate. Sorry. I was in a car accident.' He held his hand up, palm forward, as the noise suddenly increased, with her mum, Jenny and Richie asking what happened and if he was okay. 'I'm fine, really, but that's not the reason I'm here. The reason I've come round, uninvited, is to tell you all why I was travelling down to see you, Richie.'

'I thought we were going for a beer and a catch-up.' Richie frowned.

'No.' Jackson cleared his throat. 'I was coming to tell you that I've fallen in love.'

'Are you sure you're okay? That bump on the head...' Jenny reached up to her own forehead.

Laura froze, her breath caught in her throat, the yellow counter in her hand. Was he going to do, say, what she thought he was?

'I wanted to tell you all, we both did...' He caught Laura's eye. '...when we came for the roast dinner, but I chickened out and it's my deepest regret, as I'm pretty sure I've messed up the best thing to happen to me.'

'Jackson, bud, come and sit down. You're making no sense.' Richie shifted along the sofa, making room for him.

Taking a shuddery breath, Laura's eyes darted from Jackson to her brother and back again. Richie had no idea what his best mate was about to tell him.

'No. Thanks, but no. This is something I've got to say.' He

turned to Ruth and Phil. 'I love your daughter. I'm in love with Laura. We didn't plan this, but it's the way I feel and the way she felt too, until I messed things up.'

Laura dropped her counter, the small yellow piece of plastic clipping the coffee table the loudest sound in the suddenly silent room.

'This is a joke, right?' Richie stood up slowly, shifting Ava in his arms. 'Laura's not in love with you, mate. She's just had her heart broken by some idiot.'

'That idiot is me.' Jackson spoke quietly but clearly. 'And for that, I'm truly sorry.'

'Laura, that's not true, is it? You and Jackson?' Richie looked from his sister to his best mate and back again.

Laura's mouth turned dry. He'd really told them. He'd told her family, Richie, that he loved her. That meant he did, didn't it? He wouldn't have said that, said anything, if he wasn't sure how he felt. All the mistrust and worry about whether something was going on between him and Evie melted away. Him telling her family as he just had was all the confirmation she needed – he did love her. He loved her! Taking a deep breath in, Laura nodded, her voice a whisper. 'It's true.'

'But...' Richie shook his head, trying to clear the confusion. 'How long have you been seeing each other?'

'Just since she moved here, but I've felt this way about her for years.'

'No, you—'

'I have too.' Standing up, Laura cleared her throat. 'I love him and I have for years, too.'

'You still love me?' Jackson locked eyes with her.

'I still love you.' The room, her family, faded into the background as she walked the few steps towards him and sank into his arms, feeling his lips on her forehead. She'd almost lost him.

She'd almost let what Harry had done cloud her judgement but now she was sure. She was more sure than she ever had been that Jackson was telling her the truth. 'I love you.'

'Laura, I'm so sorry. I shouldn't have chickened out on telling everyone.' Jackson cupped her cheeks and leaned down, their lips meeting.

'Eurgh!' Tammy's voice shattered the silence, the moment passing.

Pulling away from him, Laura looked around the room and, as if Tammy's voice had broken the spell, she blinked as her family gathered around them. She could feel her heart racing as she waited with bated breath for her family to react. She swallowed and reached for Jackson's hand, gripping his clammy palm with her own. This was the moment of truth, the moment they'd both been dreading.

'At least we know you'll look after her, Jackson, love.' Her mum pulled Jackson towards her and kissed him on the cheek before turning to Laura. 'And I don't doubt you'll look after him, too.'

'I can't believe you two are together! This is crazy!' Jenny held her hands against her cheeks before drawing them both into a hug.

Laura nodded as her dad, Jane and Rob congratulated them until the only person left was Richie. She met his eyes. 'This wasn't planned.'

'No, it really wasn't. I'm sorry, mate, but I can't lie to you, to myself, to anyone any longer.' Jackson shifted position.

Turning, Richie handed Ava to Jane before looking at them both and shaking his head slowly.

'I really will look after her, Richie.' Jackson's voice was firm.

Sighing loudly, Richie ran the palm of his hand over his face. 'I don't know what to say... apart from this is going to take some getting used to.'

'I get that.' Jackson nodded.

But then, stepping forward, Richie wrapped his arms around them, Laura with one arm and Jackson with the other, before releasing them. He pointed at Jackson. 'But if you *ever* make her eat cookie dough ice cream again, we'll be having words.'

'Cookie dough ice cream?' Jackson frowned.

'It doesn't matter.' Laura laughed and hugged her brother again. 'Thanks, Richie. Your blessing means so much to me, to us both.'

EPILOGUE

'Do you think the rain will hold off?' Laura looked up at the clouds as she placed Vivienne's famous fruit cake on the trestle table beneath the gazebo. Up until now, this year's May had been all sunshine and warmth. Trust her to choose the only day this month which was forecast to rain, to officially open Pennycress Inn.

'Oh yes. The sun will shine down on you today. I can feel it.' The older woman smiled as she placed the hummus next to the carrot sticks.

'I can't quite believe this day has come.' Laura shook her head and looked around the garden, the willow tree standing proudly surrounded by a ring of daffodils. She'd been looking forward to the grand opening of the inn ever since she'd arrived in Meadowfield, but now it was here, she couldn't help but feel a little nervous. What if she didn't do Pennycress justice, what if she couldn't live up to Vivienne's, or her own expectations?

Vivienne joined her and looked across at the inn. 'It'll be fine. You'll do a grand job.'

Laura laughed. 'Sometimes I wonder if you can read my mind.'

'Ah, no, but I remember feeling just as nervous when I opened Pennycress for the first time myself.' Vivienne rubbed Laura's forearm.

'I just don't want anything to go wrong. I don't want to let anyone down.' She pointed up to the window of the middle bedroom. 'See what I mean? I can't even open the curtains right, they're all wonky.'

Vivienne chuckled. 'Pah, you worry too much. Now, enjoy the day.'

Laura shook herself from her thoughts. 'You're right, what's one wonky curtain?'

'Exactly. I'll go and fetch the fruit punch and then I think we'll be ready.' Turning, Vivienne retreated into the inn.

'There you are.' Jogging up to her, Jackson wrapped her arms around Laura's middle and drew him to her. 'I'm so proud of you and all that you've achieved.'

'Ha, I haven't even welcomed my first guests yet.' Laura reached up and smoothed back a wayward curl out of Jackson's eye before running the pad of her forefinger across the scar on his forehead, a permanent reminder of all that she'd almost lost.

'You will and everything will run smoothly.' Jackson kissed her on the lips. 'Think positively.'

'Yes, you're right. I do need to be more positive.' She grinned as she pointed to the open gateway leading from the small car park at the back of Pennycress into the garden. 'Besides, it's too late for any more worrying. Our first guests have arrived.'

'Auntie Laura!' Tammy grabbed hold of Toby's hand as they both ran towards her.

'Hello, you two.' Bending down, Laura waved her hand,

encompassing the empty garden. 'Look, you two are the very first guests at Pennycress Inn.'

'We are?' Toby widened his eyes.

'Yes, you are, buddy.' Jackson grinned and pointed towards the lawn and the large garden games Laura had bought – a huge chess set, a Connect 4 and Snakes & Ladders. 'Have you seen what's over here?'

'Can we pay Snakes & Ladders? It's our favourite game in the whole wide world!' Gripping hold of Laura's hand, Tammy jumped up and down.

'Haha, I know it is. Of course you can.' She watched as they ran towards the game before turning to greet Jenny and Rob. 'Morning. Welcome to Pennycress Inn.'

'This is looking amazing, Laura.' After drawing both her and Jackson in for a hug, Jenny turned on the spot, taking in the garden. 'Did you do all of this?'

'Oh, you know me, Jenny. I'm terrible at gardening and that's not changed and probably never will. No, Jill has worked her magic.' Laura looked out across the garden. It never failed to amaze her how Jill had transformed the once overgrown ramshackle garden into the landscaped delight which it was today. Over the last couple of months Jill had worked tirelessly to return it to the beautiful place she had told her it was when Vivienne had been in charge.

'Your gardener? The lady you told us about?'

'That's right. In fact, she's just arrived with her family now.' Laura waved towards Jill and her husband as they walked through the gate, their four young children immediately running towards the games. 'Hey, Jill.'

'Hi. How are you feeling? It's a big day today!' Jill hugged Laura.

'Good, thanks. Jill, meet Jenny, my sister. She was just

admiring your gardening skills.' Touching them both on the arms Laura backed away. 'I'll catch you later. Enjoy and help yourself to some Buck's Fizz.'

Walking past the tray of drinks, Laura took two glasses and proceeded towards the decking, which ran around the side of the inn. She'd spotted someone she wanted to talk to. As she climbed the stairs, she glanced across towards Jackson, who raised his eyebrows at her. Laura nodded and gave him the thumbs up in response before he turned back to the conversation he was having with Richie and Jill's husband, Gerald. 'Hello, Evie. Glad you could make it.'

Evie Taunton walked the few short steps towards her, her high heels clipping against the wooden decking. 'Laura. Thank you for the invite, although I've got to admit I was a little surprised to receive one.'

Laura held out a glass. 'I couldn't not invite the one person who made this all possible.'

'Thank you.' Taking the glass, Evie lifted it to her lips and took a small sip.

'After all, if you hadn't shown me around Pennycress or submitted my offer to Mr Yates, then we wouldn't be standing here today.'

'I suppose not.' Evie gave a slight nod of her head.

'I'd like to propose a truce.' Laura held her glass towards Evie and held her breath. Although she'd seen Evie around the village since the whole hospital ward incident, this was the first time they'd spoken.

Evie took another sip of her bubbly, eyeing Laura as she did so.

Shifting on her feet, Laura twisted the stem of her glass in her fingers, determined not to give in so easily. They both lived Meadowfield, and ignoring and avoiding each other was just ha work. If they could at least be civil to each other, both their lives would be easier. 'We both live in the same village. We can't avoid each other forever and I'd like us to get along. To start afresh.'

Tilting her head and staring at her, seemingly thinking, Evie finally lifted her glass and clinked it with Laura's. 'A truce.'

Breathing a sigh of relief, Laura grinned. 'Fantastic.'

'Auntie Laura!'

Turning, Laura heard Tammy's voice before she spotted her running towards them.

'There's someone to see you and she has a big gold chain around her neck. Toby thinks she's a pirate, but I told him she probably just really, really likes jewellery.' Tammy jumped from foot to foot in front of her.

'Oh, that will be the mayoress, Miss Cooke. Thank you, Tammy. I'll come down and speak to her.' Laura looked at Evie and smiled. 'Thank you again for coming.'

'Do you like Snakes & Ladders? Will you come and play with us?' Tammy gripped hold of Evie's hand and began pulling her down the steps towards the garden.

Laura stifled a laugh as she watched Evie teetering on her heels in an attempt to keep up with Tammy's pace. That was one thing she didn't think she'd ever see: icy Evie Taunton playing Snakes & Ladders.

'Ah, there you are.' Miss Cooke joined Laura on the decking.

'Hello. Welcome to Pennycress Inn.' Laura finished with a flourish of her hands.

'I've got to say, Laura, you're a credit to our village, you are. It will be wonderful to have Pennycress open and hosting local events again, not to mention the extra business your guests will bring to the village. You've done a fabulous job.' Miss Cooke placed her hands on her hips and surveyed the garden.

'Thank you. That means a lot. Of course, I couldn't have done it without all the help from Jackson and Jill's amazing gardening skills.' She grinned. The journey to transform Pennycress from the run-down state the inn had been in to how it was today hadn't been easy and there had been many obstacles along the way – the pipe she'd burst in the hallway, the broken banister... the list was endless – many of which had led her to question her decision to buy Pennycress in the first place, but she was glad she'd stuck it out. Now the inn was freshly decorated and everything in place to welcome her guests, Laura felt a great sense of pride that she hadn't given up on her dreams and vision for Pennycress.

'I've been speaking to Vivienne's daughter, Nicola. She told me you're pretty much booked up from now until the end of the summer?'

'Yes, that's right.' Laura nodded. She didn't know what she'd have done without Nicola's expertise these last few weeks in the run-up to opening. Over the couple of months since Vivienne had introduced them, Nicola had become a firm friend as well as helping her out so much with the website and ideas for future events, and then last week Laura had officially welcomed her into the Pennycress team – her first proper member of staff. 'The new website and social media accounts Nicola has made for the inn have had a really positive impact.'

'Well done. Oh, and congratulations.'

Congratulations? Laura shook her head. 'Thank you.'

Nodding, Miss Cooke retreated down the stairs to mingle with the other villagers who were turning up.

Leaning her elbows on the wooden railing encompassing the decking, Laura looked out across the garden. Amidst some unfamiliar faces, she recognised a lot of the guests – among them her darts teammates, Catherine, Dan and Terry, Mrs Pierce from the bakery, Pat, Mrs Pritchard and, of course, her family who had driven down to celebrate the opening with her.

She grinned. A few short months ago she'd have never even dreamt that she'd have been capable of buying, restoring and opening an inn as beautiful as Pennycress.

She straightened her back as Nicola hurried towards her.

'Laura, our first guests have arrived.' Slightly out of breath, Nicola clapped her hands. 'They're here!'

'The Oakleys?'

'Yes. They're at the front desk. I asked them to wait whilst I came to get you. I hope that's okay? I didn't want to check them in without you.'

Laura squealed. 'I can't believe it, our first guests. Come on, let's go and get them checked in.' Placing her glass on one of three rattan table and chair sets positioned on the decking, Laura gripped hold of Nicola's shirt sleeve as they made their way through the back door and into the hallway.

'Morning, you must be Mr and Mrs Oakley. Welcome to Pennycress Inn.' Laura held her hand out and welcomed them. 'I'm so sorry for the delay. It's our grand opening today and you're our first ever guests!'

'No problem.' Mrs Oakley smiled as she placed her handbag down on the reception desk.

'Right, let's just get you both checked in and then we can show you to your room.' Laura clicked the booking-in form on the computer as Nicola joined her behind the desk. 'There we go. All done. I'll show you the bedroom now and talk you through the breakfast options.'

'Oh, lovely.' Mrs Oakley picked up her handbag as Laura walked around and picked up their suitcase.

'I'm happy to carry that.' Mr Oakley indicated the luggage.

'Thank you, but no, it's all part of the service.' Laura grinned, making a rubbish attempt at hiding her excitement.

'Well, thank you. And you serve breakfast?'

'We do indeed and I may be biased, but I wholeheartedly recommend the French toast,' she called over her shoulder as she led the way up the stairs, grateful that the suitcase was relatively light. 'I hope you enjoy your stay. And please join us in the garden for the opening party if you'd like to.' Laura smiled as she shut the bedroom door behind her.

Pausing at the top of the landing, she resisted the urge to do a little celebration dance – the inn was officially up and running!

'All settled?' Richie took the stairs two at a time to join her.

'Yes.' She grinned. 'And I think they liked the room. Or else they said they did.'

'That's amazing.' Richie led the way back down. 'Jackson is looking for you.'

'Oh, right.' She nodded.

Richie paused halfway down and looked back at her. 'I'm proud of you, you know.'

'I know.' She flicked her hair back over her shoulder before laughing.

'And I think you and Jackson make a great team.' He rubbed the back of his neck. 'You make a great couple.'

'Aw, thanks. I know you weren't particularly over the moon when we got together, but I appreciate you being supportive.'

Richie nodded slowly. 'That was only because I was worried about what would happen if you broke up, but I can see that you're meant to be, now.'

'Thanks, Richie. That means a lot.' She joined him on the step below and wrapped her arms around him. 'I really do love Jackson.'

'I know.' Richie grinned. 'And he's still waiting for you, so we'd better go out to the garden now.'

Laura nodded and slipped her arm through her brother's. 'Are you and Jane still coming to stay next weekend?'

'Absolutely! There's French toast on the breakfast menu, right?'

'There is indeed. Though I don't know how Jackson will keep up with cooking breakfast here and then working at the pub, alongside finishing up renovating next door.' She smiled. Jackson had been happy to put his own renovations on hold whilst he'd helped Laura here, but now, she was looking forward to helping him for a change and putting some of her newly discovered DIY skills to the test once more.

As they walked through the hallway towards the back door, Laura frowned. She couldn't hear any of the laughing or chatting that there had been when she'd left the garden party. People hadn't gone home already, had they?

Stepping in front of her, Richie threw the back door open before standing aside.

Laura froze in the doorway. Jackson was standing on the decking in front of her, their guests gathered around the steps, all quietly watching and waiting. 'Jackson?'

'Go on then. Go to him.' Richie chuckled and nudged her forward.

Glancing back at her brother, Laura turned back to Jackson and walked slowly towards him. He held a small burgundy box in one hand. He wasn't, was he? He wasn't about to propose? She swallowed.

'Laura.' Taking her hand in his, Jackson knelt down, one knee on the decking. 'I've dreamt about this for a very long time now and can hardly believe the moment has come.'

He was! He really was! She squeezed his hand as she spoke, her words coming out in a whisper. 'Nor me.'

'You are kind, funny, genuine, beautiful. You are my soulmate.' Jackson glanced down at the ground before shaking his head and opening the ring box to reveal a platinum band, a small but perfect diamond, sitting delicately in the middle. 'I had a whole long speech prepared, but what I want to say is: you're my other half and will you do me the honour of marrying me? Please?'

Bringing her free hand to her face, Laura wiped at the happy tears and nodded. 'Of course.'

'Phew!' Carefully taking the ring from the box, Jackson slid it on her finger before standing and drawing her in towards him as the silence around them filled with applause, whoops, and a chorus of 'congratulations!'

Tammy's voice suddenly rose above the noise as she came hurtling up the steps towards them, her arms wide ready to hug them both. As she squeezed their waists she looked up and grinned, the gap from the front tooth she'd lost earlier in the week giving her a lisp as she spoke loudly. 'Auntie Laura, I told you that you and Jackson should get married. Didn't I?'

Laura laughed as she hugged her niece back. 'Yes, you certainly did. And I think it was a great idea of yours.'

'Me too, Tammy.' Jackson chuckled as he high-fived Tammy before watching her race back towards her mum.

'I don't think this day could get any more perfect.' Laura looked down at her ring before placing her hand on Jackson's cheek and looking him in the eye. 'I love you so much and I can't wait for us to be husband and wife.'

'I love you too.' Jackson lowered his lips to hers and kissed her before stepping back and nodding towards the garden and the guests. 'Shall we?'

Laura nodded as they began descending the steps to the garden. 'This is everything I ever dreamed of.'

'I—' Jackson's reply was punctuated by a series of screams.

With her eyes widening, Laura looked across the garden quickly locating the cause of the interruption to the party. She and Jackson both looked at each other. 'Claudette!'

'Away, away! Get away!' Jenny screeched as the sheep raced through the garden and propelled itself into the game of Connect4, giant plastic discs raining down around her fluffy white fleece as she headed towards the trestle table covered with sandwiches, cakes and snacks.

Within a split second, the party had divided, some people running to the back of the garden to escape Claudette's rampage whilst others made a beeline for the trestle table, racing to rescue plates and bowls of food before Claudette ran head first into it. With an almighty noise, the trestle table shuddered before collapsing and landed in a heap on the ground, the food which hadn't been saved raining down across the lawn, the guests and the sheep.

Balancing Vivienne's famous fruit cake in one hand and a tray of cupcakes in the other, Laura watched as Claudette, seemingly unfazed by the drama, squeezed through a gap in the hedge, leaving behind the chaos and destruction. She looked anxiously at Jackson, who was standing next to her clutching a now empty serving dish in his hands and wearing a covering of cheesecake across his shirt. 'We'd better be on the lookout for the others.'

Blinking, Jackson knitted his eyebrows together. 'The others?'

'Yes, the other sheep! I can't remember all the names listed at the first village meeting I attended, but Gertrude, Florence and the others. If Claudette has come through the hedge, the others might be following her!'

Laying the empty serving dish on the mound of plates and ruined food, Jackson doubled over and laughed.

'What?'

'There's only one escapee, people just have different names for her.' Jackson managed.

'Oh.' All this time, she'd assumed there was a whole flock of sheep on the loose and yet there was only one. She looked around the garden. The group of people who had rescued the food were taking it inside, whilst the rest of the guests were either getting back to their games or laughing, chatting and talking amongst themselves. Passing the cakes she'd rescued to Jenny, Laura laid her hand on Jackson's back and began to giggle.

His bout of laughter finally coming to an end, Jackson straightened up and chuckled. 'Is this the opening day you were hoping for?'

Grinning from ear to ear, Laura shook her head. 'No, it's better. Much better.'

ACKNOWLEDGEMENTS

Thank you so much for reading *Welcome to Pennycress Inn*. I hope you've enjoyed reading about Laura's fresh start in Meadowfield and her journey to find love with Jackson as much as I did writing it.

A massive thank you to my wonderful children, Ciara and Leon, who motivate me to keep writing and working towards 'changing our stars' each and every day. Also thank you to my lovely family for always being there, through the good times and the trickier ones.

And a huge thank to my brilliant editor, Francesca Best – thank you. Thank you also to Jade Craddock for copy editing and to Shirley Khan for proofreading *Welcome to Pennycress Inn*. Thank you to all of team Boldwood!

ABOUT THE AUTHOR

Sarah Hope is the author of many successful romance novels, including the bestselling Cornish Bakery series. Sarah lives in Central England with her two children and an array of pets and enjoys escaping to the seaside at any opportunity.

Sign up to Sarah Hope's mailing list for news, competitions and updates on future books.

Follow Sarah on social media here:

facebook.com/HappinessHopeDreams
x.com/sarahhope35
instagram.com/sarah_hope_writes
bookbub.com/authors/sarah-hope

ALSO BY SARAH HOPE

The Pennycress Inn Series

Welcome to Pennycress Inn

The Cornish Village Series

Wagging Tails in the Cornish Village

Chasing Dreams in the Cornish Village

A Fresh Start in the Cornish Village

Happy Days Ahead in the Cornish Village

Escape to... Series

The Seaside Ice-Cream Parlour

The Little Beach Café

Christmas at Corner Cottage

BECOME A MEMBER OF

THE SHELF CARE CLUB

The home of Boldwood's
book club reads.

Find uplifting reads,
sunny escapes, cosy romances,
family dramas and more!

Sign up to the newsletter
https://bit.ly/theshelfcareclub

Boldwood

Boldwood Books is an award-winning fiction publishing company seeking out the best stories from around the world.

Find out more at www.boldwoodbooks.com

Join our reader community for brilliant books, competitions and offers!

Follow us
@BoldwoodBooks
@TheBoldBookClub

Sign up to our weekly deals newsletter

https://bit.ly/BoldwoodBNewsletter

Printed in Great Britain
by Amazon